STABLE

An Inspiring Blend of History and Fiction

attributed

to

Sappheire

⁃⁃⁃

transcribed

by

Daniel Greene

FAMILY FUSION PUBLICATIONS
ROSEVILLE, CALIFORNIA 95678

THE STABLE
by Daniel Greene

Published by
Family Fusion Publications
P.O. Box 148, Roseville, CA 95678

Biblical words and phrases filled Jewish conversations in the first century B.C. The Sacred Scrolls were read every week in the synagogues and used as textbooks by every Hebrew school. *The Stable* includes Scripture in conversational, rhythmical, and previously copyrighted formats. Mary's songs are rhythmical renditions of Scripture, not direct quotations. All direct quotations from an English translation of Scripture are displayed in *italics* and taken from the New International Version of the Bible published by The Zondervan Corporation. Notice of Copyright is as follows:

ISBN 978-0-9906743-0-6

Printed in the United States of America

1 2 3 4 5 6 7 8 / 20 19 18 17 16 15

Cover Design by Dave Aldrich

CONTENTS

This novel is dedicated to my family,

Suzanne, Christina, David, and Jonathan,

and to many friends who partnered with us

in telling this story in Brazil and the USA.

FOREWORD

Jerusalem, circa 46 A.D.

A fashionable carriage, drawn by a pair of well-groomed horses, stopped in front of a large home in the upper city of Jerusalem. A pleasant-looking couple stepped down and knocked on the door. They identified themselves as travelers from Syria and inquired if the home belonged to the mother of John Mark.

The servant girl who opened the door confirmed that it did and disappeared inside to notify the owner. Moments later, she opened a gate and beckoned the passengers and driver to enter a spacious, central courtyard with their carriage. Soon, a kindly, gray-haired woman appeared and introduced herself as Mary, John Mark's mother. The man replied,

"We are delighted to meet you, Mary. I am Luke from the city of Antioch in Syria, and this is my wife, Sappheire. Your son and his cousin, Barnabas, have become good friends of ours since they arrived in our city. When we told them about our plans to visit Jerusalem, they urged us to contact you first. They thought that you would like to know the purpose of our trip and might help us get started.

"We have been expecting you, Doctor Luke," replied Mary. "Welcome to Jerusalem! And Sappheire, how good of you to come, too. I want to thank you both for the generous aid that all of you in Antioch sent to the community here of Jesus' followers during the recent drought and famine. I don't know how we would have survived without it. Do you have any recent news about Mark and Barnabas?"

"Yes, we do," answered Luke. "They just left Antioch with Saul of Tarsus. We put them on a ship to Cyprus where they plan to spread the news about Jesus. Their departure coincided with a request I received from Theophilus, a Roman official in Antioch. He asked me to come to Judea and research Jesus' life and teaching. Eventually, he would like a comprehensive report in the Greek language."

"The first thing we would like to do while we're here is meet with some members of the Way. I believe that's what you call this growing movement of Jesus' followers. I want to introduce myself and explain the mission that several of us from Antioch have undertaken. Would you be able to contact some of them for us?"

"I would be delighted to do that, Doctor Luke."

The following evening, Luke addressed a sizeable gathering of participants in the Way. Among them were several of the twelve messengers whom Jesus selected and commissioned to take the message about God's new kingdom to other nations.

First, Luke introduced Sappheire and two scribes who came with him from Syria to help in the process of conducting interviews. He then explained the request of Theophilus, the Roman official who was sponsoring their travel to Israel and would receive their final report.

Luke spoke with remarkable ease in Aramaic, the popular language of Israel under Roman rule. When questioned about something in Greek, his extensive vocabulary and precise answers portrayed an even greater fluency in that language. Greek was common to a wide range of political and educational discourse throughout the Empire.

While explaining how he and Sappheire came to faith in Jesus, Luke credited the encouraging words of Barnabas and the compelling testimony of Saul of Tarsus. The audience smiled knowingly. An item of news that was especially interesting was the fact that residents of Antioch were now referring to the believers as Christians, meaning "followers of the Messiah."

No one wanted Luke to stop, but his description of the multiracial community of believers in Antioch generated some worried looks and furrowed brows. It sounded like traditional, God-fearing Jews who believed in Jesus were now eating and socializing with Greek believers. That was a striking departure from traditional Jewish behavior.

In the end, Luke's amiable disposition, his mastery of language, and the fact that he had set aside his career in medicine to search out the truth about Jesus won over many in the audience. He seemed to be a gifted spokesman of Jesus' message for the Greek-speaking world. Several pressed forward to introduce themselves and offer their support. Others appeared skeptical and held back.

One, amiable listener, with a short beard and headband around his curly, gray hair, sat for some time on the floor as he rested his head against the stone column behind him. Slowly, a subdued smile of inner resolve spread across his face. When most of the others had departed, he sprang up. Adjusting his tunic and mantle, he approached the Greek physician and said enthusiastically,

"Welcome to Jerusalem, Doctor Luke. It's an honor to meet you. My name is John. I really enjoyed hearing how you and your family came to faith in Jesus."

"When you explained that you have come here to investigate the life of our Master at considerable, personal expense, I began to wonder if the time had come for me to reveal a matter which I have carefully guarded for sixteen years. This report that you are writing for Theophilus, what do you think he will do with it?"

Luke, pausing to arrange Sappheire's return by carriage to the guest house where they were staying, suggested that he and John walk together as they continued the conversation.

"With respect to your question about Theophilus," Luke began, "he has been disseminating scrolls of historical and medical value throughout the Empire for some time. If my report convinces him that Jesus was a credible embodiment of God and not merely another Jewish revolutionary intent on overthrowing Rome, I believe he might sponsor a significant distribution of the report. First, he wants to know the facts. Tell me, John, aren't you one of Jesus' twelve messengers?"

"Yes I am," responded John. "And I am eager to help you out in any way I can. Concerning your report, I feel like I should mention that there is a breathtaking story about Jesus that has never come to light publicly. If this story is ever circulated, it will fill the hearts of its hearers with wonder and celebration. It will help people of all nations understand that Jesus really is God's Messiah for everyone."

"Please go on, John, you have my full attention."

"Here is how I learned of it. Something happened on the day Jesus died that I was not expecting at all. Those hours that Jesus hung on the cross are still seared into my mind with deep, unforgettable emotion. All of us were scattered and demoralized. One by one, we emerged from the crowd and approached Jesus in shock and disbelief. A group of women gathered at a distance, weeping and mourning. I was standing near the cross when all of a sudden Jesus' mother, who is also named Mary, together with her sister, stepped out of the group of women and approached."

"I can still remember thinking, 'Mary, how did you know to be in Jerusalem today?' Jesus looked down at his mother from the cross and said about me, 'Dear woman, here is your son.' He then turned to me and said, 'Here is your mother.' We agreed to his request, of course, but didn't have time to discuss it at that time."

"On the third day, some women woke us up with the news that Jesus was alive. Complete pandemonium broke out. We could hardly believe our ears. I personally saw him alive that very evening along with nine of the twelve messengers. We thought he was a ghost, but then we touched him. He talked with us and showed us the scars in his hands and side. He even ate a piece of fish. He finally disappeared from sight, just like he had appeared. I don't recall when his mother saw him, but I know she did."

"I spoke with her again after Jesus' final appearance and told her that my family and I were delighted with the possibility of her moving to our home in Capernaum or even to our second home in Jerusalem. She said that she wanted to stay in Jerusalem, but needed to visit Nazareth once more to explain to Jesus' siblings why their brother was crucified and that he was still very much alive."

"After moving to our home here in Jerusalem, Mary began to tell me about a series of miraculous events that occurred at the time of Jesus' birth. Her husband, Joseph, and all the others who knew of these matters had passed away by that time, and she was the only one left who could reveal them."

"Hold the conversation right there, John. Here is our guest house. Would you feel comfortable joining me on the rooftop? This is so fascinating. I'd like to invite Sappheire to join us."

Soon the three were seated around some flickering oil lamps on the rooftop and the conversation continued.

"Please go on, John," urged Luke.

"Thank you for joining us, Sappheire. I was telling Luke about Jesus' mother and some events she witnessed at the time of Jesus' birth. Mary has contributed as much as any person I know to the growing faith of women in this movement we call the Way. I eventually realized that she was ahead of all of us in understanding her son's identity and mission when he was alive. She was very discreet about it, though, and waited for us to discover for ourselves who he was."

"One of Jesus' reasons for assigning her to my guardianship may have been to give her a safe place in the middle of the Judean church. It has been dangerous here, and as Jesus' mother, she could easily have been a target for interrogation or imprisonment. Did you know that King Herod Agrippa had my brother, James, killed by the sword just three years ago? When that happened, Mary moved to Capernaum to be with my mother and to comfort her over the loss of James. Mary is sixty-nine now and probably won't be coming back to Jerusalem anymore."

"I have no idea what it is that you might tell us about Jesus' birth," exclaimed Luke. "But I have come to know John Mark quite well. He showed me the outline of an account of Jesus' ministry that he plans to write. I don't think he includes anything about Jesus' birth. Is it possible that he doesn't even know about these events?"

"He probably doesn't. Mary and Joseph never disclosed them publically because Mary conceived Jesus when she was still a virgin and only engaged to Joseph. By Jewish law, she should have been stoned to death. To protect the reputations of all three, Joseph and May kept these events hidden from everyone in Nazareth, except for Mary's parents. Not even Jesus' brothers and sisters thought he was anything more than their naturally born, older brother."

"Listen to this!" added Luke. "Mary was given proof at Jesus' birth that all the angels in heaven were celebrating his arrival on earth. The story gives me goose bumps whenever I think about it. She was also shown that her son would be God's salvation for people of all nations. That news would not have been well received by the Jewish leaders and helps to explain why neither she, nor Joseph, nor Jesus, spoke publicly about these miracles. Mary told me everything and asked me to advise her about making them known."

"Luke, if you will come with me to Capernaum, we can ask Mary for permission to put Jesus' birth story into your report. If she agrees, then I will tell you all that she passed on to me. She may even wish to tell you the story herself."

After planning out the interviews in Judea, Luke left his two scribes to carry on without him. Taking John with them, he and Sappheire traveled north to Capernaum. This thriving, commercial town was located on the Roman highway known as the Via Maris, as it passed by the northern edge of the Sea of Galilee. Mary had already been informed of their pending arrival and was waiting for them.

"Hello Mary. It's wonderful to see you again," John said warmly as he, Luke, and Sappherie entered the room where she was seated.

"I brought with me some special guests from Antioch of Syria. This is Luke, a physician, and his wife, Sappheire. They are from the growing community of Jewish and Greek believers we have been hearing so much about. Luke wants to write a biography about Jesus' life in Greek. A Roman official of the province of Syria has asked for a comprehensive report, and if he finds it credible, he may even distribute copies throughout the Empire. It occurred to me that this could be the right time for you to let the full story of Jesus' birth become known publicly."

"Doctor Luke and Sappheire, how kind of you to come. Please, sit down. I can still remember the first foreign dignitaries who came to see Jesus. He was eleven months old and some Parthian scholars from Susa showed up with a caravan of camels and armed soldiers. I was just eighteen years old and barely knew how to conduct myself with educated folks."

"Tell me, Sapphiere, do you have children?"

"Yes we do. Thank you for asking. We have four children. Two are married and two are taking care of our home while we are on this trip."

"Mary, I would like to say something about meeting you today," continued Sappheire. "This encounter is beyond all my expectations. We are here today because of your son. What Barnabas and others told us about him went right to our souls; we had never heard of anyone like Jesus. Eventually, far away in Syria, I came to love and believe in your son, just like you do. Today, here you are, the mother of Jesus. I can talk with you, touch you, and hopefully become your friend."

Mary stood up and, with tears of joy, the two embraced each other warmly.

"What thoughtful words, Sappheire. Yes, you will be my friend. Tell me, Luke, where did you meet this precious woman?"

"We met in Athens," explained Luke. "I was studying medicine there and occasionally went to see plays at the indoor theaters. The first time I saw Sappheire in a stage presentation, I was immediately captivated. Today she writes plays and coaches younger actors and actresses. I hope that doesn't shock you, Mary."

"Shock me?" laughed Mary, her eyes glistening with delight. "Not in the least."

"You won't believe this, Sappheire, but that's exactly how Joseph and I met. I was only fourteen and participated in this singing group in Nazareth. Joseph happened to be in the audience watching a play one day and he couldn't get me out of his mind."

"Luke, I will let you include the story of Jesus' birth in your report on one condition. You must let Sappheire stay with me for a while as you travel around taking interviews. If you agree to do that, then John can tell you everything. I am sure that you and he will get the facts right. But I want to share with Sappheire some of the emotions I was experiencing at the time. Women need women to listen to them."

"By the way, John," Mary concluded. "Your co-worker, Matthew, is also thinking about writing an account of Jesus' life with an emphasis on Joseph and his royal ancestry. You and Luke should talk with him about which miraculous interventions he should include and which ones Luke should include. Just make sure they add up to eleven."

Two months later, the time came for Sappheire and Mary to say goodbye. They realized that they would probably never see each other again in this life. With tears running down their faces, they held one another in a tight embrace. As they separated, each one raised her hands, fingers extended, and touched the other's. Luke sensed that something very meaningful was being communicated but didn't inquire further.

Luke and Sappheire traveled by carriage to Caesarea where they embarked on a Roman vessel to Antioch. During the free hours aboard ship, Luke asked Sappheire what she planned to do with the information she had gathered about Jesus' birth.

"Above everything else, I am inspired by Mary's love for God and knowledge of the Hebrew Scriptures. A song she wrote about magnifying the Lord has stirred my spirit in a new way. She taught me the joy of humbly receiving the gift of God's Son as my Savior, even though I have nothing to offer to God in return."

"I can't keep all of Mary's treasured memories of Jesus' birth to myself. Initially, I was thinking of writing a short story about her early years with Joseph - where they grew up, when they met, and how they fell in love with each other. *Love Worth Waiting For* is the title I would give to it. But now I think I'll leave that until later."

"What I want to do first is to tell this extraordinary story of Jesus' birth through a series of plays. To start with, I will write out separate accounts of the eleven miraculous events that surrounded Jesus' birth. I didn't write everything down like you do, so I will use my imagination to fill in the conversations and emotional drama of all that Mary shared with me."

"From these narratives, my colleagues and I can create plays and write scripts. The series of plays should begin with an opening scene that puts the birth story in historical and political perspective. It should end with a closing scene that carries the audience to Mary's greatest discovery of all about her son."

"My goal will be to awaken in audiences an appreciation for Jesus of Nazareth and a desire to know more about him. Hopefully, some will even come to love him like I do. No one should ever dismiss him as merely another, short-lived Jewish prophet. He is so much more."

"What do you think of that approach, Luke?"

"It's very imaginative, as I knew it would be. Think of the impact on all of us in Antioch, and on the actors themselves. I can hardly wait to see the first play."

Back in Antioch, Sappheire lost no time in getting started. The sheer irony that God chose a simple animal shelter for his arrival on earth led her to give the unpublished collection of miraculous stories the title, *The Stable*. To the end of her days, she attributed to Mary the insight that God's presence on earth was no longer in temples but in the stables of humble, human hearts.

OPENING SCENE

Once in Nazareth

Rebekah paused briefly to catch her breath as she stepped onto the rough, stone doorstep of her adobe brick home. Glancing back into the shallow valley that cradled Nazareth, she could see the clump of trees where a natural spring provided water for the villagers. The limestone block synagogue and a few, two-story homes rose above the open marketplace where street vendors had erected their canopies that day.

Lifting her gaze to the southern outlet of this elevated natural basin, Rebekah looked across the Valley of Jezreel and saw the Carmel Hills in the distance. A sense of peace and pride welled up as the often repeated words of Rabbi Jediah came to mind and brought a smile to her face,

"Cup your hands together and imagine a small spring of water in the middle. That's what God did when he created Nazareth."

Resting her load against the wall, Rebekah swished each sandaled foot back and forth in a basin of water and splashed them with clean water from a clay pitcher nearby. As she pushed the door open, her right hand instinctively brushed over the mezuzah, a small case on the doorpost containing Hebrew Scripture. She crossed the outer room, dropped the bundle of washed clothing onto a straw mat in the corner, and straightened her back with a sigh of relief.

A distant exchange of lighthearted good-byes and the patter of running feet alerted Rebekah that her daughter, Teresa, had finally caught up. The nine-year-old burst through the open door and breathlessly announced that she and her friends had seen three Roman soldiers riding into Nazareth on the road from Sepphoris.

"And does that disturbing news exempt you from washing off your feet before you come inside?" Rebekah inquired.

"Oh, yeah, mom, I forgot. Sorry." was the well-worn reply as she whirled around. From the doorway, she continued to recount all the excitement of racing up the road with her friends.

Rebekah turned her attention to thank her eleven-year-old son, Aaron, for staying with his grandmother and to tell him to get ready for his afternoon Hebrew lesson at the synagogue. A peek into the back room assured her that her mother was resting comfortably. She told Teresa to change her wet tunic while she lightly mopped the irregular stone floor and left the door ajar for fresh air to pass through.

The rainy season was well underway in the region of Galilee, but a couple of warm sunny days was just the break that Nazareth's housewives needed to gather at the rock-lined pool below the village cistern and wash their families' clothes. The animated greetings, the latest gossip, the outbursts of laughter, and the frolicking daughters splashing in the water all turned this burdensome task into a highlight.

Planning to immediately hang up the wet clothes in the rare afternoon sun, Rebekah caught the reflection of her face in a piece of polished bronze fixed to the wall. She loosened her hair and stroked it quickly with a hanging wooden comb. As she held it tight and retrieved a ribbon from between her teeth, a shadow from the doorway suddenly darkened the walls. She glanced behind her and froze. A roughly-shaven, muscular Roman soldier wearing a crested officer's helmet filled the doorway and inquired in heavily-accented Aramaic,

"Are you alone?"

"I'm here with my two children and my mother," Rebekah answered nervously.

The soldier stared too long and finally told her to finish her hair. Rome's army in Israel was less than a legion in size but moved around the country at will. It was the twentieth year of the reign of Emperor Augustus Caesar. His brilliance as a military commander and politician had ushered in an era of international peace known as Pax Romana.

Far more numerous and oppressive in Israel were the soldiers of King Herod. Not a Jew by birth, Herod had formed an army thirty years earlier from his own people, the Idumeans, and from other foreign mercenaries. He commandeered the Jewish State with approval from Rome and crushed all opposition. For many years, Herod taxed heavily the livestock and agricultural produce throughout the land. Besides that, he forcefully recruited tens of thousands of laborers for his prodigious building programs.

Rebekah's family was relatively new to this part of Israel. In the turmoil of Herod's campaign to capture Jerusalem, her parents fled north from Judea and settled in Nazareth, a safe and unpretentious village in the region of Galilee. Nazareth was a place of hard work and modest income. Its inhabitants were farmers, sheep and goat herders, orchard keepers, weavers, carpenters, metal workers, and traders.

Just an hour away was Sepphoris, a walled city of significant political influence. Its two-story, cut stone homes with mosaic floors and columned streets contrasted sharply with the humble dwellings of Nazareth. It was likely that this Roman officer had left Sepphoris earlier in the day and was passing through Nazareth on his way south.

"Do you have anything to feed three, respectable keepers-of-the-peace?" queried the officer as he glanced outside and back again to Rebekah.

Her eyes swept through the cooking corner of her small house and she thought of her husband, Heli, with their oldest son, Levi, somewhere on the road from Capernaum. She imagined them coaxing their donkey along as it pulled a cartload of salted fish, spices, kitchenware, linen cloth, farming tools, and pottery. She knew they would be starved for the lamb and potato stew that was wrapped up on the lower shelf.

A little provoked by the officer's "peace-keeping" quip, Rebekah said nothing of the stew and answered, "I have some fruit and cheese and can get fresh bread from my neighbor."

Sensing his approval, she pulled Teresa from behind the wall and said firmly, "Go to Aunt Joanna's. Tell her I need three loaves of bread for the soldiers. She lowered her voice and whispered in Hebrew, "Tell Mary to hide!"

Picking up a wooden stool from inside the house, Rebekah moved toward the door and said, "My mother is not well and is sleeping. May I serve you outside?" A small table for Heli's street market sales sat against the front wall. As the officer stepped back, Rebekah set out a jug of water and three clay cups.

A hundred yards away, Joseph was fitting a window header into one side of his new home. The clay packed roof and adobe brick walls were nearly complete, lacking only a couple of barred openings for light and fresh air.

A few months earlier, Joseph had completed his tenth and final year of forced labor in the new port city of Caesarea. The city had become a showpiece of Herod's architectural genius and a doorway into the world of international trade crossing the Great Sea.

Joseph encountered Mary and her family three years earlier while traveling from Caesarea to his hometown of

Bersabe in Northern Galilee. One year later, their parents met, and a year after that, he and Mary were pledged to one another in the traditional ceremony of Jewish betrothal. A wedding was planned for the following spring when Joseph's new home would be completed and his carpentry profession established.

Mary was the delight of Joseph's heart. Just an hour earlier she and her cousin, Rafaela, had hurried by, singing lightheartedly. Just past his house, Mary dropped back a step, glanced his way, and strummed her fingers in his direction as if touching an invisible harp. Joseph would happily work the rest of the day on the inspiration of that little sign of affection.

As he rounded the corner and glanced toward Mary's home, he froze in his tracks. Three horses with Roman military harnessing were tethered to the oak tree in front of her house. Two soldiers rested with their backs to the tree while one seemed to be conversing in the doorway. A blur of thoughts led him to an instantaneous decision.

"Get over there now with a good excuse."

Joseph hastily gathered up a bundle of short wooden poles. Into the middle of the roll, he slid a Roman short sword that he retrieved from the false bottom of his toolbox. He shouldered the load, grabbed a carpenter's saw, and dashed behind an irregular row of houses that led in the direction of Mary's home.

Reaching the last house, he slowed to a casual walk and headed straight toward the soldiers. With a calm nod to the reclining soldiers, he approached the door and called out,

"Hello, Rebekah...Joseph here."

Joseph recognized the officer to be a centurion. He calmly looked into his eyes and said in Latin,

"Good afternoon, Sir."

While the officer was sizing up this confident newcomer with his neatly trimmed beard, sturdy tanned limbs, and short pony tail, Rebekah appeared at the door.

"I brought some wooden legs to measure for the new shelf in your kitchen," Joseph offered casually.

"Oh, thank you, Joseph," she said with obvious relief. "I really need that as soon as possible."

"Heading for Jerusalem?" Joseph queried of the officer.

"Our business is our own, Carpenter," responded the officer, "but where did you learn to speak Latin?"

He was trying to reassert his control over a situation in which this confident, young Hebrew had suddenly inserted himself. Rebekah wasn't following the conversation fully and hurried out with a bowl of fruit and a small knife.

"I worked for ten years on the palace and port facilities in Caesarea," responded Joseph as he swung his bundle to the floor inside the door.

Just then, Teresa came running up with the three loaves of bread, gave them to her mother, and disappeared inside. As she slipped by Joseph, she touched his forearm with a sense of relief. He was already pulling out some medium size poles from his bundle and leaning them against the wall. Rebekah cut the loaves into smaller pieces and carried them outside with a plate of sliced cheese.

"Will that be sufficient?" she questioned in Aramaic.

"Of course," responded the officer as he adjusted his stool against the wall. All three hungrily started to eat.

Next door, things were in a stir. Rebekah's sister, Joanna, and her husband, Ebron, lived in a slightly larger stone home about thirty yards away. The two houses were joined by rock walls in front and in back. The enclosed area contained a vegetable garden, pens for poultry and goats, a donkey shed, and a storage room for the dry goods that Heli sold at regional street markets.

Mary was at her aunt's home, spinning thread from a pile of shorn wool with her thirteen-year-old cousin, Rafaela, and caring for little Nina, Rebekah's youngest. Joanna's children had already reported the presence of Roman soldiers on the street. Joanna gathered all of them together to pray for God's protection when suddenly Teresa appeared at the door. The warning for Mary to hide carried an ominous undertone of danger that was real but unexplained.

Nazareth was a village without walls or security of any kind. The residents' primary protection was the obvious lack of anything worth stealing. Most of the men worked the fields and vineyards by day, leaving the women with little more than their wits and prayers to handle the demands of passing soldiers. The outright abduction of a teenage girl was not unheard of. As single daughters matured, they were a tremendous source of help to their families, but parents knew that, for their own protection, young women needed to marry and start their own families.

Mary whispered to Rafaela, "I won't tell you where I'm going so you won't have any secrets to hide. But at the ninth hour, go to the well and draw water. Someone will meet you there and ask if I can come home, okay?"

Joanna promised to take full responsibility for Nina as Mary borrowed an old mantle and lifted a clay water pot to her shoulder. She then slipped out the back gate and was gone.

Zig-zagging her way through the village, Mary came to a broad street that separated the Jewish and non-Jewish sectors of Nazareth. She paused to wrap her scarf tightly around her face and, when no one was in sight, disappeared into the non-Jewish, gentile neighborhood. A couple of turns later, she headed down a side street and paused under the open shutter of a small window, high on the wall of a small, nondescript house.

"Hadasha," she whispered out loud. The front door opened just as Mary turned the corner, and in the blink of an eye, she was inside.

"Mary! What a surprise to see you! I'll never forget that day when I twisted my ankle at the pool and none of the

Jewish women would help me carry my laundry home, except you. And then you got in trouble for doing it."

After a long hug, Mary pulled off her scarf and explained about the Roman soldiers. "I have no idea what's going on," she admitted, "I was next door but mother sent me a message that I should hide. No one will ever look for me here."

"But won't you get in trouble again for coming into our...what do you call it...our 'unclean,' gentile home?"

"Hadasha, believe me, staying out of foreigners' homes is not one of God's rules. We are supposed to love foreigners as much as we love ourselves. Our sacred writings point to a time when all races, all peoples, and all nations will praise God together. I am so sorry that my people insist on hiding their faith from your people. We were supposed to tell you about God, not turn our backs on you."

"Oh Mary, I know you are not like that." She gave Mary another long hug and then asked, "How can I help you? Shall I hide you in our bedroom?"

"No, just let me stay inside for a while. No one will come. If you would go to the cistern at the ninth hour, my cousin, Rafaela, will be there and she can tell you whether it's safe for me to return. There is so much I want to tell you, but first I think we should pray that God will convince the Romans to go away. My fiancé, Joseph, is building our home nearby and I don't want him to get involved. I have no idea what he might do."

"Honestly, Mary, I don't even know which God to talk to. So you pray and I will listen. Then, I want to hear all about Joseph."

Mary knelt down, placed her scarf over her head again and looked up. Words of love and adoration flowed out so freely that Hadasha felt compelled to kneel beside her. When Mary had finished, Hadasha added thoughtfully,

"Mary, if I were God, I would give you everything you asked for. But why are you so sure he hears you? You pray like you are talking to someone right here beside us. Is that possible?"

"Yes it is, Hadasha! Our creation story says that in the beginning, God said, 'Let's make people just like us.' I have a lot to learn about God but I know he's into relationships. He is loving, fair, forgiving, and truthful. And that's what we are supposed to be like, too. Hadasha, if I believe anything about God it's that he wants us to talk to him just like we talk to each other. Yes, I believe he is right here with us."

"I wish I could believe like you, Mary. But just because of a creation story? Aren't there lots of them? How do you know that yours is the right one? My father taught us some Greek stories about chaos and spirit gods who wanted to have sex with women, of course. But I don't know of any message from the gods that they made people like themselves or even care about us. Of course, the Greeks have temples for their gods and they have priests who do whatever it is that priests do. I don't know Mary. You are actually the best evidence I know of that God is there and cares about me. Now tell me about Joseph."

"Joseph is from Bersabe in the northern hills of Galilee. At seventeen, he was forced into Herod's labor pool at the port city of Caesarea. On an annual home leave, he stopped in Nazareth and saw the play where I sang and danced. He told my father he was interested in me and would return in a year. When he found us after we had moved and convinced my father that he was serious, his parents came to Nazareth to meet us. One year later, we were engaged. I was doubtful at first, but Joseph is really persistent. He's building a house for us and we plan to have a wedding in the spring."

Back at Mary's house, the soldiers had devoured most of their food and began to banter back and forth about the absence of pork in the Hebrew diet. The officer raised his voice and called out to Joseph,

"Hey, Carpenter, have your ever killed a man?"

"Five at one time, sir," responded Joseph without the slightest hesitation.

"And with what weapon?" the officer added.

"With a saw blade," interrupted one of the soldiers. The two snorted with laughter.

"Oh, I'm pretty good with an ax," said Joseph.

Among Roman soldiers, exaggeration and bluffing were the normal course of conversation. Rome ruled over the Mediterranean world with an iron fist and the legions were the backbone of its power. Military commanders sparred for the toughest assignments and the soldiers swaggered with arrogance. With little else to conquer, they turned to conversational skirmishes. The citing of imaginary feats of strength and prowess evoked laughter from fellow soldiers and provoked even rowdier claims in return. This insignificant Jewish carpenter was right in step with Roman bravado and had just scored a point.

Sensing it was his move, the officer called out,

"Carpenter, come out here."

As Joseph stepped outside, the centurion slid his short sword out of its sheath and handed it to Joseph, handle first.

"This is a real weapon, Carpenter, do you know what to do with it?"

Joseph took the weapon and respectfully examined the small insignia etched into the base of the blade. Admiringly, he said, "It's Italian, forged in the foundry of Etruscas on the Rubicon. An excellent sword, sir."

Joseph took a step back, bowed to its owner and said in Latin, "At your service, sir, by life or by death." He then whirled around and dropped into a fighting position, sword fully extended toward an unseen opponent.

The Romans were dumbfounded. These were a soldier's opening words in a competitive training exercise that marked the final graduation from basic training for the legions. Instinctively, the officer slammed his hand onto the wooden table and barked, "Go!"

Joseph exploded into a series of lightning blows, a powerful thrust, parries left and right. Suddenly, he pulled the blade high with both hands to thrust down on an opponent, but it was a feint. His back foot shot forward into an imaginary shield with a powerful kick.

Landing like a cat with the sword in the opposite hand, he repeated the entire series of blows, thrusts, and parries. Then, without warning, he dropped to the ground, slapping the dirt hard with his free hand and forearm. At the same instant, one foot swept with vengeance across the space to his front, upending an unseen opponent.

Back on his feet in a flash, Joseph struck at more opponents to the left and to the right. Then, with a final burst forward and a shout of victory, he threw the sword a full two strides ahead, burying the blade into the lone oak tree. All three horses lurched back against their tethering, eyes wide with fright.

The two soldiers swore by the gods with delight while the officer nodded grudgingly. Joseph wrenched the sword free from the tree trunk, laid it across both hands, and respectfully offered it back to its owner.

"That's a magnificent sword," said Joseph, "one of the best."

Dropping the sword back into its sheath, the officer queried,

"Where in the world did you learn that, son?"

"In Caesarea, sir, while working on the palace and other projects. Tribune Tavius Justus took three of us to work on his new home. One day he told me he needed my services privately as a sparring partner for his two small sons who wanted to learn sword fighting. As they improved, he enrolled me in basic sword training as a member of his private security force."

Joseph had obviously scored another point, and a big one at that. The officer stood to his feet and said,

"Carpenter, why don't you get on with your bench building. I have a final matter to discuss with the lady of this house."

Rebekah was completely shocked by Joseph's display of fighting skills. He had surprised her a number of times, but this was beyond comprehension. Sensing that the situation was now somewhat in her favor, she stepped out the door and asked,

"How may I be of help?"

"Just a small matter of business", the officer said. "I need a new housekeeper in Jerusalem. I pressed the beggar at the entrance into Nazareth for the names of any attractive, young women who might like to start new careers. He mentioned that one of Nazareth's most talented maidens was a girl named Mary. He said that she lives right here. Is Mary around?"

Rebekah's confidence drained away in an instant and she stuttered,

"She...ah, she's not here, and I'm not sure where she is."

Sensing that the officer might ask Rebekah to go and find Mary, Joseph rolled the dice one more time. "Truthfully, sir, Mary is my fiancé. We've been engaged for a year and plan to marry as soon as I finish building our home. I'm sure there are many other excellent possibilities for a housekeeper in Jerusalem."

The two soldiers listened quietly to see how this new duel of words would turn out.

"Well," said the officer, "Let's call her. I'll explain my offer and she can decide for herself. Or, maybe I'll decide for her. The beggar described her as a talented dancer and attractive young woman."

"Oh that she is," countered Joseph, "both inside and out. She's very religious, however, and would want you to convert to the Jewish faith. You know our priests forbid us from entering the houses of uncircumcised foreigners."

At this, the soldiers grimaced with suppressed laughter. One blurted out,

"This Hebrew is pretty handy with the sword, sir. He could probably perform the circumcision today."

His partner countered,

"Or maybe even use his saw."

They both roared with amusement. Trying to somehow cover for the officer's predicament, one soldier pushed the other forward and blurted out,

"And you are going to be first!"

Again they both broke into open laughter. The centurion's plan had degenerated into comedy. In a final attempt to regain his superiority, the officer turned to derision and disgust.

"Carpenter, stay here with maid Mary if you like and scratch out a miserable life under your Jewish laws. Or, wake up and embrace Rome. You have a future. Don't waste it on counters and table legs. Join Rome!"

At that he stormed off, mounted his horse, swore at his subordinates to get moving, and trotted through the village to the south. As the three passed Joseph's partially finished two-room house, the officer sneered again.

"Look, the carpenter chose this over a marble mansion with Tribune Tavius in Rome. Poor fool!"

Inside Rebekah's house, Joseph dropped to his knees and raised his hands above his head.

"Almighty God, thank you!"

Rebekah stood beside him with one hand to her chest. She gasped for breath and blurted out,

"Joseph, God bless you. Oh my goodness, thank you, thank you."

As Joseph stood to his feet, Rebekah grabbed his tunic with both hands and questioned,

"What's this about you killing five men and where did you learn all that sword stuff? Do I even know who you are and you want to marry my daughter?"

Joseph broke into a chuckle.

"Oh, that's just a soldier's form of entertainment. Whoever tells the biggest story wins. And the sword drill? I was planning to keep that secret. You know we aren't even allowed to own a sword under Roman law."

"I'm going to find Mary," declared Rebekah. She doesn't know how close she came to the end of her dreams today."

"Wait a little, Rebekah. Roman soldiers play a game of leaving and then doubling back to watch from a distance. We need to stick to our story."

Rebekah gave way to some pent-up feelings and recounted the fear and surprise she felt at each new turn of events in this Roman intrusion. In her mind, Joseph had risen to a whole new level of competency as the future protector of her daughter. Suddenly, Rebekah was on her feet again and blurted out,

"I can't wait any longer. I've got to find Mary. She is taking care of Nina, you know."

As she hurried out the side door and down the well-worn path to her sister's house, Rebekah's mind raced through various places that Mary might be hiding.

"Joanna," she called out, barely stopping at the door of her sister's home. "Where did Mary go? Oh, I'm so glad you have Nina," she said, swooping up her baby girl into her arms.

"Are the soldiers gone?" inquired Joanna as she stepped back from her kneading bowl.

"Yes, they're gone, thanks to God and thanks to Joseph, too." replied Rebekah. "But I don't know where to start. Tell me, do you know where Mary is?"

"No, we don't. She asked Rafaela to go to the cistern at the ninth hour and said that someone would meet her there."

"Oh my," complained Rebekah, "she doesn't know how close she came to being taken away. If Joseph hadn't been there, I don't know what we would have done. Let's go and find her right now."

"Rebekah, I think it would be better to follow Mary's plan. She's a bright girl and knows what she's doing. All of us waiting anxiously at the well could only make it harder. Why don't you and I go and hang up your laundry while Rafaela waits at the cistern."

Side by side, the two sisters walked along the path to Rebekah's home, each with a hand on little Nina who fell limp on their arms as they swung her back and forth. After Rebekah had recounted the dramatic events of the last two hours, she felt considerably relieved. The conversation moved on to their eldest sister, Elizabeth, who was married to a priest in the hill country of Judea.

"We haven't heard any news from Elizabeth this year, have we?" asked Joanna. I wonder if she and Zechariah are well. How old would she be now?"

"She will turn sixty next year. I'm sure that she is still struggling with the disappointment of not being able to conceive."

An hour passed and the two had barely finished hanging up the wet clothes when Rafaela and Mary stepped through the back gate.

"Mary," exclaimed Rebekah. "Where have you been? You don't know how close you came to being abducted today. Bartholomew told this Roman officer and his soldiers about your dancing and singing. He wanted you for a house keeper in Jerusalem! Oh my child, my daughter, whatever you are, I was so afraid until Joseph…"

"Until what, Mother? Did Joseph hammer some sense into their heads?" interrupted Mary as she and Rafaela broke into laughter.

Once again, Rebekah dramatically recounted the whole story, expressing her moments of greatest despair and utter surprise at Joseph's casual response to everything.

"It was like David slaying the giant!" she gasped as they paused together at the door.

A short ways away, Joseph was approaching with a thick, wooden plank on his shoulder. As he slid it gently to the ground, his eyes passed over the four and settled on Mary. A faint grin of success settled on his face, but he didn't know what to say.

"Mother," said Mary, "may I give Joseph a hug?"

"Well, okay," replied Rebekah. "After all, you owe him your freedom today."

Mary stepped up to Joseph and grabbed his tunic chest high with both hands, pulling him closer.

"Joseph," she said with her eyes locked on his and her face beaming with admiration, "Mother told me what you did today. Thank you for saving my life!"

Joseph's hands slid around her back and crossed until she was tightly snuggled in his arms. Three sets of feminine eyes were drinking in this moment of physical affection so rarely allowed publicly in Jewish culture, even among betrothed couples. Mary rested her head on Joseph's chest. He was lost in the bliss of their embrace as he closed his eyes and buried his face in her dark, cleanly-scented hair.

"Okay, Okay. That's enough. The victory has been celebrated," interrupted Rebekah.

As Joseph and Mary disentangled themselves, he announced,

"That was worth fighting a whole cohort of Romans for, Mary. I think I'll go out and find one right now!"

"Oh, no you won't," replied Rebekah firmly. "The party is over and I want my new counter finished."

FIRST MIRACLE

Zechariah's Vision

The sun had just peaked over the horizon when Zechariah and Elizabeth stepped into the cool morning air, secured the door of their two-room house in Beth Hakkerem, and headed toward Jerusalem. Their steps were slow and deliberate as they passed through the terraced vineyards surrounding their village and entered the main thoroughfare from the hill country to Jerusalem.

"Shalom," meaning "Peace," was Zechariah's simple greeting to the younger merchants and vendors that hurried past them on their way to the city. At sixty-five, Zechariah was feeling good about life. Born and trained to be a priest, he counted himself privileged to be a member of the tribe of Levi and a descendent of Moses' brother, Aaron. His eyesight had deteriorated, but his memory was keen and his convictions were strong. Zechariah even still enjoyed teaching lessons from memory in the Hebrew school at Beth Hakkerem's synagogue.

The time had come for him to help out once more at the temple in Jerusalem. He belonged to a division of priests by the name of Abijah. Twice a year, each division gathered its members in Jerusalem for a full week to carry out the exacting tasks of worship in the temple. After a lifetime in the priesthood, Zechariah and Elizabeth were well acquainted with the routine.

"You are amazing, Zechariah," observed Elizabeth, as a break in the commercial traffic enabled her to move up beside her husband. "Fifteen years ago you were supposed to retire from temple duties, but since they allow you to continue helping out wherever you can, we have never stopped coming. I am glad you still have the strength to do it. For me, this trip is always a fresh opportunity to pray and leave my personal expectations with God."

"Yes, dear, I know what you mean," replied Zechariah as he reached for her free hand and held it briefly. Five years younger than Zechariah, Elizabeth carried inside her a deep sadness for she was barren. All her married life, she had longed to have a baby to love and to care for. As other women in the village bore children, Elizabeth held them, fed them, and played with them, but she had none of her own.

One of the scrolls in the Jewish collection of sacred Scriptures, recorded the story of a childless woman in Israel named Hannah. This woman was a source of inspiration to Elizabeth because she had promised to give her child back to God if he would enable her to conceive. God had answered Hannah's prayer with a son, and the child became a great prophet by the name of Samuel. Elizabeth's prayers, however, remained unanswered.

With advancing age, Elizabeth knew that her childbearing years had long passed. Nothing short of a divine intervention could fulfill her deepest, inner yearning now. Maybe this time she would be able to fully let go of her disappointment and turn her longing into words of loving submission to God.

As she dropped back a few steps behind Zechariah, her heart turned to one of the Psalms that was written for worshippers heading for Jerusalem and the temple. Quietly, she prayed,

"Out of the depths I cry to you, O LORD; O Lord, hear my voice. Let your ears be attentive to my cry for mercy... I wait for the LORD, my soul waits, and in his word I put my hope. My soul waits for the Lord more than watchmen wait for the morning."

The sun was directly overhead when they reached the main road between Galilee and Jerusalem. Here they paused to rest under a tree. Elizabeth looked to the north and spoke of her younger sisters, three days away in Nazareth.

"How I would love to see Joanna and Rebekah. The last time was five years ago when Heli, Rebekah, and their children came to Jerusalem for Passover. We all stayed in Eldad's home."

Eldad was Elizabeth's younger brother. He was a priest, a respected scholar in Jerusalem, and a member of the Sadducee religious party. The Sadducees managed the temple and dominated the higher ranks of the Jewish religion. Zechariah and Elizabeth were looking forward to staying in Eldad's spacious home again, in spite of his air of condescension toward Zechariah, a common, country priest with no advanced education.

"Let's see," continued Elizabeth. "Levi would be eighteen, Mary sixteen, Aaron eleven, and Teresa nine. I remember it as if it was just yesterday...stroking Mary's head in my lap during that visit. The whole family was seeking comfort over the death of little Anna, Rebekah's youngest child at the time. Mary had such a good spirit but she couldn't understand why God would let Anna die. So I told her,

'I understand how you feel, Mary. God let Anna die and he never let any of my children be born. So, I am learning to trust Him, too, just like you are.' Mary sat up at that moment. She looked into my eyes and said, 'Oh Auntie, I never thought of it that way.'"

"We held each other for a long time," recalled Elizabeth as her eyes moistened and a tear rolled down her cheek. Reaching into her travel bag for a cloth, she prayed,

"Dear God, I would love so much to see Mary again."

The first glimpse of Jerusalem in the distance brought fresh energy to the tired travelers. Twelve years earlier, King Herod had begun to rebuild the Jewish temple on a grand scale. The enormous courtyard that surrounded the temple covered one sixth of the inner city. The temple itself was an awe-inspiring masterpiece of gleaming white sandstone and marble. It's sacred, central structure was complete and religious services were performed regularly. Zechariah couldn't help feeling excited about serving one more time in this magnificent setting.

By mid-afternoon, the aging pair had entered Jerusalem and was slowly pushing through the throngs of worshipers and commercial operatives. The city seemed more congested than ever. New shops of exotic, foreign articles had squeezed in between the traditional tailors, shoemakers, butchers, and bakers. Foreign languages and currencies added to the confusion.

Exhausted as she was, Elizabeth made a mental note of some places she wanted to visit while Zechariah checked on his assignment for the next day. His name was not on the list of priests who would carry out the morning sacrifice, so he could stay the first night at Eldad's home.

They were welcomed warmly by Eldad and his wife, Abigail. Their two-story home actually possessed a guest room with water drainage. After washing away the dust and tiredness of their journey, Zechariah and Elizabeth sat with their hosts and chatted over a light dinner. The conversation brought them up to date on Eldad and Abigal's children and then turned to their relatives in Nazareth.

"Our son passed through Nazareth four months ago," said Abigail. "He learned that Mary is engaged to a young man in his tenth and final year of forced labor in the port city of Caesarea. His name is Joseph and they say he is a bold and God-fearing member of the tribe of Judah. They plan to be married next year."

Zechariah and Elizabeth slept well that night and during the next two days, Zechariah assisted in an assortment of daytime tasks in the temple. On the third day he was thrilled to discover that he had been assigned to the ceremony of sacrifice and prayer the following morning. At dusk, he left to spend the night in the temple and Elizabeth promised to be there when the temple gates opened in the morning.

Together with his colleagues, Zechariah was reminded that the services they were going to perform the following day represented all Israelites everywhere. Their speech and conduct should be blameless and prayerful at all times. Following these instructions, they were allowed to rest a few hours until they were awakened in the pre-dawn darkness by an attendant to wash and dress themselves in clean garments.

After conducting an inspection of the temple courts by torchlight, the visiting priests gathered to receive their assignments. A random selection was made by drawing lots.

At the blush of dawn, one group of priests was selected to ascend the long ramp in front of the temple, to stir up the coals on the elevated altar of burnt offering, and add fresh wood. Then, a second drawing of lots selected others to carefully examine the sacrificial lamb, take its life, and lay it on the altar of burnt offerings.

Suddenly, a three-fold blast of silver trumpets reverberated through the courts of the temple and rang out over the walls and into the neighboring streets. Immediately, the main gates were opened and a wave of scurrying worshipers rushed across the Court of the Gentiles and congregated at the inner gates leading into the Court of Israel. Elizabeth had arrived early but was barely able to keep her footing in the surge across the enormous courtyard.

Before the inner gates were opened, a third lot was drawn for the highly honored assignment of entering the temple and placing sweet smelling spices on the altar of incense. This solemn task was only allowed once in a priest's lifetime. The incense represented the totality of Israel's prayers offered up to Almighty God. If there was ever a sense of united approval among the visiting priests about the one who was selected, it was that very morning. For the chosen priest was none other than Zechariah.

Over the years Zechariah had longed to be chosen for this task. Feeling a quiet stamp of divine approval, he felt elated and humbled at the same time. He quickly selected two long-time friends to accompany him. One left immediately to obtain a container of fresh coals from the altar of burnt offerings while Zechariah himself went to pick up the golden censer which contained the incense.

Moments later the inner gates were opened and the courtyard rapidly filled with morning worshipers. Elizabeth had tried her best to keep up with the men who rushed through the women's court and up fifteen steps to the large, brass-plated doors that led into the Court of Israel. On each side of these doors was a portico from which a few women could see the men, the priests, and the doors into the temple. Pressed against a column at one side, Elizabeth looked out across the kneeling men and searched for Zechariah.

Priests were ascending and descending the ramp to the altar of burnt offerings but Zechariah was not among them. Her search paused as two priests bound the feet of a small, white lamb and took its life. The lamb neither struggled nor cried out as its blood poured into a basin. Elizabeth closed her eyes but couldn't hold back her tears of compassion. She felt indebted to the lamb as it quietly surrendered its life. Should she not surrender herself and her expectations to God in the same way? Words of Scripture came to mind.

"Though he slay me, yet will I hope in him."

"Yes, God, I will trust you," she whispered.

Three priests were approaching the doors into the Holy Place, the first of two rooms inside the temple. The prolonged, low reverberation of a fixed air horn echoed throughout the temple mount, calling all to pause as Israel's prayers were symbolically offered up to God. Elizabeth needed only a glance at the three before she exclaimed,

"Oh my, Zechariah, you have been chosen!"

Her heart leaped and her eyes rose to the sky as she thanked God profusely. The doors to the Holy Place opened, and Zechariah disappeared inside with his two colleagues. Soon one returned bearing the previous day's ashes. Then the other, having placed bright new coals on the altar of incense, also returned and closed the door.

Zechariah waited for the signal to be given to approach the golden altar and spread incense across its glowing coals. Light flickered gently from the seven-branched candlestick to his left. To his right was the table of showbread. Outside in the men's court, worshipers were lying prostrate and silently whispering their most fervent prayers. Elizabeth offered her own prayer of gratefulness to God and desire to release to him her deepest disappointment.

"God Almighty, thank you for this gift to Zechariah. I reaffirm my surrender to the life you have chosen for me."

At the discreet ring of a bell, Zechariah approached the altar and spread incense across the coals. A cloud of sweet smelling smoke arose, creating a faint, rising glow. He bowed in worship and started to back away.

Suddenly, a commanding, angelic figure enveloped in vivid, white light appeared to the left of the altar. Intense fear gripped Zechariah as he fell to his knees. He would have prostrated himself but the voice of the angel demanded such immediate and total attention that he could neither move nor look away.

"Don't be afraid, Zechariah, your prayer has been heard. Your wife Elizabeth will bear a son and you are to name him John. He will be a joy and delight to you and many will rejoice because of his birth, for he will be great in the sight of the Lord. He is never to take wine or other fermented drink and he will be filled with the Holy Spirit even from birth. Many of the people of Israel will he bring back

to the Lord their God. He will go on before the Lord, in the spirit and power of Elijah, to turn the hearts of the fathers to their children and the disobedient to the wisdom of the righteous - to make ready a people prepared for the Lord."

It was Zechariah's turn to respond and he was completely overwhelmed. Every imaginable blessing God could give him had just been promised. But the whole crescendo of supernatural predictions seemed to rest on one fragile down beat. He and Elizabeth were to have a baby. And that wasn't just difficult, it was impossible! Regrettably, instead of saying, "Yes" or "Thank You," out came an expression of doubt.

"How can I be sure of this? I am an old man and my wife is well along in years."

Having, perhaps, never been questioned or even doubted by a human being, the angel identified himself.

"I am Gabriel…"

Zechariah knew the biblical record and knew Gabriel to be the "Might of God," the angel that God sent to Daniel to explain the future and predict the arrival of God's Messiah.

"If I could just take back my words," thought Zechariah as he dropped his head to the floor in complete abasement.

"I stand in the presence of God," continued Gabriel in a firm, ringing tone, *"and I have been sent to speak to you and tell you this good news. Now you will be silent and unable to speak until the day this happens, because you did not believe my words. They will be fulfilled at the right time."*

By now the crowd outside was stirring. Many were up on their knees, some even stood. The priest should have reappeared. Something was wrong. Elizabeth was up on her knees, too, and she feared the worst. Did Zechariah have a stroke? Had he erred in his duties? Did God strike him down? She grabbed the column beside her and pulled herself to her feet.

Inside, Zechariah opened his eyes, raised his head, and realized he was alone. Picking up the golden censer, he stood to his feet, and backed away from the altar. As he reached the door, he turned, pushed it open, and stepped out in view of the crowd.

Zechariah knew the priestly benediction by heart, but when he raised his voice to project it, no sound came out of his mouth. He tried some hand signals describing an angel, his inability to speak, and some wonderful news. No one understood anything.

Quickly, some supervising priests approached and escorted him down the steps while another gave the benediction. It was on that fateful walk that Zechariah understood the totality of his discipline. He could neither hear nor speak!

Elizabeth had gone through an array of emotions by this time. First came a wave of relief when Zechariah finally appeared, walking normally. Then came the shock that he was unable to speak. When other priests approached him, he seemed oblivious to their questions, as if he wasn't even hearing them. Was he deaf, too?

As they led him away, Elizabeth worked her way through the crowd of women and ran out the door of the women's court. Hurrying around to the side, she came to an entrance into the priests' quarters and knocked repeatedly. Finally, an attendant appeared and agreed to look inside for information about Zechariah. Eventually, she was ushered into a back room where a physician was examining her husband.

Elizabeth rushed to Zechariah, and he embraced her with complete recognition. He was totally unresponsive to her questions, however, and she quickly perceived that he was both deaf and dumb. The physician asked who she was and then explained his initial findings.

"Elizabeth, I haven't found any signs of injury or trauma. Zechariah's pulse rate is moderately faster but his temperature is normal. At this moment, I'm assuming that he had an age-related seizure that has affected his speech and hearing. My suggestion is that we let him rest for a few hours right here. Why don't you come back for him at noon."

As Elizabeth was leaving, she turned at the door for a final look at Zechariah. Oddly, he was looking straight at her and smiling broadly. His hand pointed to her, to him, and back to her.

"Something about us," she thought to herself. "It's a nice gesture, but why now?"

Mystified, Elizabeth turned away and left the priests' quarters. Feelings of surprise, perplexity, and doubt spiraled randomly through her mind as she traversed the city and entered Eldad's home. Abigail was there and provided the kind and listening ear that Elizabeth so desperately needed.

Back at the temple, Zechariah indicated that he wanted to write something. They brought him a page of papyrus, and he wrote in large letters,

"I had a vision. An angel appeared. He said my wife will have a son, and my son will be a great prophet."

By this time, the high priest had heard about the incident and came to see Zechariah. He inquired into Zechariah's education and history of service. It was evident that he was a commoner, a "rustic" priest from the countryside.

The high priest directed an assistant to write back to Zechariah, "Anything more?" When Zechariah penned the words, "The angel's name was Gabriel," the high priest expressed began to doubt the authenticity of Zechariah's vision. As a Sadducee, the high priest didn't regard Daniel's scroll as inspired Scripture and thought that Daniel's references to archangels named Michael and Gabriel were more reflective of Babylonian mysticism than of genuine Jewish revelation.

When the high priest learned that Zechariah's wife was barren and past the age for childbearing, that ended the matter. An angelic prediction that someone too old to have a baby would soon conceive was preposterous. Zechariah had obviously been caught up in the emotion of his assignment, suffered some kind of seizure, and was mixing together reality and imagination.

Elizabeth returned at noon as directed, and Zechariah was released to her keeping by the physician with instructions that she should bring him back the next day for further examination.

"Amazingly," observed the physician, "Zechariah exhibits no loss of memory or body control. He can't hear or speak, but responds normally to people around him. He recognizes his friends and can write their names on a tablet."

"I think I should tell you Zechariah's explanation of what occurred, Elizabeth. He has written to us that the angel, Gabriel, appeared to him and told him that you will give birth to a baby boy. In view of that, I would like to ask your age, if you don't mind."

"I am fifty-nine" responded Elizabeth. "But, wait. Are you saying that God sent an angel to tell my husband that I am going to conceive and bear a child? That has been my plea to God for forty years, so please tell me the truth!"

"Ma'am, all I am saying is what Zechariah wrote down. Whether it's true or not, I don't know. The high priest is inclined to believe that he suffered a seizure and is imagining the part about the angel and the baby. I am also telling you that his impairment is not like any seizure that I have treated before. Help him get some rest and let me know tomorrow if you observe anything new."

As soon as Zechariah was released by the physician, he took Elizabeth to an empty chamber in the temple and began mouthing words and gesticulating energetically. Little by little she pieced together his story. An angel had appeared in the temple and given him the message that she was going to have a son who should never take wine or fermented drink.

Elizabeth could hardly believe what she was learning. The angel's message had a lot to do with her! It was a dramatic affirmation that God had heard their prayers for a child and he was answering them. She desperately wanted to believe, but why was such a wonderful message obscured by Zechariah's senseless disabilities?

Elizabeth knelt and bowed to the ground with her face in her hands; she had no choice but to believe. When she could feel the presence of a baby in her womb, she would gladly display a fuller expression of excitement and gratefulness to God. Pregnancy at her age would be an amazing miracle for all to see.

A day later, the high priest gave his report to the Sanhedrin, a ruling body of seventy priests who were allowed by Herod to manage the Jews' religious and social affairs. A decision was reached that priests above the age of fifty could not participate in any of the special assignments for which there was a drawing of lots.

The permanent priests in Jerusalem maintained a strict hierarchy of position and privilege. They were well educated and well remunerated. As a favor to the outlying members of their tribe, they made several medical and hygienic services available to those who came each week to carry out the work in the temple. There was even a fund that priests could draw on to replace worn-out garment or sandals.

On the morning after Zechariah's vision, he seemed perfectly normal except for the complete loss of speech and hearing. He indicated his wish that Elizabeth accompany him to the temple where he led her to a room designated "Visiting Priest Services". First of all, he had his hair and beard trimmed and then led Elizabeth to a counter where funds were provided for the purchase of clothing. Elizabeth spoke to the attendant,

"I believe he would like to purchase a new mantle and tunic."

When the appropriate currency was produced, Zechariah signaled, "Not one, but two!" Somehow his energetic insistence and clean-cut appearance convinced the attendant that he had no choice but to double the request.

Zechariah led the way to a clothing shop where he picked out a new mantle and tunic. Then, to her surprise, he steered Elizabeth to the women's section and indicated that she should pick out a garment as well. Elizabeth disagreed but Zechariah simply shrugged his shoulders and pointed to his ears. He couldn't be argued with.

As they were leaving, a table of children's clothing caught Elizabeth's eye. She paused to hold up a little boy's outfit and a fountain of repressed feelings welled up, moving her to tears. Zechariah could only watch sympathetically as she held it close and whispered,

"Oh, God, after forty years, has my time really come?"

Sensing the deep significance of this moment, Zechariah took the item to the attendant, pointed to his ears, shook his head, and handed the man his coin purse. At that, the shop owner, who had been watching from a distance, stepped in and carefully folded up the outfit. He closed Zechariah's purse and handed both the outfit and purse to Elizabeth. As he ushered them to the entrance, only Elizabeth heard him say,

"We are so sorry for your loss ma'am. Please accept our condolences."

Age and wisdom brought a tender smile to Elizabeth's tear stained face. She accepted his kindness, knowing that no amount of explanation could even begin to clarify their real situation.

That evening and the next day were the Sabbath, so the two attended the morning sacrifice together. Elizabeth had no idea what Zechariah was thinking but she liked his enthusiasm. She was slowly embracing the idea that he really did see an angel, and her heart was shifting from doubt to gratefulness and joy. In the women's court, she lifted up her hands in prayer and surrendered herself to be a willing recipient of God's goodness, including the miracle of a son. She wanted to shout the news to the entire courtyard, but realized that she didn't have the freedom yet to share this news with anyone. For now, it was a secret.

Back home in Beth Hakkerem, Zechariah and Elizabeth began a new chapter in their lives. As word spread through the village that Zechariah had suffered some kind of impairment in the temple, the villagers came by to have a look at him and convey their sympathy.

Oddly, with his hair cut and beard trimmed, Zechariah looked perfectly healthy. He was quickly bored with visitors though, and looked for some physical task to perform while Elizabeth conversed with their friends. Strangely, Elizabeth seemed almost too happy, considering the gravity of her husband's loss of speech and hearing.

Zechariah was dismissed from all teaching activities at the synagogue. He came every day, however, set aside his mantle and took on every cleaning assignment he could find. At home, he wore short-sleeved tunics, worked in the garden, milked the goats, and helped Elizabeth with her daily chores. In the early evening, you could find the two strolling in the surrounding hills, stopping here and there to act out some idea, and then laughing about it.

"How romantic," commented the other women in the village, "Could a seizure do this for us?"

One morning, Elizabeth felt some light nausea and stayed in bed for a couple of hours. She blamed it on something she had eaten and soon the symptom passed. The next morning, the nausea returned, and with it, a sense of sluggishness. On the third day, it happened again but she got up to work through it. A feeling of dizziness immediately came over her and she was forced to lie down.

That afternoon, Elizabeth went to see a good friend who was knowledgeable about women's illnesses and described her symptoms.

"How old are you Elizabeth?" the friend asked.

"Fifty-nine," she replied.

"Well," said her friend, "you can rule out pregnancy, although those are exactly the symptoms. I think you simply have a light case of the flu; there is always something going around."

Elizabeth rushed home. Seeing Zechariah in the garden, she ran in his direction calling out,

"Zechariah, I am pregnant!"

Zechariah didn't even look her way, so she grabbed his face with both hands and slowly mouthed the words,

"I have a baby!"

Bewilderment crossed his face, followed by a look of curiosity. Elizabeth patted her stomach and rocked her two arms in front of her.

Zechariah completely lost his composure. Leaping up and down, he threw the hoe aside and tried to shout but nothing came out. He danced in circles and then knelt in front of Elizabeth. With his ear to her abdomen, he raised his hands and mouthed the words,

"It's true, it's true. Thank you, God, thank you."

Their celebration lasted into the evening. Zechariah had one last jug of wine left from the previous season and he filled two cups, but Elizabeth shook her head.

"No, thank you. My son will be a Nazarite, and that means no fermented drink for him or for me."

Perceiving that her response was negative, Zechariah downed them both. His next question for Elizabeth was who they should tell.

"Eldad and Abigail?" he mouthed and pointed in the direction of Jerusalem.

"No," said Elizabeth, shaking her head.

"The high priest?" Zechariah described.

Again, "No".

"The villagers?" Also "No".

So Elizabeth wanted to keep it a secret.

"Where will you stay?" questioned Zechariah with an array of hand motions.

"Right here," Elizabeth signaled. If he understood correctly, Elizabeth wanted to stay at home, living normally, but keeping her pregnancy a secret.

"For five months," she counted out on a calendar.

"Then a big party!" she motioned by opening the door, pulling her tunic tight across her abdomen, and dancing in a circle.

The joy and amazement over God's miraculous intervention into their lives was impossible for Zechariah and Elizabeth to put into words. The most they could do was to look deeply into each other's eyes and trade an array of meaningful facial expressions and mouthed words. They knew that they were part of something bigger and it had to do with God's Messiah. It never occurred to them, however, that the angel of God might soon be approaching Nazareth.

SECOND MIRACLE

Mary's Vision

Joseph's release from service in Caesarea and arrival in Nazareth lifted the excitement and attraction between he and Mary to a whole new level. When Heli was out of town, Rebekah felt responsible to control the emotionally-charged relationship between the two.

One Sabbath afternoon, Rebekah suggested that they could have a private conversation on a bench in the vegetable garden between her home and Joanna's. She recalled that getting to know Heli before their marriage was something that simply hadn't occurred. She was only fourteen at the time and her parents made all of the decisions. She and Heli were never even allowed to be alone together during their courtship.

"Can you believe this, Mary?" began Joseph as they sat down together. "We met three years ago and today we finally have permission to talk together without someone listening. I have imagined this conversation a hundred times in my head, but now that the opportunity has come, I'm not sure where to begin."

"Well, actually we did have a private conversation the day we met," laughed Mary. "You volunteered to help me carry costumes and stuff to the rabbi's house after the play.

We didn't have permission to talk that day and I got into a lot of trouble afterward."

"I hope you'll be happy with me," continued Mary. "I'm just a country girl from Nazareth and you've had all those amazing experiences in construction work, even serving on the staff of a Roman tribune. I still can't believe that the tribune gave you his horse, Zephyrus. That's way beyond my little world, Joseph. Are you really sure about us?"

"Mary, ever since I saw you dance and sing three years ago, I've been sure about us. You are beautiful and courageous and have this quiet confidence in God. Everything I know about you makes me happy. You are a gift from God and I love you with all of my heart."

Mary enjoyed Joseph's passionate declaration of affection and instinctively watched his face. Older than most brides of her day, she had developed the maturity to measure a man's sincerity by watching his eyes more than hearing his words.

Joseph relished Mary's secure, unembarrassed composure in conversation. As a smile of trust and admiration crossed her face, he felt more captivated than ever by her sweet spirit and longed to take her into his arms. His open hand was resting on the bench between them and Mary gently placed her hand in his.

"I told mother that I might hold your hand today, if you wished. She thought it was too soon, of course, and said that she didn't hold father's hand until after they were married. If we start now, maybe it will become a lifelong habit. Wouldn't that be a shock to our culture? Tell me, Joseph, how come you are so sure of yourself?"

Joseph paused, enamored with Mary's hand nestled in his. It was so small, delicate, and perfectly formed. He wanted to lift it to his lips, but held back.

"How come I am so sure of myself? Hmmm…You know my admiration for Joseph, whom Moses wrote about in the Torah. Joseph has always been my hero. No matter how badly he was treated, he had this sense of destiny that God was going to work things out. I have tried to maintain that same confidence and God has opened doors for me that were beyond my expectations. Meeting you, for example, was an impossible dream that came true."

"The rabbi in Caesarea encouraged me to see Joseph and Daniel as models for slave laborers. He told me not to feel sorry for myself but to trust God like they did. Those two were swept up out of nowhere and placed in the service of kings. So who knows where our story will take us?"

"I like your confidence, Joseph, but it's a little scary. My world is really small compared to yours. I think my biggest adventure so far has been learning how to read and write Hebrew. My brother, Levi, let me do his homework, and mother encouraged it since father was gone a lot. Do you remember Judith, the rabbi's wife? She also knows how to read and lets me help her teach stories about women in the Scriptures to young girls on Sabbath afternoons. In fact, we are meeting later today."

"And just like you, I have a heroine in the Torah. As long as I can remember, I wanted to be a prophetess like Miriam, Moses' sister. Of course, just like you and Joseph, Miriam and I have the same name in Hebrew. When God delivered our people from slavery in Egypt, she took a tambourine and led the women in dancing and singing songs of praise to God. That's what I want to do for our people someday."

"When the rabbis read from the Torah, and from the prophets, and especially from the writings that can be sung," continued Mary, "I have always felt close to God. He is so real to me. I know he is right here listening to us. I love him deeply and want to please him. It really makes me happy when I'm singing to him."

"And when you sing, everyone else picks up your happiness, too," commented Joseph. "I can still remember all of the villagers, myself included, singing the last line of your song about Immanuel at the end of that play. We couldn't help ourselves. We sang it over and over until the rabbi stood up and stopped us. Have you thought of any new songs lately? I'm always hoping to hear you sing one."

"Now you're getting sure of yourself again! But here's one from a favorite psalm. I sing it to God every day."

"Yet I am always with you;
   You hold me by my hand.
   You guide me with your counsel
   and will take me to your glorious land.
   Whom have I in heaven but you?
   There's nothing on earth I'd rather live for.
   If my body and soul cannot survive,
   God will keep my heart alive,
   And be my portion forevermore."

"That was beautiful," said Joseph admiringly. "It gave me the impression that you are closer to God than I am. How can you be sure about me?"

"Well, I wasn't sure at first. I wanted to be like Miriam, and thought that she never married. Do you know how you won me over?" Mary asked.

"When you came back two years ago, we had lost our home and moved to the edge of town. I was amazed that you searched for us and found us. When you told me that you had been thinking about me all year long and did a lot of kind things for me, I was overwhelmed. We were penniless at the time. You had my broken sandals fixed and even bought me a new pair. That's when I began to think that maybe we were supposed to be together."

"Mary, I don't believe I have ever known a girl who is so passionate about her faith. You inspire the faith of others, too. I could see it in the faces of those young girls around you at the synagogue this morning. They love you, they trust you, and I do, too."

The conversation that day was a rare and romantic exception to the demanding pace of life in Nazareth. Mary's week was filled with homemaking activities. She and her mother shared the tasks of grinding sccds into flour, baking bread in an outdoor oven, replanting the vegetable garden with winter varieties, milking the goats, raising chickens, making clothes and buying items at the central street market. With Joseph around to share the evening meal, the challenge of preparing enough food had grown considerably.

For his part, Joseph was excited about building a house in Nazareth and launched into an ambitious plan that drew from his ten years of experience in construction. Riding on Zephyrus, he arranged for beams and poles to be sent from his family's tree cutting business in Bersabe. In the Valley of Jezreel he purchased kiln-dried bricks at one of the clay pits that supplied Herod's construction sites.

Three months flew by and one task after another fell into place to the astonishment of Heli and his friends. As the farmers were planting wheat and barley in the month of October, Joseph was applying the first coat of stucco to the adobe brick walls of his house. The tightly lashed poles on top were strong and the well-packed clay that covered them easily drained off the earlier, light rainfall. When the heavier winter rains finally came, the house was closed in.

One day, the weather broke and the sun came out unexpectedly. That was the day when the tranquility of their lives was sabotaged by the Roman centurion and two soldiers who wanted to abduct Mary. Everyone was still talking about Joseph's ability to disarm the situation and rescue Mary.

Late the next day, Heli and Levi arrived, tired and hungry from their trip. Joseph helped Levi unload the goods and care for the donkey while Heli sat with Rebekah and listened to her gripping story. Mary was cheerfully humming a song to little Nina while heating up the lamb and potato stew and placing the meal on the table.

As night fell, small, clay oil lamps were lit in the eating area of Heli's small home. Here, the hungry family gathered and repeated together the Shema, Israel's sacred confession.

"Hear O Israel: The LORD our God, the LORD is one.
Love the LORD your God with all your heart and
with all your soul and with all your strength..."

After repeating the entire confession, Heli gave thanks for God's protection and provisions. Then, everyone settled down on mats and rugs around the low wooden table spread with fresh barley bread, lamb and potato stew, olives, cheese, nuts, and dates.

"Well," announced Heli after the most urgent pangs of hunger had been quieted, "Levi and I dash off to Capernaum during a break in the weather and when we get back, everyone is talking about Joseph single-handedly rescuing my daughter from abduction by a Roman centurion."

"Joseph, I am enormously grateful. You did the right thing and have in every way earned the hand of my daughter in marriage. I can't thank you enough."

"Of course, if anyone cares to thank us, too, for trudging through twenty miles of muddy, washed out roads to sell enough goods to support our family for a week or two, you are welcome to say so."

"Daddy, I saw Joseph do this fighting stuff with the centurion's sword," burst out Teresa, sitting proudly next to Joseph. "It was so amazing! The soldier's horses got scared and almost ran away."

"Heli, you are right and we do thank you for your work," interjected Rebekah in her conciliatory fashion. "And isn't it wonderful to finally have a second man around so you don't have to worry so much about us when you are away on trading business?"

"Excuse me!" snapped Levi. "It seems to me that there are three men around this table. And who do you think guards our payload when father is off talking politics with the other traders? Last night, I single-handedly thrashed three thieves who tried to make off with some of our salted fish."

Mary glanced at her mother and caught the slight hint of amusement in her face. Earlier that day, Rebekah had commented,

"Watch the conversation tonight. We have three male egos that will be in serious competition. It's the way men are. Our job is to serve up enough food and affirmation to leave them with full stomachs and full chests, if you know what I mean."

Mary smiled knowingly at her mother's attempt to deftly affirm all the men but, after years of sibling rivalry, she couldn't resist questioning Levi's story.

"So, Levi, were these three invaders twelve-year olds, or what?"

Everyone chuckled but didn't anticipate that Aaron would step in for the kill.

"No, they were girls."

The family snickered loudly. Levi grimaced wryly and tried to even the score.

"Good one, you little scroll mole. And what did you learn in Hebrew school today? Do you even know the difference between boys and girls or does that come up in next year's lessons?"

With her wedding only a few months away, Mary was allowed to sit next to Joseph at family meals. Occasionally, their hands drifted together under the table. Aaron and Teresa were quick to spot this and accuse them loudly of an impropriety. Joseph loved the little game and vigorously defended himself and Mary.

"Come on guys," he said to his young fans one night. "I bumped into a cactus plant today and Mary is just pulling out the needles."

"Right!" groaned Aaron. "Every time you come over here you put your hand in the cactus."

"Tomorrow he's going to fall on the cactus," roared Levi.

Heli and Levi were traveling less because the roads were often impassable for a donkey cart in winter. With Joseph regularly at the table, Heli's income was strained to the limit. One day, Teresa was alone with her mother and quietly whispered,

"Mother, you know the jar where you keep your food money? Well, I saw Joseph with his hand in the jar. Do you think he took out some money?"

"Can you keep a secret, Teresa?" said Rebekah.

"Yes," replied Teresa hesitantly.

"Well," went on Rebekah, "Joseph wasn't taking money out of the jar, he was putting money into it. Do you remember how often we used to run out of money and had to borrow from Aunt Joanna or just skip eating for a day or two? Since Joseph came to town, our food jar has never run out once. Maybe tonight you can give him a big hug and he won't even know why. But you and I will know, okay?"

That night, Joseph did get a long hug from Teresa, and even Mary asked,

"What was that all about?"

That evening, the rain stopped and the clouds cleared away. Everyone stepped outside in the cold just to see the beautiful, full moon. Joseph and Mary lingered an extra minute by themselves.

"Mary, when can I take you home with me?" Joseph whispered.

"In three months," she whispered back. "When the almond trees bloom, I'll be yours."

Mary slipped back into the house and locked the door. The kitchen lamps were out already and only one small lamp flickered in the backroom. Everyone was hurriedly pulling off their outer clothes and putting on their warmest sleeping garments.

Heli and Rebekah had a raised bed in the corner, while the grandmother slept on a pallet in the middle. Each of the children unrolled a woven mat, a straw-filled cushion, and a wool sleeping pad on top of that. One by one they adjusted their bedding, pulled their thick woolen blankets over themselves, and rocked from side to side until the edges were completely tucked in. Rebekah inquired with a yawn, "Everybody ready?"

A mumble of "Good Nights" came from under the blankets and Rebekah blew out the lamp.

Mary's mind launched into a prayer of gratefulness.

"Dear God, everything I have ever wanted you have given to me. Thank you for life, for health, for family, and for Joseph. I trusted you and you have given me the desires of my heart. I offer myself and the years ahead to you. Please come, Immanuel, please come soon."

Warm, comfortable, and deeply content, Mary slipped into a quiet sleep that could have lasted until morning.

Suddenly, a subdued light penetrated Mary's head scarf, and she awoke with a start. The light was coming from the kitchen with a steady glow that she had never seen before. Instinctively, she tightened her headdress and sat up. The others were sound asleep, seven mounds of wool lying perfectly still. Mary stood up, tightened her robe, and stepped through the doorway. She immediately dropped to her knees.

An illuminated, angelic figure approached her, passing right through the low table on the kitchen floor. Mary's thoughts instantly grasped for a supernatural explanation.

"Had she died? Was she being taken up into heaven? Was this God's messenger? Was it Michael or Gabriel?"

Her heart told her yes, and she fell forward with her face to the floor. The angel touched her, lifted her to her knees again, and greeted her.

"Greetings, you who are highly favored! The Lord is with you."

Mary was troubled. To be singled out by an angel and greeted so warmly was a level of divine favor beyond anything she could imagine. Was this a prelude to being rebuked for her failings? With her hands clasped together, she began to tremble.

"Do not be afraid, Mary, you have found favor with God. You will be with child and give birth to a son, and you are to give him the name Jesus. He will great and will be called the Son of the Most High. The Lord God will give him the throne of his father David, and he will reign over the house of Jacob forever; his kingdom will never end."

Mary knew exactly what this meant. It was Isaiah's prophecy about a virgin giving birth to a son whom she would call Immanuel. Didn't every young girl from David's successive generations secretly hope for this? But she was betrothed to Joseph. Would Joseph father the child after their wedding? Somewhat perplexed, she inquired,

"How will this be, since I am a virgin?"

"The Holy Spirit will come upon you, and the power of the Most High will overshadow you. So the holy one to be born will be called the Son of God. Even Elizabeth your relative is going to have a child in her old age, and she who was said to be barren is in her sixth month. For nothing is impossible with God."

Convinced and surrendered, Mary bowed her head to the floor and responded simply,

"I am the Lord's servant. May it be to me as you have said."

A moment of silence ensued. When Mary opened her eyes, she was alone and the angel was gone. After glancing into the back room where her family continued sleeping undisturbed, Mary sat down on a stool and pinched her forearm hard. She then gathered her thoughts, fell to her knees again, and whispered a prayer,

"Dear God Almighty, what am I to think? Why would you pick me, a poor, simple girl from Nazareth to bear your Anointed One? It's beyond my comprehension. No one will believe me. I am not even sure that Joseph will believe me. But yes, I will do it. Please help me to think calmly and understand what I should do next."

Sitting in the dark, Mary retraced the words of the angel. When she was sure she could remember everything, she let her thoughts roam across the many new insights the angel had given her about the Messiah. The Messiah would be divinely conceived and have no human father. That left Joseph out. But if conception occurred outside of her marriage to Joseph, she could be stoned under Jewish law. No apparent resolution came to mind. Did God want this birth to happen quietly and in secret? Didn't the whole nation want to know about this? Again, she had no answer.

Another thing, her parents were not awakened by the angel; just her. Why would they believe her? Why would Joseph believe her? How could she prove that God's messenger had spoken to her? Was she convinced? Yes. It really happened and she could never deny it. When she conceived, she would have only one story to tell. An angel of God spoke to her this very night, in this very house.

What should she do? Wake up her parents and tell them everything? No, wait. There was Aunt Elizabeth. If she was expecting too, then a miraculous story was already underway. The angel gave her that clue for a reason. If she could just talk to Elizabeth and see the baby in her womb, all doubts would be erased.

That settled it. Somehow, someway, she had to go to Judea immediately. She couldn't reveal the vision to anyone yet, just to Elizabeth. When her own pregnancy was undeniable, she would return and tell her parents and Joseph. Poor Joseph! But Joseph had surprised her before. If any groom could find his way through this, it would be Joseph.

Mary retrieved a coal from the oven outside, lit a lamp in the kitchen, and copied down her conversation with the angel on a papyrus sheet from her father's work records. She then entered the bedroom and gently shook her parents.

"I have something important to tell you, please come to the kitchen and leave the others sleeping," Mary whispered. When they were all in the kitchen, Mary continued,

"I have been awake a long time this morning, Mother, and feel an urgent need to visit my aunt, Elizabeth. I have never felt so strongly about something like this before. You know my distrust of people who say that God wants them to do this or that. Well, this time I'm the one who is saying it. Will you help me get there?"

Doubts, concerns about the weather, dangers of traveling alone, her wedding, it all came up. But Mary was resolute. Finally, Joseph was called and he listened to Mary's explanation. Joseph loved Mary deeply and he trusted her judgment. When anyone contemplated taking a bold step in life, Joseph was inclined to be supportive. It was his approach to life and he took Mary's side. Transportation, however, in the dead of winter was another matter. Finally, Joseph spoke his mind.

"I don't trust any of these caravans with Mary. I want to take her there myself on Zephyrus. Alone, I could make the trip in two days easily. With two of us, maybe three or four days. I'll get her a space with the women at the rest stops in Nain, Scythopolis, Sychar, and Bethel. It all depends on the weather, but we'll reach the hills of Judea on the fourth or fifth day."

"Absolutely not!" declared Rebekah. "I don't trust you two on foot or on horseback. And Mary is not staying in a Samaritan town. That's entirely out of the question. What would people say here in Nazareth?"

The arguments went back and forth until finally Levi, who had been listening since Joseph came in, spoke up,

"Listen, I'll go with them. Someone will always be walking. We'll just rotate around. Joseph, will you let me ride Zephyrus alone at least some of the time?"

"Sure, I will," laughed Joseph and then continued, "I have some business to take care of in Jerusalem and need to make the trip anyway. When I'm finished, I'll have some silver denarii coins to leave with Mary."

Eventually, Joseph's plan was begrudgingly agreed to by Heli and Rebekah. Since the winter rains were falling again, the three waited until there was another break in the weather. One morning, when day dawned under cloudless skies, they packed up quickly and left.

By the afternoon of the fourth day, the travelers reached the village of Beth Hakkerem in the hill country west of Jerusalem. Levi had been to Zechariah and Elizabeth's home seven years earlier, when his family came to Jerusalem for Passover. But this time, he was unable to find it. Mary had never been there, so they inquired at the synagogue for directions and learned the exact location.

When they finally spotted the house a short ways ahead, Mary stopped the others and asked if they would let her proceed to the house alone. It was a strange request given the consensus with which they had decided everything on the trip so far. Levi objected to being denied a chance to greet his aunt and uncle but Joseph, once again, defended Mary.

So, they worked out a plan. In two days at noon, Joseph, Levi, and Zephyrus would be in front of the synagogue. Mary was to come there and let them know if she was okay and tell them what news they could take home. Joseph asked her to find out how long she needed to be in Beth Hakkerem and when he could come back to get her.

"After all, Mary," he said, "the almond trees will bloom in three months."

"Don't worry," she replied. "I'll be ready."

Mary took her bedroll and extra clothes and walked confidently up the road to Elizabeth's house. She was out of earshot, but Joseph watched her clap her hands and wait for someone to appear. The door opened and a gray-haired woman stepped out. There was a very emotional greeting as the two embraced each other for a long time. They then turned, arm in arm, and entered the house.

"Funny thing," commented Levi. "That looked like Aunt Elizabeth all right, but I had the impression that she was pregnant. But that's impossible. Mother says she was always barren and now she is too old to bear children. She must have put on some weight."

"We'll find out in a couple of days," observed Joseph. "For now, let's head to Jerusalem. I want to show you some of Herod's other architectural accomplishments aside from the temple."

THIRD MIRACLE

Elizabeth's Greeting

Seated on a wood bench at the side of his house, Zechariah
pulled a thick, wool blanket tightly around his shoulders and
leaned back against the rough, earthen stucco. The hill country of Judea was in the grip of winter, but a bright sun bathed
the eastern side of Beth Hakkerem's humble homes that
morning. Zechariah closed his eyes and raised his face to
soak in the warm sunlight.

Eventually, he reached inside his cloak and retrieved
three papyri manuscripts. After returning from Jerusalem six
months earlier, he had written out word for word the message given to him by the angel, Gabriel. The letters were
large and deliberately transcribed. Shielding his eyes from
the bright sun, he read them slowly to himself. He then slid
them back into his clothing and repeated the final line in his
mind.

"And n*ow you will be silent and not able to speak until
the day this happens...*"

"Until what happens?" Zechariah wondered. "Until
Elizabeth conceives?"

No, that had occurred and he was still impaired.
"Until John is born?"

"Hopefully, yes," he thought to himself. But if that were true, he was destined for another four months of divine discipline.

Two months earlier, Zechariah had shown the first two pages of Gabriel's message to Rabbi Shemaiah, a close friend. This man, in turn, read them to Elizabeth. When Elizabeth heard the full account, she was surprised to learn that the angel had mentioned her by name.

The message was longer than she had previously imagined and gave several details about their son and his mission to Israel. They were to name him John and, from birth, he was to keep the Nazarite vow of total abstinence from grapes and alcoholic drink. The angel's final words indicated that John would prepare a people for the Lord.

"Does that mean what I think it means?" Elizabeth wondered. This was stunning. Her son was to be a herald to the Messiah. Suddenly, it flashed across her mind that while she was anticipating John's birth, somewhere in Israel there might be another woman waiting to give birth to Israel's coming Messianic King.

"Would she be an elderly woman like herself or a young mother?"

"Why, of course," she suddenly remembered. "There is Isaiah's prophecy, known to every Jewish woman. *'The virgin will be with child and will give birth to a son, and will call him Immanuel.'* So she will be a young girl, not even married yet."

That thought gave to Elizabeth a deep, inner contentment about her own miraculous pregnancy. She was not alone. Today, however, was the day that Elizabeth had chosen to invite her friends to her home to reveal her true condition. It made her smile when she thought of the invitation she had sent them through a young niece,

"Today is Elizabeth's sixtieth birthday! Please stop by this afternoon and help her celebrate."

Elizabeth had not left her house for five months except for a few short walks after dark. When friends came by, she was often lying in bed. Her excuse was that she didn't feel well, and really, that was quite true. She had experienced both morning sickness and chronic tiredness.

"How will I ever make it through nine months?" she often wondered.

In her spirit, though, Elizabeth was profoundly affirmed and poured out her praises to God. Many times Zechariah found her sitting in their rocking chair, and a pillow supporting her lower back. With eyes closed and hands resting on her unborn child, she would be singing a favorite psalm. Her love for God was greater than ever before, and that's what kept her going.

When her friends in Beth Hakkerem arrived in the middle of the afternoon, Zechariah met them at the door and signaled for them to come inside. Elizabeth was seated with a folded blanket across her lap. The women seated themselves around her on the floor.

"My dear friends," she began. "I have not seen many of you during the last five months. Perhaps you heard that I was not feeling well or that I was experiencing exhaustion or had the flu. It's time that you all know the truth. God has graciously answered our prayer of many years and showed us that nothing is impossible with him. In my fifty-ninth year, he gave me this!"

Elizabeth pushed the blanket off, stood up, and pulled her garment tight to show her enlarged abdomen. The women gasped and clapped for joy. They encircled Elizabeth to embrace her and feel her baby. Every possible exclamation of surprise and excitement was voiced during the next few minutes.

"It's not possible," one friend exclaimed. "It's a miracle," cried another. "Why didn't you tell us?" said a third.

"Please," said Elizabeth, "let's give all the credit to God who makes the impossible possible."

Then came the questions. Elizabeth described the day in Jerusalem from her point of view and tried to downplay Zechariah's condition as a comprehensible effect of being confronted by a real angel. When she realized that she couldn't answer all their questions and the women wanted to carry the news throughout the village, she stood and said,

"Before you go, Please come to my table and help me celebrate this occasion,"

The fresh honey bread and cups of hot tea were distributed as more questions and expression of amazement continued to flow between the women.

When everyone had left, Elizabeth sat down exhausted but happy. Zechariah smiled broadly, shook his head and hands with expressions of success, and picked up the plates and leftovers.

The following days were marked by intermittent clouds and sunshine. One morning, Zechariah spent a few hours cleaning the entrance to the synagogue and observing the boys in the Hebrew classes he had previously taught. After lunch, he fell asleep in the bedroom of his home.

Elizabeth sat down to rest her back when two hands clapped in front of her house. A distantly familiar voice called her name. She opened the door and saw a young woman that reminded her of someone she might know.

"Hi, Aunt Elizabeth. It's me, Mary, from Nazareth."

At Mary's first words, Elizabeth's baby jumped inside her. Not just once, but repeatedly. A divinely guided insight swept into her mind with the astounding revelation that her niece, Mary, was the mother of God's Messiah!

"Mary," Elizabeth burst out,

"Blessed are you among women, and blessed is the child you will bear! But why am I so favored, that the mother of my Lord should come to me? As soon as the sound of your greeting reached my ears, the baby in my womb leaped for joy. Blessed is she who has believed that what the Lord has said to her will be accomplished!"

"Aunt Elizabeth," replied Mary. "You can't imagine what it means to me to hear what you are saying. I had no one to talk to and here you are confirming everything."

The two fell into a long, tight embrace. They finally separated and touched one another's faces as tears of joy ran down their cheeks. Arm in arm, they entered the house, united in an adventure of such amazing significance that they hardly knew where to begin. Mary placed her hand on Elizabeth's abdomen and baby John jumped again. When Elizabeth asked how far along she was, Mary laughed candidly.

"Oh, Auntie, I have no idea. Ten days ago an angel told me that God would surround me with his power and fill me with his Spirit. I don't have to do a thing. It's a little scary since I am still a virgin. But I feel like God is very close. It's like his wings are over me."

"You saw an angel?" gasped Elizabeth. "Why, that's what happened to Zechariah in Jerusalem. He was chosen to offer incense at the morning sacrifice and the angel, Gabriel, appeared to him in the temple saying, 'Your wife, Elizabeth, will bear a son.' We are to name him John and he is going to prepare our people for the coming of the Lord."

"Aunt Elizabeth, can you believe it? The Son of David is coming! The angel told me you were in your sixth month and that nothing is impossible with God. It's all true, isn't it? What else has happened? Please tell me everything."

"Well, Zechariah suffered some kind of impairment that day. He can't speak or hear. You'll see when he wakes up. I think he knows more than he has told me, but we can only communicate by signs. He is healthy and happy, though, and he helps me a lot. He is the father of this baby and wants to be a good one."

"Words cannot describe what it means for me to be here, Aunt Elizabeth. It's all so new. The angel, Gabriel, came into our house at night. His light filled the kitchen but my family didn't wake up. He told me that I was going to give birth to the Son of the God, the Messiah, and I should name him Jesus. Then he told me about your baby and I knew right away that I needed to come."

"I didn't tell my parents or my fiancé, Joseph, about the angel or his message. Why would they have believed me? I had nothing to show them. I told them that I was sure something had happened to you and I needed to come and help. My parents didn't believe me but Joseph was supportive. He and Levi brought me here. I don't know what Joseph will do if I arrive home pregnant? People could stone me. I know Joseph won't, but what is he supposed to think?"

"Mary," urged Elizabeth. "Don't worry. This is God's doing, not ours. He isn't going to send his Messiah into your womb and then let people stone you. Listen, Zechariah is waking up, and we need to tell him who you are. I mean, who you really are. That won't be easy."

Zechariah entered the room and looked at Mary curiously. Elizabeth used a series of hand signs to describe her birth family and her sisters in Nazareth. She then pointed to Mary and described a child growing up to Mary's size. When she slowly mouthed the name "Mary" Zechariah got it. He embraced Mary and pointed to his mouth and ears while shrugging his shoulders.

"Now," said Elizabeth. "Let's tell him the real story."

She had Zechariah sit down while she acted out a scene in which their son, John, would one day introduce Mary's son. It was so confusing that Zechariah understood nothing.

Finally, Elizabeth pointed to Mary's abdomen and mouthed the word, "Messiah." Zechariah's eyes opened wide and he sat motionless. Then he slid to his knees, raised his hands in thanks to God, and bowed before Mary.

Mary was shocked. She knelt down and tried to pull him up. Elizabeth understood her predicament.

"Mary, this is not the last time someone will do this. You just have to accept it when it happens."

"Auntie, it's all so crazy," replied Mary. "It sounds like people will either stone me or bow to me. I hope there are more options."

The next morning, Mary's thoughts returned to the song she had been thinking about on the trip from Nazareth. She had made a copy for reading but when Zechariah left for the synagogue, she shared it with Elizabeth as a rhythmic song.

"In my soul, I just magnify the Lord,
  In my spirit, I sing of God my Savior.
  When he saw my youth and poverty,
  He thought to himself, this girl can work for me.
  Every generation will celebrate my blessing,
  It's all from the Mighty One whose name I am confessing.

For those who desire to live in awe of God,
  His mercy reaches out to every generation.
  His strong arm has worked wonders of all kinds,
  He scatters those whose pride enflames their minds.
  Rulers on their thrones, he causes to fall down,
  The humble he lifts up and gives to them a crown.

The hungry he fills up with a sumptuous feast,
  But the rich he sends away with nothing at all.
  Tell Israel, his servant, that help is on the way,
  Showers of mercy, he's planning every day.
  For Abraham and all his heirs, now and evermore,
  The promise to our fathers, He will never ignore."

Elizabeth loved the song and wanted to learn it. She also wanted to hear about Mary's encounter with an angel. Having held it all inside for over a week, Mary felt immensely relieved to have someone with whom she could share everything. The visit with Elizabeth was exactly what she needed. Here, she could see a bigger picture and feel more confident about the future.

She thought about Joseph's arrival the next day and wondered how much she should tell him. It didn't seem wise to introduce him to Elizabeth and Zechariah yet. They could easily make some reference to Mary's pregnancy and that would lead to an immediate return to Nazareth.

However, she could tell him to take home the news about Elizabeth's pregnancy. Rebekah and Joanna would be shocked. Hopefully, they would come to accept it as a genuine, divine intervention and begin to get ready for the bigger surprise of her own pregnancy. At least they would know that Mary was needed to help Elizabeth through her final months.

On the second day, Mary saw Zechariah's wax writing tablet and wrote out a question. Elizabeth was surprised and wanted to know how she had learned to write. Zechariah indicated that he needed larger letters. When Mary realized that he could comfortably make out five to seven words at a time, she wrote out this question,

"Will you teach me about my son?"

Suddenly the mental clouds parted for Zechariah and, like a beam of sunlight, Mary's request illuminated a divinely appointed task. Out of all the priests in the land, God had chosen him not only to father the Messiah's herald but also to orient the Messiah's mother about the mission of her son.

For months, he had been sorting through sacred scrolls at the synagogue. He couldn't make out all the words but the blurred shape of the text enabled him to remember different prophecies about the Anointed One. His mind was bursting with insights and, now, he had a vision for what God wanted him to do. Zechariah smiled broadly, grabbed the stylus, and firmly wrote,

"Yes!"

Late in the morning of the third day, Mary excused herself to visit the street market. She stopped to wait for Joseph under a tree near the synagogue. It wasn't long before he appeared in the distance, riding with confidence and effortlessly absorbing Zephyrus' powerful strides.

Mary started to walk calmly toward Joseph, but when he jumped to the ground and spread his arms out, she broke into a run. A pace away, she stopped and put out her hand to avoid the embrace.

"Wait, Joseph, our time has almost come, but we can't have rumors circulating in Beth Hakkerem."

"Your wish is my command," returned Joseph, lightly kissing her extended hand. Together they walked toward the market square.

"Are you okay" inquired Joseph.

"Everything is fine," said Mary. "Where is Levi?"

"I left him in Jerusalem so that I could make this trip at full gallop," Joseph replied. "He'll come back with me, of course, when I come to pick you up."

"There is some astonishing news for you to take home," began Mary. "Elizabeth is going to have a baby. She was barren all these years and, now, at sixty, she is in her sixth month of pregnancy. This baby is a miracle, Joseph, a divine intervention. When Zechariah was in the temple seven months ago, an angel appeared and told him that Elizabeth would have a son. I would take you to meet them but Zechariah has suffered some kind of impairment and is unable to speak or hear. They need lots of help and I know that God wants me to be here."

"How long will you stay?" inquired Joseph.

"Elizabeth's baby should arrive in three months," said Mary. "I know that's right on top of our wedding. Do you think you can wait an extra week or two?"

"No, I can't wait an extra week or two!" steamed Joseph playfully. "But if you're not there, I guess I won't have any choice. I've waited three years for you, Mary, so I won't fight over a week or two. Levi and I will come back in eleven weeks to get you. Do you need anything right now?"

"Well, there is one more thing. Zechariah's eyesight is bad and he can't see his wax writing tablet very well. I have a lot to learn from him and the best way is with large letters and short messages on papyrus."

In the market place, they found a trader who had a small stack of papyri and some ink. Joseph inquired how soon he could obtain more. It would take a week, so Joseph paid the trader in advance for thirty more sheets. Mary purchased some salt, nuts, cheese and grain before they returned to the synagogue.

"Mary, I have something for you in the saddle bag."

Joseph reached inside and took out a small bag of coins and placed it in her hand.

"This is for whatever you might need."

"Thank you, Joseph. Thank you so much. You are always looking out for me and it means more to me than you will ever know. I'll be waiting for you."

As Joseph galloped off, Mary waved and thought to herself, "How will he feel when he finds out there are two of us waiting for him?" She closed her eyes and whispered,

"I am your servant, Lord, but I have no idea how you will convince Joseph that I am still a virgin."

A few days later, Mary woke up feeling nauseous. Not wanting to question the food they were eating, she said nothing. The problem persisted until, one day Elizabeth saw her bend over and choke back an urge to vomit.

"Mary, are you sick to your stomach?"

"I am so sorry, Aunt Elizabeth. I didn't want you to think I was ill and unable to work."

"Mary, you aren't sick. You are pregnant! I should know because I was there just six and a half months ago. Praise God, my child. The angel spoke the truth!"

After they both laughed and hugged, Elizabeth commented enthusiastically,

"There is another reason why God sent you here, Mary. How would you have explained morning sickness to your family in Nazareth?"

As time passed, Zechariah became increasingly caught up in Mary's thoughtful questions, beautifully inscribed on an endless supply of papyri. Eventually, Mary's mature and winsome presence melted away Zechariah's defenses, and he tearfully admitted to having doubted Gabriel's prediction. Quite spontaneously, she wrote out a question for Zechariah one morning.

"Can you bring home a scroll of Scripture that tells about the Son of David?"

Zechariah smiled broadly and penned confidently,

"Better than that."

He disappeared into the bedroom and returned with a leather case from which he pulled a small scroll. Elizabeth explained,

"It's a copy of the scroll of Zechariah, the prophet, for whom my husband was named. Our village purchased it for him on his fiftieth birthday. It's his most prized possession."

Zechariah gingerly unrolled the double scroll on the low dining table and stepped back. As Mary knelt down and placed her hands on the two scrolls, she felt a wave of excitement pass over her. Perhaps she was the first woman to even hold this scroll, much less read it.

The text began with familiar warnings for her people and a vision about God's predictions of peace and prosperity for Jerusalem. Not far into the columns, she encountered some lines that seemed to reach out to her.

"Shout and be glad, O Daughter of Zion. For I am coming, and I will live among you, declares the LORD. Many nations will be joined with the LORD in that day and will become my people. I will live among you and you will know that the LORD Almighty has sent me to you."

"Auntie," Mary said. "Listen to this."

As she read aloud, her attention was drawn to the titles, "LORD" and "LORD Almighty." The LORD Almighty was sending the LORD to live among his people. Weren't these one and the same? Still puzzled, Mary reached for Zechariah's tablet, wrote the two titles for God with a question mark after each one, and pushed it forward to her uncle who was kneeling in front of her, watching intently.

Zechariah paused thoughtfully. He then pointed to the words, "LORD Almighty," with his left hand and pointed straight up with the right. Next, he pointed to the title, "LORD," with his left hand and with his right hand pointed to Mary's womb. Mary sat still, eyes fixed on her uncle, wondering if she really understood what he was saying.

"Immanuel", meaning "God with us", and "Son of David" were familiar titles for the Messiah. But here, Zechariah the prophet and Zechariah her uncle were calling him the "LORD", or "Yahweh" in Hebrew.

"We use "Yahweh' meaning 'He is'," thought Mary to herself, "because, out of reverence for our Creator, we don't even dare to speak God's revealed name, 'I Am.' Is uncle Zechariah saying that my baby is 'Yahweh'?" Mary struggled in her mind for answers.

"Could God send himself to earth, clothe himself in a human body, and still remain in heaven?"

She bowed her head and covered her face with her hands as new emotions welled up inside her.

"Oh God, how is this possible?" she quietly prayed. "How much of you will be in my son? Are you and your Anointed One separate or the same?"

Elizabeth perceived her confusion and knelt down beside her.

"Mary,we are not ready for the LORD's appearing, but we have been chosen to participate. Especially you, dear one. We don't even understand a natural birth. How can we ever comprehend a supernatural one?"

Slowly rolling the ends of the scroll together, Mary stood up and signaled to Zechariah that she would like to read more the next day. He understood and returned the scroll to its hiding place while Mary and Elizabeth took a slow walk to the village square. Mary was first to speak.

"Aunt Elizabeth, since childhood, my concept of the Messiah was always a young man like David who would lead our nation in throwing off our oppressors and cleansing our land of idols and foreign gods. What Jewish girl hasn't hoped to be his mother or maybe his bride? The angel who spoke to me said, *'...the holy one to be born will be called the Son of God,'* and told me that I should give him the name Jesus. Has Jesus always been with God? Is he now taking on a new assignment here on earth? Is that what you think?"

"Mary, if we could understand God, then God would be something we made up in our minds. God will always be greater than that. Let's just enjoy him and love him and keep on learning about him. So the angel told you, *'the holy one to be born will be called the Son of God?'* We never address God as our father, but it sounds like Jesus will."

The next morning, Zechariah brought out the scroll again and Mary continued her reading. Some more lines about a "*Branch*" caught her eye.

"Here is the man whose name is the Branch, and he will branch out from his place and build the temple of the Lord... and he will be clothed with majesty and will sit and rule on his throne..."

Mary wrote out for Zechariah, "Who is the Branch?"

On his feet in an instant, Zechariah gave a sweeping display of a tree falling. Only with Elizabeth's help did Mary finally understand that David's line of Jewish kings was cut down like a tree. The prophet was predicting that the Messiah would come from David's descendants like a new branch growing out of a tree stump.

"That could be you, Mary," observed Elizabeth. "Your father is a descendant of David through his son Nathan, not through Solomon. You are having a baby without any male help at all, so your son, Jesus, is a full-blooded son of David. He is a new branch."

Close to the end of the scroll, Mary encountered a disturbing prediction.

"And I will pour out on the house of David and the inhabitants of Jerusalem a spirit of grace and supplication. They will look on me, the one they have pierced, and they will mourn for him as one mourns for an only child, and grieve bitterly for him as one grieves for a first-born son."

"What is this?" wondered Mary. "Here in the middle of God's restoration and blessing of Judah and Jerusalem, the inhabitants turn on their deliverer and pierce him. Then, they mourn for him. It makes no sense at all!"

Hoping that some interpretation of the passage would eventually dispel the dilemma of a suffering Messiah, Mary pushed it into the back of her mind and said nothing to Zechariah or Elizabeth.

One day Zechariah wrote, "We must visit Jerusalem."

Elizabeth signaled the difficulty she had with walking and Zechariah made signs that just he and Mary go. Mary's look of confusion prompted Zechariah to write more,

"Rabbi Beniah. School of the Consolation of Israel."

"Aunt Elizabeth, what is the School of the Consolation of Israel?"

"Oh, I get it, Mary," she responded. "He wants to visit the head of a school that offers a study program on the consolation of Israel. The prophet, Isaiah, referred to the coming of God's Messiah as consolation for our suffering nation. That school is for young rabbis seeking greater understanding of the Messiah. Zechariah sent a fine, young man there from Beth Hakkerem, but his health was bad and he died before finishing his course of study. I am not sure why he wants to take you there."

A few days later, Zechariah and Mary made the journey to Jerusalem. Upon arrival in the city, they stopped at Eldad and Abigail's home. Mary's explanation as to who she was brought no small excitement to Abigail, but the news of Elizabeth's pregnancy, now in her seventh month, left her speechless. Abigail immediately sent a servant to Eldad at his school of advanced religious studies to inform him of Zechariah's arrival with a niece from Nazareth and to mention that they wished to stay the night.

That afternoon, Zechariah led Mary to a study house near the temple. The inscription over the door read, "School of The Consolation of Israel." After Zechariah knocked on the door, Mary stepped up, introduced her uncle. and explained that due to his current impairment of speech, she was serving as a spokesperson. As usual, Mary's confidence and sincerity were disarming and, with little more than the name of Rabbi Benaiah on her lips, she managed to work their way into the headmaster's presence.

"Your honor," Mary began. "Rabbi Zechariah is a priest from the village of Beth Hakkerem. While offering incense in the Holy Place ten months ago, he had a vision and suffered an impairment of speech and hearing. Perhaps you are aware of this matter?"

"Yes, yes, of course...ah...young lady... and your name is...?

"Mary."

"Oh, yes, yes, Mary, I see. Hmmm, and you are from Beth Hakkerem?'

"No, your honor, I am from Nazareth."

The lines of doubt etched on Rabbi Benaiah's face only deepened. Surprised and distracted by Mary's youthful face and confidence in his presence, he searched for another question. Mary continued,

"I am Zechariah's niece. His wife, Elizabeth, is soon to bear their first child and I came to Judea to help her."

"Well," said the rabbi, "I do recall hearing something about Zechariah's vision, or seizure, or whatever it was, and I wish him well. How may I serve him?"

Mary glanced at Zechariah. His hand motions described a man and then the facial description of someone dying.

"I believe he wants to see you about a young man from Beth Hakkerem who studied here but died before completing his course of study," Mary explained.

"Oh yes, that was Benjamin, one of our best students. He was deeply dedicated to the subject of the Messiah. His intentions were to finish the course of study and then depart for the Qumran community near the Dead Sea. He developed a high fever and died rather suddenly. He was a terrible loss."

Zechariah made some hand motions that described the opening of a scroll and writing in it. Benaiah appeared puzzled until Mary questioned,

"Did Benjamin prepare a document during his course of study?"

"Why, yes," responded Benaiah. "All of our students are required to read through the Scriptures; the Law, the Prophets, and the Writings. They copy onto a separate scroll all of the references they can find to the Messiah. These scrolls provide discussion material for our course of study. Benjamin's scroll is here. Would Zachariah like to see it?"

Mary looked at Zechariah, pretended to hold a scroll, and raised two fingers to her eyes. He nodded vigorously. A short time later, Benaiah returned with a leather case that held the double rolls of a medium-sized papyrus scroll. Zechariah carefully unrolled it on a study table until he came to the end. He looked closely at the last column and beckoned Mary to come and see.

Mary bent over to read when Rabbi Benaiah interrupted,

"Can you read Hebrew, young woman?"

"Yes, your honor. Here are Benjamin's final words. 'My time has come. I dedicate this scroll to those who believe and pray for the consolation of Israel. Immanuel, Son of David, please come quickly.'"

Zechariah became agitated and signaled to Benaiah his desire to take the scroll with him. Suddenly, Mary understood the reason for this journey. Zechariah remembered that Benjamin's course of study involved copying all the prophecies about the Messiah into one scroll. He wanted to obtain this for her.

Benaiah was not easily convinced in consideration of Zechariah's age and isolation in Beth Hakkerem, but he eventually agreed. A scribe was summoned and a document prepared acknowledging the transfer of Benjamin's scroll to the possession of Rabbi Zechariah.

Unexpectedly, Zechariah wrote out a request for a smaller, blank scroll and handed the note to Benaiah. The Rabbi asked Mary if she knew the purpose of Zechariah's request. She explained that she had no prior knowledge of either of his requests. By the Rabbi's facial expression, she could tell that he was going to decline. She then suddenly remembered the coins that Joseph had given her and asked if she could purchase the new scroll.

The Rabbi agreed, took her into an adjoining room where new scrolls were stored, and mentioned the price of eight silver denarii. Taking a deep breath, Mary opened her bag of coins and discovered that Joseph had left her ten. She quickly completed the transaction and returned with a subdued but triumphant smile for her uncle.

As the two departed in the direction of Eldad's house, a smile crossed Mary's face, then a chuckle. She imagined running back to the School of the Consolation, bursting through the door, and singing,

"He is here! He is here! He is not coming someday; he has arrived! Would you like to feel him? Would you like to carry him? His name is Jesus! His name is Immanuel! Be consoled, all of you, all Jerusalem, all Israel, all nations. He is here!"

The sheer joy of what Mary knew and no one else knew, aside from Zechariah and Elizabeth, was overwhelming. Her feet began to skip and then to dance. A favorite Hebrew word meaning "Praise the Lord" welled up from her heart to her lips.

"Halleluyah, O my soul..."

"Halleluyah, O my soul..."

Hearing nothing, Zechariah wrapped his arms tightly around the two leather cases and pushed ahead through the crowd like a small ship at sea. The crowd washed to either side and stopped momentarily to stare at the young girl behind him who was dancing gracefully and singing with such abandon.

"Shalom Aleichem." "Peace be upon you," they offered as the two disappeared into the crowd ahead.

The evening discussion at Eldad and Abigail's house was no small challenge for Mary, who had to speak for Zechariah, Elizabeth, and Eldad's sisters in Nazareth. The conversation immediately turned to Elizabeth's pregnancy and it didn't take long for Mary to realize that Eldad had, for months, dismissed Zechariah's vision as merely a seizure or some other medically documented phenomenon.

As he probed Mary's testimony about Elizabeth's condition, even suggesting that she may have gained some weight and imagined it to be a baby, Mary struggled to maintain a respectful attitude. Glancing occasionally at Zechariah, she could not miss his subdued delight at Eldad's furrowed brow and pursed lips. Although he missed the entire conversation, nothing pleased him more than to see Mary's unrehearsed account of Elizabeth's pregnancy gradually pushing his educated brother-in-law into a corner of groundless skepticism.

Back in Beth Hakkerem, Mary could hardly wait to see what Messianic passages Benjamin had chosen. She knelt at the low dining table while Zechariah stood and ceremoniously pulled the double scroll from its leather case. He paused, desperately wanting to explain things like priests customarily do, but no words came. Mary sensed his frustration and bowed her head as he laid the scroll in front of her and sat down to watch.

Mary gently unrolled the scroll from right to left. The sheer quantity of Scripture carefully inscribed along the horizontal lines of pressed papyri leaves was impressive. She had no idea there were so many prophecies and references to the Messiah in the Sacred Scrolls. They came from the oldest, Genesis, and from the most recent, Malachi. Column after column was dedicated to quotes from the Psalms and the prophets, particularly Isaiah and Jeremiah.

"Aunt Elizabeth," said Mary. "May I read out loud? I am going to need your help to understand these passages about our Messiah."

"Bless you, my child," responded Elizabeth. "I was hoping you would ask. But keep your papyri sheets close by and give the hard questions to Zechariah."

As Mary began to read from the beginning, Zechariah watched attentively.

"Then God said, 'Let us make man in our image, in our likeness, and let them rule over the fish of the sea and the birds of the air, over the livestock, over all the earth, and over all the creatures that move along the ground.' So God created man in his own image, in the image of God he created him; male and female he created them."

"Now here are Benjamin's comments," added Mary.

"To whom was God Almighty speaking? Here we are at the beginning of time and Moses tells us that within the singular nature of God there exists a divine counterpart with whom the Almighty communicates. Together they created our human race and shared with us their own unique nature. No explanation is offered. No concurrence is sought. Moses records the story of creation as it was revealed to him, but someone is with the Almighty in the beginning and the reader can only wait in expectation for the prophets to reveal to us who he is and what he will do."

Mary's mouth fell open as if she was seeing the Great Sea for the first time. With unmistakable wonder, she looked at Elizabeth and exclaimed,

"Auntie, I think he is saying that Jesus was together with the Almighty in the beginning."

And that's how Mary and Elizabeth embarked on an educational program that neither had ever imagined possible. Zechariah brought out the new scroll Mary had purchased at the School of the Consolation, and included a short note.

"Mary, this is yours. Copy down what you wish."

Mary bowed, took the scroll, and whispered a prayer of thanks. She then smiled at Elizabeth and added, "Is anything too hard for God?"

Most readings ended in a short walk for the two women. Elizabeth needed the exercise and Mary needed to process what she was learning. From time to time Elizabeth counseled her,

"Mary, I want you to remember that you only have a couple of months before you will start to show. Before then, you need to return home and tell your parents and Joseph what God is doing so they can decide about your wedding. Just pick the scriptures that make the most sense to you.

A few days after that conversation, Mary began to read passages that Benjamin had taken from the Psalms.

"The kings of the earth take their stand and the rulers gather together against the LORD and against his Anointed One…I will proclaim the decree of the LORD: He said to me, 'You are my Son; today I have become your Father. Ask of me, and I will make the nations your inheritance, the ends of the earth your possession.'"

"This is amazing," thought Mary. "Some of this is a conversation between the Father and the Anointed One who becomes his Son. Has this already occurred? Will it take place the day Jesus is born? Will I hear the Father speaking to him as a baby? Will he give an answer?"

Chuckling at the thought of her baby talking, Mary glanced at Elizabeth and gave a sign of two talking hands. Elizabeth smiled and blurted out,

"Yes, Mary, let's go for a walk. But you have it backwards. I can hear you speak. It's Zechariah that needs sign language."

Both laughed at her mistake and then looked over at Zechariah. He seemed to understand exactly what had happened and grinned knowingly. And so the process went on day after day. Mary could hardly believe all that she was learning about Jesus. A profound love and longing to hold him in her arms was growing inside her. On a walk with Elizabeth she blurted out,

"Auntie, I never went to a day of Hebrew school but now I feel like I have been enrolled in the School of the Consolation of Israel in Jerusalem. I only came here to help you. Well…actually I came here because the angel sent me, if you know what I mean. It's all turned out to be so much more that I could have ever imagined."

"Yes, Mary, and guess what? God has enrolled me alongside you. I am the oldest student they ever had. I'm eight months pregnant and can't even read or write. How is that for breaking all of the rules? Oh, my dear child, isn't God wonderful. He turns everything upside down, just like your song about magnifying the Lord."

When early signs of Mary's pregnancy began to appear, Elizabeth insisted that Mary could not wait any longer. She needed to break the news to her parents and to Joseph as soon as possible.

The next morning, Zechariah and Mary made the six hour trip Jerusalem. They encountered a priest and his family who were headed for Cana in a covered horse drawn wagon. The driver agreed to look for riders in Cana and pass through Nazareth on his return trip, so Mary was welcome to ride along. She explained this in a short note to Zechariah, allowing him to return home worry-free.

During the trip, Mary unrolled her scroll just enough to read one column at a time. Quietly meditating on the prophecies about her son, she began to commit many of them to memory. Five days later, she descended near her home in Nazareth. With bedroll and travel bag in hand, she prayed quietly,

"Almighty God, I'm arriving home a different person than when I left. Whether I succeed or perish is in your hands. May it all happen to me as your servant, Gabriel, said three months ago, right here in Nazareth."

FOURTH MIRACLE

Joseph's Dream

On the day that Joseph said goodbye to Mary and galloped out of Beth Hakkerem, he was thinking to himself,

"Mary is caught up in this incredible story of an angel in the temple and a miraculous pregnancy, but she doesn't seem particularly shocked or surprised about it. It's as if she knew somehow that this was going to happen."

Two hours later, he met Levi in Jerusalem and the two began the trip north to Galilee. On the second day, a rainstorm slowed their progress. Woven reed shields kept off the worst of the pelting rain and cold wind but by late afternoon they were soaked to the skin. Between the towns of Sychar and Sebaste, in the region of Samaria, Joseph guided Zephyrus into a shelter marked, "For Jews Only."

Samaria was inhabited by a mixture of Jews and other ethnic populations deliberately placed there centuries earlier by conquering foreign empires. The full-blooded Jews of Judea and Galilee refused to socialize or worship with Samaritans and basically regarded them as heathen.

The enterprising owner of this shelter charged Jewish travelers five mites each to spend the night near a series of small fires where they were able to dry out and escape the wind and rain from the west. Conversation that night with travelers from Caesarea sparked Joseph's interest in seeing the famous port city again.

"Levi, if the weather clears tomorrow, what would you think of going home through Caesarea? You could see the Great Sea and the new world of international trade."

Actually, Levi was already feeling homesick, but not wanting to show any sign of weakness to his future brother-in-law, he agreed. Arriving in Caesarea at dusk the next day, Joseph found beds and a shower in the dormitory for Herod's construction crew managers. He then took Zephyrus to the Roman stable. The handlers knew the horse well and were delighted to board him for a couple of nights.

The next day the two walked out on the magnificently engineered sea walls that circled the harbor. Inside these walls were protected, cargo platforms for arriving and de-parting vessels. Joseph pointed out the companies of laborers who were slavishly loading and unloading the ships.

"That's where my training started, Levi, moving lumber and hauling stone."

Just then a Roman warship entered the harbor with two rows of long, heavy oars dipping smoothly into the water in absolute unison.

"Look, there's a command ship," Joseph observed. "It's like the one I took to Alexandria with the tribune."

Their next stop was the construction management head-quarters. The director of all building projects in Caesarea was a Grecian architectural genius by the name of Gregorios Farsala. He was both surprised and pleased to see Joseph again.

"Well, Joseph, when are you coming back to work?"

"Thanks for the offer, sir, but in three months I am going to marry the most beautiful girl in Galilee."

"Not a problem," retorted Gregorios. "Just marry the girl and bring her with you. With the tribune gone, I can work you all day and for some decent pay, too. Herod has invited more delegations to come for games and festivities this year and he wants more housing for his guests of honor."

"To add to my problems, Herod has finally reached an agreement with the Sanhedrin to carry out the Emperor's enrollment decree this year. Every Hebrew adult in Herod's kingdom will need to register in his city of origin. So, all Jewish workers get an extra week off. Joseph, I really need your help!"

"I'll keep you in mind," said Joseph. "But I can't miss my own wedding!"

Next, they headed for the synagogue to visit Rabbi Elim. The rabbi was glad to see Joseph and delighted to meet someone from Mary's family.

"Welcome, Levi. According to Joseph's reports, your sister must be the most wonderful girl in all of Galilee."

"Oh, ah...well, she's okay, I guess," muttered Levi. "It will be nice when she moves over to his house."

"Joseph, I want to tell you something," continued the Rabbi. "Before the tribune left town, he came by the synagogue with his wife. They had read the five scrolls of scripture in Greek that you bought for them in Alexandria, and wanted to know if faith in God, like you have, is what God has in mind for all people."

"What could I say?" continued the rabbi. "It's ironic, actually. I was against the Scriptures being distributed in Greek. But maybe the words of God in Greek will be the pathway to faith for people of all nations. If our mission as Abraham's descendants was to bless the whole world with faith in our Creator, we have failed miserably. We loathe the Romans, we despise the Greeks, we dislike the Syrians and Persians, and we hate the Idumeans. Curse them all for enslaving us! But that's just how I feel about it."

Caught up in his emotion, Elim was nearly out of his chair. He then slumped back, as if defeated by his own arguments, and said,

"Think of it, Joseph, these foreigners have been pouring into our land for centuries. Somehow you had the right idea with the tribune and his family, and maybe I helped a little, too. I counseled you to encourage their faith in God outside of our Jewish religion, but I never imagined that I would get involved personally. In the end, I gave them my blessing and told them, 'Go in Peace, may God be with you!'"

The next morning, Levi and Joseph were on the road early. Zephyrus was energized by two nights in his old stable and he trotted tirelessly northward. They made excellent time and by evening of the second day, arrived in Nazareth. Heli and Rebekah were glad to see them. When Elizabeth's pregnancy was brought up, the discussion intensified dramatically. Rebekah sent Teresa next door to get Joanna. The two could not believe their ears. Elizabeth, their oldest sister, at sixty, was pregnant?

"Why, Joseph, that's impossible! Are you sure you got it right? Did you see her? And why didn't Mary let you go into their house?"

Joseph found himself on the defensive and unprepared for the onslaught of questions.

"Look, I am just telling you what Mary said. She told us that Elizabeth's baby was a miracle from God. Zechariah was in the temple seven months ago and an angel appeared. The angel told him that Elizabeth would bear a son. That's what Mary said. Their baby is a boy. How would they know that unless God told them?"

"I did think it was strange that Mary didn't take me up to the house on the second visit," continued Joseph. "But she said that Zechariah lost both his speech and hearing in the encounter with the angel. That was a little odd, I agree, but I trust Mary. You know her; she is the most honest person I have ever met. If I can't trust her then who can I trust? That's all there is to it."

"Well, okay," concluded Rebekah. "But there is still something about this whole story that I don't understand. All that urgency about going to visit Elizabeth, where did that come from? Then you three go there and she wants to greet Elizabeth by herself? That's odd! If Elizabeth is expecting a baby in two months, Mary was right to stay and help. But isn't this going to delay your wedding plans? How do you feel about that, Joseph?"

During the month of March winter began to lose its grip on Galilee. The temperature rose steadily and the intense downpours gave way to lighter occasional showers. Joseph took Zephyrus out of town to run free on the hills one morning and noticed that the buds on the almond trees were beginning to swell. In another week, they would burst open. Then he would go and bring Mary home.

The next day, he worked on a set of chairs until dusk. As he was cleaning up for dinner, there was a hard rap on the door.

"Joseph, I need to talk to you."

It was Heli. As Joseph opened the door, he continued,

"You need to come with me right now."

Sensing considerable urgency in Heli's voice, Joseph quickly dried his hands and stepped outside. Heli was already heading home and Joseph had to run a few steps just to catch up.

"What's going on, Heli?"

"Mary is home," was the curt reply. "She arrived about an hour ago."

"Is everything okay? inquired Joseph.

"No, it's not," replied Heli bluntly. By then they were approaching the door of Heli's home. Heli was frowning, his voice...ominous.

"Joseph, Mary is pregnant."

Stunned, Joseph stopped in his tracks and threw his head back as if he had been hit by a low-hanging tree limb in the dark. The news was utterly incomprehensible. Heli entered the door and there was nothing for Joseph to do but follow. He stepped inside and stood still. Mary was seated quietly on a stool while Rebekah stood in front of her talking hysterically. Mary did not appear to be pregnant. She looked at Joseph searchingly and then refocused on her mother. Dumbfounded and in disbelief, Joseph approached Mary and took a seat next to her.

Rebekah was beside herself but Mary was attentive and respectful. Joseph glanced at her face and saw nothing of fear, shame, confusion, or defensiveness. Quite to the contrary, her natural demeanor of calmness and maturity seemed stronger than ever. This moved Joseph to pause and wait for more information. Maybe Heli had jumped to a conclusion; maybe he misunderstood something.

Heli had the good sense to ask Rebekah to sit down and let Mary tell her story to Joseph.

"Joseph," she began. "I couldn't wait any longer to tell you everything, so I came back early." Resting her hand on his arm, Mary looked straight into his eyes.

"I need you more than ever before."

Whatever thought Joseph had of hammering her with an outburst of shock and confusion faded as their eyes met and searched one another deeply.

"Mary, until now you have never disappointed me. So I refuse to believe anything until I hear it from you."

"Thank you, Joseph. The night before I told you I needed to visit Elizabeth, I was asleep here with the family. Early in the morning I was awakened by a light in the kitchen. When I stepped into the doorway, I saw a vivid, angelic figure standing right here. His presence was so frightening that I fell to my knees."

"The angel said to me, *'Greetings, you who are highly favored! The Lord is with you.'*"

Mary was holding a small, papyrus sheet in her hand. She glanced down and continued.

"*'Do not be afraid, Mary, you have found favor with God. You will be with child and give birth to a son, and you are to give him the name Jesus. He will be great and will be called the Son of the Most High. The Lord God will give him the throne of his father, David, and he will reign over the house of Jacob forever; his kingdom will never end.'"*

"What's that in your hand, Mary?" snapped Rebekah. "What are you reading?"

"I wrote down the angel's message that very morning before waking you up," answered Mary. "It's what the angel said and I wanted to record it correctly."

"Joseph, I had no doubt that this was an angel from God and I wanted to know what I should do next. So I asked the angel how this would happen since I was a virgin."

"The angel explained, *'The Holy Spirit will come upon you and the power of the Most High will overshadow you. The holy one to be born will be the Son of God. Even Elizabeth, your relative, is going to have a child in her old age, and she who was said to be barren is in her sixth month. For nothing is impossible with God.'"*

"I bowed my head and said, *'I am the Lord's servant. May it be to me as you have said.'* My eyes were closed and my face on the floor; when I looked up, the angel was gone and the room was dark."

"I looked behind me," Mary recalled, "and everyone was still asleep. The first thing I did was light a small lamp and write down the angel's words. I then put the lamp out and sat there for a long time, just thinking about the vision."

"Would you have believed me, father, if I had told you? Would you have believed me, Joseph? I couldn't offer any proof that I was pregnant. In fact, I don't think I was pregnant yet. No one else saw the angel and I had nothing to hang on to except Elizabeth. She could prove that it was all true and she might even need my help. That's why I insisted on going."

Heli was listening hard, trying to find a flaw in Mary's story. Feeling pressed to say something, he asked,

"Mary, none of us saw this light or heard voices. How do you know this wasn't just a dream instead of a real angel from God? And are you sure you are pregnant? You don't look pregnant?"

"While you were gone, I checked Mary closely," Rebekah interjected. "She is beginning to show and is experiencing all the typical effects. I believe she is pregnant; I just don't believe her story yet."

"Tell me, Joseph," cut in Heli. "You took Mary to Beth Hakkerem. Be honest with us, please! Are you the father of this child?"

"If I was, I would be the first to tell you," Joseph replied, "and I would gladly assume the consequences. No, I am not the father of this child."

"Mary," pleaded Joseph, down on one knee beside her, "If someone has touched you, threatened you, or done this to you in secret, tell me. I will get revenge. I will take you away and we can start our life together somewhere else. I know you wouldn't have done this willingly."

"Thank you, Joseph," responded Mary. She reached out and gently touched the side of his face. She then looked into Joseph's eyes with all the honesty and compassion she was capable of and added,

"I came home to find out what you think I should do. I believe God wants us together. I believe that somehow this child is our mission, not just mine. But I can't force you into anything. The only thing I can prove is that the angel's message about Elizabeth is true. She will give birth to her son in a week or two. After you have heard everything, Joseph, please tell me what I should do. I believe God will guide me through your decision."

Joseph sat back and was quiet for a while. He was torn between two decisions. He had been thinking of the shame this would bring on Mary and her family as soon as it became known. Some would even want to stone her. He thought of the ridicule and humiliation it would bring on him, too. But he loved Mary and he wanted her to survive.

Perhaps he should break off the engagement and send her back to Beth Hakkerem before anyone in Nazareth saw her. She could have the baby there. Apparently, Zechariah and Elizabeth knew all about this and would be supportive.

On the other hand, Mary was sticking to her story. Could she really be the virgin chosen to conceive the Messiah? The prophecy was well known and Elizabeth's pregnancy was strong evidence.

And then, there was the plea she just made. It showed spiritual strength beyond her years and that was one of the reasons Joseph loved her so much. She trusted in God without fear and now she was willing to do whatever he decided. Before he reacted impulsively, or took sides, he needed to hear everything and ask God for more insight.

"Heli and Rebekah, with your permission I suggest that we refrain from questioning Mary's story until tomorrow. She has been traveling for five days and needs rest. What she is telling us is what our people have waited for, prayed for, and sung about for centuries. We just never imagined it could happen to us."

"Since you have given Mary to me in a binding contract of marriage, and she has asked me to tell her what to do, I want to withhold judgment until we have heard everything about Elizabeth and Zechariah. Let's set tomorrow aside to listen, pray, and contemplate this new circumstance in our lives. After that, I will tell you what decision I will make as her betrothed husband."

"Are Aaron, Teresa, and Nina next door? I know that Levi is traveling, but are the others still unaware of your return, Mary?" She nodded affirmatively. Joseph continued,

"No one knows about this accept us and no one was expecting Mary today. Let's keep all of this confidential until we know what she should do."

"Mary, I cannot hide my shock and disappointment," concluded Joseph. "But I promise you that I will give you a fair hearing and treat you with love and respect. Your arrival in Beth Hakkerem didn't make sense to us but now we know why. I still love you; I just feel betrayed."

Joseph dismissed himself for a walk but quickly returned to address the question of how to keep Mary's presence in Nazareth a secret. They finally agreed that Rebekah and Mary should spend the night in Joseph's house while Joseph stayed with Heli and the children. The children were called and told that their mom was caring for someone who had arrived from out of town. This person had some personal issues to resolve and needed Rebekah's full attention for a couple of days.

The next morning, the four reopened their discussion. Heli and Rebekah expressed again their confusion and doubts about Mary's story so Joseph led them all in a prayer to God for wisdom and guidance. When Mary followed with a prayer of confidence and gratefulness to God for choosing her to conceive and give birth to God's Messiah, Heli couldn't contain himself any longer.

"Mary, this just doesn't make sense. I know the prophet said that Immanuel would be born of a virgin, but to our family? We understand that you have always had this fixation on the prophetess, Miriam, and you love the scriptures, but look at us! We're just poor, simple folks from Nazareth. The Pharisees call us uneducated commoners. Don't you think God would have the good sense to pick someone wealthy or educated to bring his Messiah into the world?"

During the next few hours, Mary told them everything that happened to Zechariah in the temple. She also explained how Elizabeth and her baby reacted to her arrival.

"Joseph, the reason I didn't want you to meet Elizabeth that day was my fear that she might know I was the mother of the Messiah. Sure enough, she said it right out. How could she have known that?"

Everyone concurred that Elizabeth's greeting was a supernatural intervention that was humanly impossible. Their chief concern was what to do next. If Mary stayed and a wedding was held in a month, people would soon realize that Mary's baby was conceived before the wedding. There would be shame for them and threats against Mary. Mary would lose many of her civil and religious rights while Joseph would look foolish and lose respect.

By the end of the day, Joseph found himself leaning toward the idea of Mary returning immediately to Beth Hakkerem and living somewhere in the vicinity of Zechariah and Elizabeth until she had her baby. He would privately rescind the contract of marriage, sell his home, and move back to Bersabe. Then, he would check in on Mary and decide what to do next.

No one liked this solution, least of all Mary. Deep inside her, the joy of God's favor was turning into shame and rejection. Was this the best they could do for God's Son whose kingdom was going to last forever? Tears emerged and ran down her face. Joseph felt utterly miserable. Finally, he announced that he had not reached a decision and would wait until morning. Mary dried her face, knelt, and prayed in front of them all with commitment and surrender.

"God Almighty, your servant, Gabriel, spoke to me on this very spot, and I willingly entrust myself to you and to your servant, Joseph, for the decision that needs to be made. I can never thank you enough for the privilege of bearing this child and I will never deny the message spoken to me by your angel, Gabriel."

The children were called to see their sister and spend the night at home. Back in his own house, Joseph, normally confident and strong, wept in defeat.

"God, I don't know what to do. I want to believe Mary. I want to help her welcome your child into this world, but I don't know how to do it."

He sat for a long time on his bed, trying to think of a solution. He eventually fell asleep. An hour later, he was dreaming and found himself trapped in the same emotional dilemma over Mary. Unexpectedly, an angelic figure permeated with light approached him.

"Joseph, son of David, do not be afraid to take Mary home as your wife, because what is conceived in her is from the Holy Spirit. She will give birth to a son, and you are to give him the name Jesus, because he will save his people from their sins."

Joseph woke up with a start and reflected on the details of his dream. He repeated to himself the words of the angel and perceived that they contained the answer he was looking for. God wanted him to be known as the father of Jesus and whatever creative measures he needed to take to conceal Mary's pregnancy were up to him.

"Would that be so hard?" he asked himself. The cloud of doubt and defeat lifted and he was suddenly set free. He pumped his fist in the dark and said out loud,

"Yes, God, yes! I get it! Mary was right all along and I just needed to believe her. Thank you so much, Almighty God, thank you!"

It took just a moment to fasten his sandals and rush down the street to Mary's door. As he reached out to knock, he remembered that the children were also asleep inside. The adults really couldn't talk about this until daylight.

Returning to his house, Joseph was wide awake. He started a fire to make some tea and with a wool blanket wrapped around his shoulders, sat on the front doorstep of his house and thought about ways to conceal Mary's pregnancy. In the middle of his contemplation, the conversation with Gregorios Farsala in Caesarea came to mind.

Gregorios had offered him a job and wanted him to start as soon as possible. That job would give them a good excuse to leave Nazareth right after the wedding and spend a few months in Caesarea. Everyone would agree that a chance to make some money in Caesarea was a good thing.

Secondly, there was the news about a census that Caesar Augustus had decreed for the Roman world. All adults of

Hebrew descent would need to register in their cities of origin. For the families of both Joseph and Mary, that was Bethlehem and they would undoubtedly make the trip during the dry season. Joseph and Mary could go later in the year and have their baby in Bethlehem. They would stay out of sight for a few months and eventually return to Nazareth without any suspicion of impropriety.

As the morning light spread over the hills to the east, Joseph finished off his third cup of tea and stood up with a fresh sense of confidence and excitement. Mary was right. What an amazing young woman she was. What an indescribable honor to share with her the task of parenting the Messiah. And now he had a plan! Maybe it wasn't a perfect plan, but it proved that they could take the necessary steps to preserve Mary's reputation. Joseph liked challenges and he was up for this one.

At sun up, he went to the small window above the kitchen area in Heli and Rebekah's house, and gave a cheerful greeting.

"Hello, anybody home?"

"Are you up early today, Joseph?" responded Rebekah. "Or have you been walking the streets all night?"

"Just tell Heli that I have some good news. When you are able to talk, let me know, okay?"

As he walked away, he heard Rebekah shaking Heli awake. "Heli, get up. Joseph says he has some good news."

It wasn't very long before there was a knock on Joseph's door. He opened it and there stood Levi, Mary, Aaron, Teresa, and Nina. Mary explained,

"Levi came home last night so we had a little party after you left. He is going to stay here with the others while we finish yesterday's conversation. My parents said I could come over and walk you back to our house."

"I hope you have some food here, Joseph," grumbled Levi. "Apparently it's so important for you guys to have more weird talks that we're supposed to skip breakfast."

"Don't worry, Levi. You'll be coming back faster than you think," laughed Joseph.

As they started off, Mary looked intently into Joseph's face, trying to read his thoughts. There was hope in the air but what was it? She couldn't wait any longer. Grabbing Joseph's arm with both hands, she burst out,

"Joseph, what are you thinking?"

A smile broke across his face.

"I'll sum it all up for you in two sentences. God sent an angel to me last night with an unequivocal message. He said, 'Joseph, marry the girl now!'"

"Joseph!" cried out Mary. "Are you teasing me?" She could hardly believe that all the dreadful options of the night before had disappeared in an instant.

Standing in the middle of the street, Joseph took both of her hands in his.

"Mary, I am so sorry that it took an angel to get through to me, but I swear to you, one appeared in my dream last night. He told me your baby was the work of God's Holy Spirit and that we should get married now. There is nothing in life I would rather do than marry you. We can set a date today."

Such a wave of emotion swept over Mary that she completely forgot where she was and who might be looking. As her words of surprise, joy, and relief poured out, she jumped up and grabbed Joseph around the neck. Hearing Mary's outburst, Rebekah rushed outside and waved her arms vigorously, trying to get the two off the street. All Joseph could do was stand where he was and hold Mary tightly to his chest.

A minute passed, maybe more, before Mary relaxed her grip and Joseph was able to set her down. Approaching Rebekah, Mary simply said,

"Sorry Mother, but my whole life was just resurrected from the grave."

"You two are unbelievable!" blurted out Heli. "How can you go from hopeless defeat to celebrating in the street in one short night?"

"Well, sir," answered Joseph as he entered the house, "God intervened last night and put me on the right path. I didn't have a vision but I did have a dream. And in my dream, an angel told me to stop wasting time and get married because Mary's baby is the work of God. We are to name him Jesus because he will save people from their sins."

"I woke up and realized that God wants me to be known as the father of Mary's baby, even though I am not. It means that we need to have a wedding as soon as possible."

"Now wait a minute, Joseph. Do you think everyone is going to close their eyes when Mary walks by? Do you think they're going to forget how to count when a baby arrives three months early?"

"Heli, I have been thinking about that for the last three hours and perhaps it won't be so hard to conceal the age of Mary's baby," stated Joseph. He then calmly shared his plan to leave Nazareth and take a job in Caesarea.

"That's okay for the time being, Joseph, but what about the baby's birth? That's the moment of truth, you know."

"Yes, sir, you are exactly right," answered Joseph. "But apparently God already thought of that. We all know about the Roman census and the fact that Jews are to register in their ancestral towns. So, all of us have to go to Bethlehem at some point this year. You and all our relatives are likely to go during the dry season, but we will wait until later in the year and go to Bethlehem by ourselves."

"We'll stay there until the child is born. I can find work for a few months and when we return to Nazareth no one will know his birth date except us."

Mary gasped, "Joseph, did God tell you this or did you think of it on your own?"

"What do you mean?" Joseph replied.

"Well, at Zechariah and Elizabeth's house, I saw what the prophet Micah wrote about the Messiah's birthplace. I wrote it down in my scroll...wait...look, here it is!"

"*'But you, Bethlehem, Ephrathah...out of you will come for me one who will be ruler over Israel, whose origins are from of old, from ancient times.'* Then Micah added, *'Israel will be abandoned until the time when she who is in labor gives birth.'*"

"Can you believe that? It might mean something else but it sounds like the prophet was talking about Jesus and his mother! And this was written down hundreds of years ago. It's like God knows everything ahead of time!"

"Oh, Mary, you are way beyond me," said Rebekah. "You should probably check that out with the rabbi. What I do know is that we need to have a wedding. Did Micah say anything about a wedding? Like maybe in two weeks? How do you feel about that, Mary?"

"I'd prefer three months ago, Mother, but yes, two weeks is fine. The sooner the better is the way I feel about it. And guess what, Joseph?" Mary added with a twinkle in her eye, "In two weeks the almond tree blossoms will still be in full bloom."

Joseph broke into a broad smile.

"Well, let's start the celebration right now," burst out Rebekah. "I've been waiting for this moment for three years. "Halleluyah! Halleluyah!" she cried out. She grabbed Mary and the two fell into a whirling circle of dancing feet and flying hair. No sooner had Joseph pushed the table aside when two hands reached out from the whirling circle and pulled the men into their ring of celebration.

"*Halleluyah! Halleluyah!*" rang out the happy foursome in a traditional Jewish wedding dance.

Hearing the commotion next door, Joanna couldn't stay away. She soon appeared at the side door followed by her entire family. Mary ran up the street to Joseph's house, pushed the door open, and blurted out,

"Come on home. We are going to have a party and the last one there has to serve!"

A wild dash ended with Mary carrying Nina and the others reaching the house first. Everyone was shouting and jumping around. As soon as Mary entered, Heli grabbed her hand, along with Joseph's, and shouted above the rest,

"This is an official announcement, folks. Mary's wedding to Joseph of Bersabe will take place two weeks from today. You may now greet the bride and groom and wish them well."

A fresh round of cheers, congratulations, and dancing broke out, both inside and outside the house. Neighbors appeared and a party ensued that devoured every scrap of food and every drop of wine in the house. By noon, the excitement had subsided and Joseph whispered to Mary,

"We need to talk."

With a new sense of freedom, they made their way to the wooden bench in the garden. After a long embrace, Joseph sat down, grabbed Mary's hand, and began,

"Mary, I am so sorry for putting you through all that turmoil. I fully accept your baby as our child and our mission from God."

"Shhhhhh," she answered quickly, placing her finger on Joseph's lips. "Not even a whisper about the baby. This is our secret and the appearance of the angel is, too. I can't wait to tell you everything I learned in Beth Hakkerem. God sent me there to strength my faith, to help Elizabeth, and to learn about our son. He is far greater than anything I have ever imagined."

"I can't wait to hear what you have learned," observed Joseph, "because up to now, the supernatural side of our story has been revealed to you alone. I love your courage, Mary. You said yes to the angel, yes to visiting Zechariah and Elizabeth, and yes to facing your parents and me. Now, an angel has spoken to me too, so I can't simply ride along and passively let you make all the decisions about Jesus.

I, too, need to step out and be an enthusiastic participant in God's plan for us and our child; or should I say, his child."

"Please go on," said Mary, visibly moved by his words.

"Well, in case you didn't know, a wedding pretty much means one thing to a man, and that is physical intimacy. But we have a special situation with you carrying God's Son. I really don't want to say this, but I think we should refrain until after Jesus is born. Do you agree?"

"I agree, totally. The angels didn't ask this of us, but I know it's right. And Joseph, in these three years since we have known each other, I don't think I ever respected you more than I do right now."

FIFTH MIRACLE

Zechariah's Recovery

On the morning that Mary left Beth Hakkerem and began her journey back to Nazareth, she and Zechariah assisted Elizabeth out of her home and over to a favorite rest area under the sprawling limbs of an old terebinth tree. With one on each side, they maneuvered her to some comfortable wooden chairs the villagers had placed on this site which marked the beginning of the Way of the Synagogue.

Mary dropped an armload of pillows onto one of the chairs and arranged them into a comfortable seat as they eased Elizabeth down. The sun was just above the horizon to the east and its rays pierced the cool, spring air with a promise of warmth to follow. Mary saw the frown on Zechariah's face as she knelt down to wrap a favorite wool blanket around Elizabeth's legs and feet.

"Zechariah is none too happy about leaving you out here while we head for Jerusalem," Mary observed openly. "And I am even more unhappy about saying goodbye."

"Oh, nonsense," replied Elizabeth. From here I can call any of our neighbors if I need help. Just take him by Leah's house on your way out of the village so he can see that she is planning to come here shortly. Right now, I want to be alone with God. I want to enjoy this beautiful morning, to sing my favorite hymns, and to pray for your safety. Come, dear one, let me embrace you one last time."

Mary was still kneeling as Elizabeth took her head in her hands and pulled her close. Elizabeth's plentiful gray hair fell over Mary's thick black tresses, now pulled back and clasped behind her head. Zechariah stood mesmerized by the two women he loved most.

"Your departure is going to leave an enormous hole in my life, Mary. You have been with me every day through my most difficult months. We never stopped marveling at the sheer wonder of what God was doing and at the cloak of secrecy he has placed around us. No one on earth knows what we know and we needed each other just to grasp it all. What a precious time! You read to me the words of the prophets and filled my heart with amazement and praise. Some things about God's Messiah we clearly understand and many we don't. It takes my breath away just to think about it all."

"Auntie," responded Mary, "I am so young and unprepared for this. You and Zechariah have been my mentors. You gave me a chance to learn about my son and to read the prophecies about his arrival. You listened to my questions, my fears, and my confusion about everything. Now my faith is stronger and I'm ready to face Joseph."

"Please remember that my pregnancy is a secret between the three of us," added Mary. "When Zechariah regains his ability to hear and speak, remind him once again to wait for God to announce my son's identity. Does that make sense?"

"That makes perfect sense," replied Elizabeth. "You are young but you have wisdom beyond your years. You are an inspiration to me and I want to love and trust God like you do. Joseph has a big task ahead, too, and it sounds like God has selected him for it. I will pray every day for you both and I will keep your secret!"

"Okay, dear one. It's time for you to go. Zechariah will find transportation for you to Nazareth. I know in my heart that you can't wait another day."

Elizabeth's eyes dampened as she looked up and clasped Mary tightly.

"Almighty God, carry this sweet servant of yours safely to her home. We have neither the strength nor the wisdom to fulfill your plans on our own. We release ourselves to your control."

As Zechariah shouldered one of Mary's travel bags and started walking, Mary picked up the other and paused to wipe away her tears. With a final exchange of kisses and clasping of hands, she tore herself away and ran a short distance to catch up. Elizabeth let her tears run freely down her face and kept waving goodbye until the two disappeared around the bend near the synagogue.

The early morning sun bathed Elizabeth's face below the outstretched arms of the great tree. She sat motionless and let a cloud of precious memories pass through her mind like mist rising from a rain soaked valley.

Somewhere behind Elizabeth, the rapidly approaching clatter of small sandals on hard earth and the high-pitched giggle of children's voices brought a knowing smile to her face.

"Hi, Aunt Elizabeth! Hi, Aunt Elizabeth!" panted two young girls as they raced up to each side of her chair.

"Yaffa and Yarona, my favorite grandnieces. Let me look at you," burst out Elizabeth with obvious delight.

"Yaffa the beautiful, and Yarona the songstress, like flowers and birds of spring you are. Come, let me kiss you."

"Auntie, we brought you some fresh raisin bread. Our mother baked it this morning," gasped Yaffa, still catching her breath. Holding up a small, woven reed basket, she continued, "Mother wants to know if your baby is coming today."

"Can Mary come out and play, Auntie?" asked Yarona.

"Well, well, well, so many questions to answer. First of all, Mary has just left for Nazareth. She is engaged to a young man named Joseph and they are going to be married. Very soon, I hope! And no, my baby isn't coming today. Maybe next week, though. I can hardly wait."

"Yaffa, please run into my house and bring me the small kitchen knife so I can share this bread with you. Mmmmm. Doesn't it smell good?"

In the days that followed Mary's departure, Zechariah slipped back into his private world of silence all too readily. He missed Mary. In his mind he returned to the many abbreviated dialogues with her on papyri. He thought about the day when he had penned a query to Mary,

"Why you? Why me? Why Elizabeth?"

Mary had seemed to understand the deeper significance of Zechariah's question and retrieved the song she had shared with Elizabeth on the second day of her visit. For Zechariah, she wrote it out in large letters,

"In my soul, I just magnify the Lord, In my spirit I sing of God my Savior…"

As Zechariah had pondered the lyrics, he could see that Mary had the answer. God delighted in turning things upside down. He wanted to entrust his plan of moral restoration for the human race to the lives of humble peasants. They were his delight and he would reward their faith in Him. If God preferred to bypass the rich and famous, would his Messiah be the same? A line from the first of Isaiah's songs about the Messianic Servant came to mind.

"He will not shout or cry out, or raise his voice in the streets. A bruised reed he will not break and a smoldering wick he will not snuff out…"

Then there was the day that Mary had written out a challenging request for Zechariah.

"Uncle, please write a song about God's salvation and about your son?"

"Impossible!" Zechariah had written back with a frown. But Mary insisted and her enthusiasm was contagious. The very next day, he began to write.

"Praise be to the Lord, the God of Israel, because he has come and has redeemed his people..."

When he had finally finished, Mary rewrote it as a rhythmic song and sang it to Elizabeth. Zechariah had received such a tender, loving embrace from Elizabeth that he could still remember it long after John was born.

Elizabeth's friend, Leah, and other women from the village came by regularly to check on her condition. In anticipation of the pending delivery, one of them sent her teenage daughter to stay in Elizabeth's home at night. Sure enough, just ten days after Mary's departure, Elizabeth woke up the young girl in the early morning, and told her to call the midwives. She was beginning to feel some contractions.

The midwives brought a birthing chair, checked on the baby, and talked with Elizabeth. They explained that more time was needed but said they would stay with her. Hearing nothing and unable to speak, Zechariah retreated to his neighbor's house. As the day dawned, more women showed up with words of encouragement and humorous birth stories to tell.

It was mid-morning when Elizabeth's contractions reached the next level of strength and frequency. Eventually, she lost control and cried out. She later remembered being helped into the birthing chair, but all the advice about breathing, relaxing, and biting on a tightly wrapped towel became a blur in the face of her pain.

"Push, Elizabeth, push!" she heard. "Just one more time, push!"

At the moment she thought she had literally turned inside out, it was over. The women helped her back to her bed where she lay utterly exhausted as the midwives washed off baby John and rubbed him down with salt.

"*Mazel Tov*" "It's a boy", the midwives shouted to the women outside. Elizabeth already knew that but she had no strength to respond. She heard the baby's cry and whispered that she needed air. As soon as the baby was tightly wrapped in a fresh cloth, he started a bumpy ride from woman to woman around the room. Finally someone turned to check on Elizabeth but she was unresponsive; she had passed out. More confusion ensued and a midwife shouted,

"Get out! get out! Elizabeth needs air!"

As the women rushed back outside, Elizabeth's baby was carried right out the door with them. His cries drew nothing but admiration, kisses, and gentle, rocking embraces. Then another instruction came,

"Zechariah wants to see his son!"

Back went the newborn from bosom to bosom, until he was placed in the arms of his exuberant father. Secretly hoping that this was the moment of restoration, Zechariah lifted his eyes to heaven and mouthed words of praise and thanksgiving, but no sound came. He hid his disappointment and worked his way into the crowded bedroom to kneel beside Elizabeth. Barely revived, she was propped up on some pillows. Without a word, Zechariah placed John in her arms and kissed her damp hair.

The next few days were all about the baby. To her utter joy, Elizabeth felt her breasts filling with milk, and with a little practice, she began to nurse her child. Framed in loose gray hair, her face expressed a level of peace and fulfillment that Zechariah had never seen before.

The first ceremony in the life of a Jewish male is circumcision. On the morning of the eighth day, the friends of Zechariah and Elizabeth gathered to witness this event, which officially inducted their son into the Jewish race. He would be given a Jewish name and obligated to keep the laws of Moses. Zechariah had always planned on performing the circumcision. However, due to his poor eyesight and Elizabeth's insistence, a Mohel, one who was skilled in performing circumcisions, was called from a neighboring village.

The house was filled with all the guests it could hold while others stood outside. In the bedroom, the infant was passed from Elizabeth to the chosen godparents, relatives of Zechariah. They entered the front room, welcomed by an enthusiastic chorus of blessings, and placed the child in the hands of Zechariah's good friend, Rabbi Shemaiah.

Zechariah tapped a neighbor on the shoulder and signaled to him that the chair he was sitting in should be left empty. It was a custom that symbolized the presence of the great prophet Elijah, who, in his day, chastised the Israelites for forsaking the ritual of circumcision.

Shemaiah placed a few drops of wine in the baby's mouth and loosened his wrapping. Then, the Mohel raised his hands and prayed,

"Blessed are you, Lord God, Ruler of the Universe, who has sanctified us with your commandments and directed us to bring this child into the covenant of Abraham, our father. As he enters the covenant, may he enter into the study of the Torah, into marriage and into the exercise of good deeds."

"Amen," responded the guests vigorously.

The Mohel sat down as Shemaiah finished unwrapping the baby and placed him in his lap. The women closed their eyes and winced as the men grimaced and leaned forward to watch closely. What some of them had performed in their own houses, the Mohel accomplished with a single, firm stroke of his razor sharp knife. In efficient, memorized steps he quickly wrapped a small tight compress around the offended organ. At the baby's cry, Elizabeth stirred. Shemaiah had barely begun to replace the loosened cloth when she was at his side, hands outstretched. She wrapped her son tightly and hugged him to her chest. She then sat down quietly.

The Mohel stood again and prayed,

"Oh, God of our fathers, raise up this child to his father and mother, and let his name be called in Israel, Zechariah, the son of Zechariah…"

Elizabeth had just begun to discreetly nurse her son when it occurred to her that the angel's instructions regarding John's name had never been discussed with the Mohel. So she interrupted him and spoke up,

"No! He is to be called John."

Everyone was surprised and a neighbor said to her,

"There is no one among your relatives who has that name."

"Ask his father," responded Elizabeth.

Zechariah had been accompanying everything with great interest and noticed that Elizabeth had spoken to the Mohel. The neighbor turned to Zechariah, made a motion of writing with one hand, while pointing to the baby with the other. Zechariah signaled for a writing tablet. With the stylist, he wrote on the waxen face in large letters,

"His name is John."

The nearest person read the phrase out loud and a small commotion of surprise circled the room. But that was only the beginning. Something was stirring in Zechariah. He stood to his feet and shouted out loud. "Yes, his name is John and I am Zechariah his father! I heard you talking about John's name and suddenly realized that God had set me free from my handicap. I can hear and speak again!"

Elizabeth stood with surprise and rushed to Zechariah. Tears of joy welled up in their eyes as they embraced. Baby John was jarred loose from Elizabeth's breast and cried out.

The Mohel was unable to finish his prayer of dedication because the excitement over Zechariah's deliverance turned everyone's attention from son to father. A divine intervention had just occurred and the impairments of Zechariah's speech and hearing were clearly gone. He was completely coherent and bursting with a spirit of praise and thanksgiving.

As soon as Elizabeth managed to provide fresh comfort to baby John, Zechariah asked for everyone's attention as he offered his own blessing for the miracle child in their arms. His words poured out with such profound insight and authority that the guests all stopped talking and listened with amazement. In his enthusiasm, Zechariah recited Mary's rhythmic version which was easier to remember,

> "Praise be to the Lord,
> The God of Israel.
> He has come to visit us,
> To redeem and make us well.
> Like a horn, this Mighty Savior
> Has sprung up from David's line.
> He'll fulfill the prophets' forecasts
> Written down by God's design…"

Everyone was stunned at Zechariah's conviction and clarity. It sounded like he had personal knowledge of the Messianic events he was describing. Toward the end of his song, Zechariah turned to his newborn son and added,

> "And you my little son,
> One day you'll be God's spokesman.
> To wake them up and get them ready,
> To point out God's Salvation.
> With mercy offered and sins forgiven,
> Heaven's light will spread abroad.
> Pulling us from death and darkness
> Into a path of peace with God."

Elizabeth knew all about Zechariah's song of praise and blessing. Mary returned to Nazareth with a copy of it in her travel bag. The rhythmic version was eventually lost but Zechariah's original prose survived in Mary's possession.

When Zechariah had finished, Elizabeth recalled Mary's candid comment,

"Auntie, isn't God wonderful. It's like he stopped Uncle Zechariah right in his tracks and gave him a year off to court his wife, father his child, and contemplate the coming of our King. When his voice returns, he's going to have such a story to tell."

That thought suddenly jarred something else loose in Elizabeth's memory. Dropping baby John into the arms of her good friend, Leah, she broke into the exuberant circle of guests crowded around her husband and whispered,

"Zechariah, please come quickly into the bedroom; there is something I have to tell you." Once inside, she continued,

'The last request Mary made as she was leaving was that I would ask you to keep her pregnancy a secret once your speech returned. She believes that God wants to bring his Anointed One into the world unnoticed. She wants us to wait for God to choose the time and place for him to be revealed."

"It's a good thing that you called me, Elizabeth, because I was right on the verge of telling our neighbors that Mary is the Messiah's mother. I mean, she is the living proof of everything."

"Yes, she is, Zechariah, but think of Mary. She is unmarried and we have no idea how Joseph has responded to her pregnancy. If we tell people who she is, someone is bound to run up to Nazareth and start talking. Let's keep Mary's secret and trust God to make the announcement. Besides, isn't that John's task when he is older?"

Zechariah agreed, but his enthusiasm was undiminished. Fueled by his son's birth and the secret presence of God's Messiah in the womb of his beloved niece, he could hardly contain himself. Both at home and in the synagogue, he quoted Messianic Scriptures with such confidence that he stirred many of the villagers to new levels of faith and religious practice. A week after John's baptism, Elizabeth brought up some of the pending events in the near future.

"Zechariah, Passover is just a week away and I don't think that John and I are ready for the demands of an extended trip to Jerusalem. Why don't you go by yourself, and after you return, we all need to visit the temple for John's dedication and my purification ceremony. While you are there for Passover, would you ask Abigail if we can stay with her when we arrive with baby John?"

Zechariah agreed and left a week later with the Passover worshipers from Beth Hakkerem. Elizabeth was not a bit lonely during his absence since Leah and the other women felt free to come by more often. When Zechariah returned, he was amazed to find his wife looking healthier and happier than before.

With baby John wrapped up on her back or riding alongside in a reed basket, Elizabeth had spent considerable time working outside, hoeing and planting a variety of seeds and seedlings in their vegetable garden. With a light tan on her face and arms, she looked fresh and invigorated. She sang and chattered away to her son, nursing him regularly, and carrying him with a new spring in her step. Zechariah was energized just to see her and excitedly launched into his own report,

"Elizabeth, you would not have believed the look on Abigail's face when I knocked on the door and said hello. She acted like I had risen from the dead. I stopped by a second time to see if Mary or any of her family had come for Passover and she said she hadn't seen them. All we can do is assume that Mary's secret was not disclosed in Nazareth, that she and Joseph got married, and that everything is working out fine."

Ten days later, Zechariah and Elizabeth proudly traveled to Jerusalem with their son and stayed at Abigail and Eldad's home. The excitement of the two sisters-in-law was irrepressible. Elizabeth eagerly described her delivery and

Abigail affectionately cradled John while trying to decide who he looked like. Eldad had no other recourse than to give his hearty congratulations.

Awakening early, Zechariah and Elizabeth went to the temple. He attended the morning sacrifice while she nursed John outside the women's court. Zechariah then took John in his arms and proceeded to a temple chamber where fathers were presenting their firstborn sons to God as required by the Law. The line was already quite long and a number of the men were awkwardly trying to quiet their infant sons who missed the familiar voice, smell, and embrace of their mothers. Nearly all were young men. Zechariah's wrinkled face and white beard created a notable contrast with the others, drawing muted smiles, raised eyebrows, and a few whispered comments as the line moved along.

The ceremony was brief. A priest took John in his arms, requested his name, and greeted him as the firstborn son. He then recited a short blessing while Zechariah placed the redemption fee of five shekels into a box. Returning the child to his father symbolized God's wish that he be raised by his parents.

Elizabeth had departed to the women's court with other mothers whose childbirth had occurred at least forty days earlier. There, she participated in a ceremony of purification, indicating that she had recovered fully from the physical effects of childbirth. In this group, there was no one who approached Elizabeth in age. She relished the startled looks and, in short, quiet conversations, extolled the kindness of God Almighty. As a member of the poorer class, Elizabeth presented two bound doves to be sacrificed on the altar of burnt offerings. Upon completion of the purification service, the women were pronounced ceremonially clean and free to partake in the sacred formalities of temple worship.

That evening, the two sat with Eldad and Abigail and reviewed the events of the last eleven months. Eldad had no other choice than to admit his unbelief.

"Well I must apologize for any doubt that I expressed about your vision in the temple, Zechariah. Your son is evidence that God has intervened and given the two of you a blessing, the likes of which we have never seen before. How was your recovery, Zechariah? Was it a gradual improvement?"

"No, it was quite sudden," he replied. "I hate to tell you this, but my response to the angel's message in the temple was one of doubt, knowing that our childbearing years had passed. The angel was displeased and said that because I doubted him, I would be unable to speak until the day his words were fulfilled. I was deaf and dumb until the day of our son's circumcision. The moment I wrote on a tablet that his name was John, my speech and hearing were completely restored. It was the third miraculous intervention that we have witnessed."

"And what was the second?" pursued Eldad.

Zechariah glanced at Elizabeth knowing that he had just opened the door to recognition of Mary as the mother of God's Messiah. Elizabeth's hand gently slipped across her neck like a cutting blade. Zechariah wasn't sure what to say, so Elizabeth came to his rescue,

"Oh, we call it a miracle. A friend arrived and we had this intense conversation about the coming of the Messiah. Baby John gave me a jolt in the womb, so we call it a miraculous moment."

"Yes, that happens a lot here at the temple," replied Eldad. "People find themselves in awe of God and suddenly everything seems like a miracle. I suppose there is no harm in it. However, when the day of the Lord arrives, according to the prophet Malachi, he will appear suddenly in the temple. Evil doers will be consumed and we will trample them under the soles of our feet. Pardon me, Elizabeth, but that will be more than a leap in the womb. Elijah himself will return and prepare us for his coming."

A wave of anger passed through Zechariah. Eldad had just belittled Elizabeth and he had no idea that her baby jumped because Elizabeth was embracing the Messiah's mother. Of course her baby jumped! Unfortunately, none of this could be revealed. Eldad's final comment, however, got Zechariah's attention.

"Elijah!" thought Zechariah to himself. "Why didn't I make the connection? The angel said about our son, 'He *will go on before the Lord, in the spirit and power of Elijah, to turn the hearts of the fathers to their children and the disobedient to the wisdom of the righteous – to make ready a people prepared for the Lord.'* And those are the closing lines in Malachi's scroll, the last of the Jewish prophets!"

"Yes," reflected Zechariah, lost in thought. "Elijah does come first. Everyone knows that. But they don't know that he might be a new prophet *'in the spirit and power of Elijah.'* A new Elijah has arrived and Immanuel is coming right behind him.

"Hello! Are you still with us, Zechariah?"

Eldad was standing in front of Zechariah waving his hands in his face.

"It seemed like you checked out of the conversation a bit ago, Zechariah. Are you having a new vision or do you need to retire and get some rest?" frowned Eldad as he crossed his arms.

"Don't worry," interjected Elizabeth from her seat. "I know the look. He is merely processing some new thoughts and sorting them out. He'll be okay."

At that moment, Zechariah sprang to his feet.

"My apologies, Eldad. I'm fine. Your comments about the reappearance of Elijah brought some fresh insights for which I am deeply grateful. But you are right, tonight we need to prepare for our journey home."

The next day, after the early morning rush of horses, camels, and commercial wagons had subsided, the elderly couple said their goodbyes and began the trip home to Beth

Hakkerem. Elizabeth carried baby John in a large scarf bound over her shoulder and across her back. Zechariah had a similar load of morning purchases, including food and water for the day's journey.

Their hearts were light and their minds filled with new insights into the privileged role that God had given them in the arrival of his Messiah. Unlike the other husbands and wives on the road, they walked side by side that day, buried in conversation.

"So," began Elizabeth, "Last night after we wiggled past Eldad's question about the second miracle, you seemed to disappear into some deep contemplation about Elijah. What were you thinking?"

"Somehow I had not grasped that the angel's description of our son coming in the spirit and power of Elijah was a coded reference to him being the Elijah who is to come. I was angry at Eldad's dismissive remarks about John's leap in your womb. He didn't have the faintest idea that you were embracing the Messiah's mother. He doesn't even know that the unborn Messiah has been in his home! Can you believe that?"

As the day wore on and an exceptionally pleasant rest under a tree lulled all three into a comfortable nap, the travelers realized that home was not far away. Their pace was relaxed as Elizabeth thoughtfully asked,

"Zechariah, we haven't talked very much about this last year. Tell me, what will you take away from a year of divinely imposed silence?"

"My, what a question!' reflected Zechariah. "Well, there is this thing of secrecy that surrounds the coming of God's Anointed One. I would never have predicted that. Silence was imposed on me because of my unbelief. Mary was forced into secrecy by a pregnancy outside of marriage. People like Eldad are left out by their own skepticism. When the Messiah arrives, hardly anyone will know about it!"

"Another thing," continued Zechariah, "watching Mary read through Benjamin's scroll, I realized that the Scriptures are flooded with references to the Messiah. During Passover, I attended a lecture at the temple by Rabbi Benaiah. He told us that the rabbis have identified four hundred and fifty-six references to the Messiah in the Scriptures. Silence has enabled me to start learning again."

As the late afternoon sun began to set behind the hills to the west, the travelers reached their door and affectionately touched the mezuzah as they entered.

"Oh, John, my precious little rider," chuckled Elizabeth, "you have now been to Jerusalem and back. Come, let's change your clothes so you can swing a while in your basket."

"Zechariah, I haven't given a moment's thought to eating tonight and there isn't a scrap of food in this house. Shall we just go hungry until morning or do you want me to ask for something from our neighbors?"

Just then, in the distance, there was a rapidly approaching clatter of small sandals on hard earth and the high pitched giggle of children's voices. A knowing smile passed over Elizabeth's face and she announced expectantly,

"Why don't we just wait a moment and see what God provides."

SIXTH MIRACLE

Jesus' Birth

Mary's eyes opened to a panorama of rolling hills that spilled onto a broad, coastal meadowland she knew to be the Plains of Sharon. In the wake of the rainy season, wild flowers were bursting through a rich, green mantle of grass around her. The cool morning air, fresh and delicately scented, lured her to draw in a slow, deep breath, followed by another.

She eventually she pushed off the warm wool blanket, still damp with dew, and sat up. Joseph was sitting quietly close by, drinking in her tangle of shiny, black hair and her first, sleepy stretch of the morning.

"Good morning, my bride. Is this the bedroom of your dreams or have you been abandoned in the wilderness?"

"Oh, you're so poetic," Mary yawned. "Listen to those birds singing. Aren't they beautiful? So this is where you camped on your trips home from Caesarea?"

"It is. And I always wished for someone to share it with."

Mary crawled over and sat next to Joseph. She pulled the wool blanket over them both and gazed out across the sloping hills before them.

"Is that the Great Sea off in the distance?" she asked.

"It is, and I thought we would be there by midmorning," mumbled Joseph with his face buried in her hair. "But now I'm not moving until noon."

This was the third morning since their final wedding celebration in Nazareth. The out-of-town guests were still asleep when Joseph and Mary loaded up Zephyrus in the predawn darkness, whispered goodbye to Mary's parents, and hurried out of Nazareth into the Jezreel Valley. Slowly, the nagging fear that someone might discover Mary's pregnant condition began to subside.

A hasty departure to Caesarea, however, became the occasion of their first argument. Joseph wanted to push hard through the Jezreel Valley and into the Carmel Hills, so they could reach his old camping spot. Mary was exhausted from the wedding and wanted to stop sooner for rest and time to talk.

Eventually, Joseph gave in and rented a room for the first night. When Mary slept until noon the next day, he realized his selfishness and apologized profusely. They resumed their journey into the Carmel Hills more casually and still managed to reach Joseph's old campsite at dusk.

The two chatted on until Mary began to hum. Joseph listened quietly and then asked what she was singing.

"Just a verse from one of David's psalms," she said and sang it for him,

"Let the morning bring me news of your unfailing love
With all my heart, I'm trusting your control
Show me now the steps that I should take
For to you, my LORD, I'm lifting up my soul."

The words so perfectly captured the moment that Joseph joined in and together, with eyes closed and faces lifted, they sang the verse repeatedly. Joseph finally changed the subject,

"How about some fig cakes to start our day?"

Mary grimaced as the thought of figs sent a wave of nausea through her.

"Anything wrong?" questioned Joseph, sensing her queasy response.

"Don't mention fig cakes for a while," she replied. "I had too many of them at our wedding. Now the mere thought of figs gags me. What I am craving for is a bite of juicy melon. Maybe I can squeeze some lemon juice into a cup of water for now?"

Interrupting her own thoughts, Mary asked, "What is that wall that runs along the beach as far as I can see?"

"It's an aqueduct that carries fresh water from a spring on Mount Carmel all the way to Caesarea. I spent most of my second year in Herod's service on that project and helped to slide many of those huge stone blocks into place."

Joseph whistled to Zephyrus who trotted up from where he was grazing. He held out a leather bowl filled with water while Mary groomed the horse with a small leather brush. They strapped the saddle securely in place and fastened their clothes and blanket behind it. As they rode off together, Joseph requested,

"Please tell me more about your time with Zechariah and Elizabeth? I know you learned a lot there, and I'd like to hear about it."

"Honestly, I don't even know where to begin," Mary answered. "This little baby of ours is far beyond anything I ever imagined. It was as if Uncle Zechariah struck the rock and truth about Jesus came pouring out. You've seen my little scroll. It has my gleanings from a larger scroll, which contains gleanings from all over the Scriptures."

Mary explained about the School of the Consolation of Israel, Benjamin's scroll, and how God placed both her and Elizabeth in what they affectionately called "God's divinity school for women."

"And guess what," laughed Mary, "Our professor was brilliant. He wouldn't give us the answers, instead he made us dig out the truth by ourselves."

"God is writing out a story in our lives, Joseph, and it's full of surprises and secrets. The angel, Gabriel, burst into my life and said, 'Surprise, Mary, the Messiah is coming and you are going to be his mother! If you have any questions, talk to your Aunt Elizabeth.' When I got to Beth Hakkerem, I found Zechariah and Elizabeth buried in surprises and secrets too. Zechariah couldn't speak and Elizabeth couldn't read. But God placed them right in the middle of this story."

Joseph slid off Zephyrus to stretch his legs and continued on foot while Mary rode alone.

"So how did you learn from Zechariah when he couldn't hear or speak?"

"He brought me scrolls. I read them out loud and Elizabeth helped me understand them. Sometimes I wrote out questions for Zechariah and he wrote down his answers."

"We started with a scroll written over five hundred years ago by the prophet, Zechariah. While reading it, I learned that Jesus has been with God from the beginning. He is the one we call Yahweh and it has always been his plan to come and live among us. He is the LORD and the LORD Almighty will send him to us."

"One day I wrote "LORD" and "LORD Almighty" on Zechariah's writing tablet with a big question mark. He pointed to the LORD Almighty with one hand and with the other pointed up to heaven. He then pointed to the LORD and with the other hand pointed to my stomach. How do you suppose that made me feel?"

"Whoa!" blurted out Joseph.

Zephyrus stopped instantly, snorted and shook his head. Mary and Joseph broke out laughing as she pulled herself up off of Zephyrus' neck.

"What I meant to say was 'Hold everything Mary.' Are you asking me how I think you felt when Zechariah said the

LORD was inside you? Maybe you felt like you had been buried by an ocean wave and needed someone to pull you up for air. Since the LORD is our way of writing Yahweh, your baby is carrying God's most revered name.

"Exactly, Joseph. Did I tell you what Elizabeth said when she first saw me? You and Levi were watching from a distance, but she said right out,

'Why am I so favored that the mother of my Lord should come to me? As soon as the sound of your greeting reached my ears, the baby in my womb leaped for joy... '"

"The mother of her LORD, Joseph! That's what she called me. Now we have to keep that a secret. I could get stoned for saying my baby is the LORD, but I can't deny it either. Do I understand it? No. But I believe it, Joseph, I really do! God is in Heaven and his Anointed One is here in my womb at the same time. Jesus is the Holy One of Israel, a divine image of God Almighty, who was with him in the Creation."

"And there is more! King David wrote in the Psalms that the Anointed One will be our King and will fulfill a decree that God made about him. The Almighty said, 'You are my Son. Today I have caused you to be born of a woman. If you ask me, I will make the nations your inheritance, and the distant reaches of the earth your possession.'"

"When did God make that decree, Joseph? Has he said it already, or will he say it on the day that Jesus is born? Do you think that we might hear him say it?"

"Mary!" burst out Joseph. "How do you keep track of all these Scriptures? Do you memorize them?"

"How could I not memorize them, Joseph? They are about my son! In Beth Hakkerem, I copied as many of them as I could into my little scroll and I read them every day."

By now, Mary was leaning so far out of the saddle to peer into Joseph's face that she let go of the reins, wrapped her arms around Joseph's head and fell into his arms. Completely taken by surprise, Joseph staggered momentarily, caught her awkwardly, and slowly lowered her to the ground.

"Okay, my sweet bride!" he exclaimed, laughing. "God is taking us on an adventure that is beyond anything I ever imagined. I'm all for it. If this decree you spoke of describes Jesus' relationship to the nations, then maybe some time in Caesarea is just what his parents need."

Caesarea was Mary's first immersion into the world of Rome and the international cultures that circled the Great Sea. After showing her the harbor with its seawalls, ships, and loading platforms, Joseph took her by Herod's palace, the outdoor theatre, the hippodrome, and the new temple to Augustus Caesar. Arriving at the multi-stepped entrance to an unmarked stone building, he asked her to wait with Zephyrus while he went inside.

Mary watched men arriving and departing by chariot and on foot in Syrian, Roman, and Grecian garb. They all seemed pressed for time and carried themselves with an air of importance. Placing her free hand on her stomach, she spoke softly,

"Jesus, here is a crossroads of the nations that you will one day rule. Like Zechariah predicted, you have '*roused yourself from your holy dwelling*'. You are '*coming to live among us*' and '*many nations will be joined with you in that day.*'"

"I have no idea what that will look like, Jesus, but as a daughter of Zion, I promise you that I will '*shout and be glad*'."

Joseph suddenly appeared on the steps accompanied by a robust, heavily-bearded man in a striped knee-length tunic, a broad waistband and matching headband. As they approached, Joseph stepped ahead, gathered Mary tightly to his side with one arm and announced enthusiastically,

"Gregorios, this is Mary of Nazareth who has joined me in marriage. Now there are three of us as she is expecting our first child. Mary, this is Gregorios Farsala, the architect and overseer of Herod's building program in Caesarea. He says that I am the first Jew to ever offer to work a day more than the required ten years in Herod's service. And he plans to reward me handsomely!"

"Well, well, well, so this is the flower of Galilee that captured your heart, Joseph," interjected Gregorios. "Rarely do I empty a flask of wine with my managers without at least one toast to Joseph of Bersabe, the Jew who turned down Roman citizenship and the Tribune's daughter to marry his Hebrew love."

Gregorios reached forward with both hands, gently shifted Mary's headscarf behind her, and announced,

"Your reputation has gone before you, young woman, and I can see it is justly deserved. How am I going to compete for Joseph's time when he has you to go home to each night?"

"Sir, I am honored to meet you," Mary replied brightly. "Your construction achievements are beyond anything I have ever seen, aside from our temple in Jerusalem. If we are competing for Joseph's time, you will probably win, but if we are competing for his heart, I will never lose."

Gregorios stepped back and crossed his arms. He started to say something and then stopped. His countenance softened and he looked wistfully at Joseph.

"You were entirely right, Joseph, she is wonderful." Then he bowed and said,

"Mary, Caesarea welcomes you and your child. Whatever you need, you shall have. May the peace of your God rest upon you."

Joseph couldn't wait to introduce Mary to Rabbi Elim. The rabbi was delighted to meet the young woman about whom Joseph had talked incessantly over the last three years.

"So, Mary of Nazareth really does exist! Joseph has told me all about you. You are gifted in song and dance and even taught yourself how to read. So, what draws a young woman like you to the Scriptures?" the rabbi asked.

"Well, sir, the Scriptures tell me that God is very, very close. When I hear them read aloud, I believe God is speaking to me. And there is so much about the coming of the Anointed One, the Son of David. Do you think he will be coming soon?" Mary asked without hesitation.

"Well I certainly hope so," mused the Rabbi thoughtfully. "And which scrolls do you enjoy the most?"

"The Psalms and the writings of Isaiah and Jeremiah are my favorites. Would it be possible for me to read one of them sometime?"

"You are the first woman who has ever asked. When one of those scrolls is not in use, I will let you know."

As Mary passed into the fourth month of pregnancy the morning sickness disappeared and Mary felt renewed energy and enthusiasm. One Sabbath day, the Rabbi mentioned that the scroll of Isaiah was available and if Mary wished to read it, she should come to the study house, better known as the Bet Midrash. The following afternoon, he escorted her into one of the smaller study rooms and left her with the large Isaiah scroll.

Three hours later, when Joseph happened to be at home, Mary burst through the door beaming with exhilaration.

"Joseph, you won't believe what I discovered while reading Isaiah's scroll. God was really angry with our people, but he promised them that a special day was coming when he would make things right. In that day, God will send us *'the Branch of the LORD.'* That's like a new shoot from among David's descendants."

Mary put her hand on her abdomen and added, "the Branch is right here!"

"After predicting the coming of the Branch, Isaiah couldn't stop his prophecies from pouring out. He spoke of a virgin bearing a son and calling him Immanuel. He promised that a Great Light would dawn in Galilee. He envisioned a child being born who will be given God's names and will reign on David's throne. That was my first song, the one that caught your attention at the play. Do you remember?"

"I do remember, Mary. How could I ever forget?" replied Joseph, glad to get a word in.

"Well, Isaiah didn't stop there. He got so excited that in the eleventh column of his scroll, he wrote a song of praise on the theme of In That Day. I paraphrased it in a rhythmic form and here is how it goes,"

> "I will praise you, LORD,
> In that wonderful Day,
> When the anger I deserve
> Will all be turned away.
>
> God is my salvation,
> And the LORD is my song.
> Like water from the well,
> He sustains and makes me strong.
>
> Let's give thanks to the LORD,
> And call on him in that Day.
> Tell the nations what he's done,
> And put his name on display.
>
> Sing to the LORD of his glorious deeds,
> Tell the world. Let Zion lead the way
> With shouts of praise and songs of joy,
> God's Holy One has come to stay."

"Can you believe it, Joseph? That Day has come! Can you feel the excitement and joy? Do you like my song?'

"Yes I do, Mary! And I like even more the happiness I see in your face. The next time you go to the Bet Midrash to read, I want to go with you. I won't tell Gregorios where I'm going because he will want to come, too, and bring a flask of wine, of course."

Months five and six passed quickly. Mary glowed with the health and vigor of a young woman perfectly adapted to pregnancy. She and Joseph were enjoying their temporary home, which featured a second floor sleeping room and a balcony that looked out over the Great Sea. One night Mary asked Joseph how he was handling their restrained relationship.

"I would never say I like it, because I don't. But I'll tell you a little secret. Abstinence makes the heart grow fonder. I never thought I would admit that, but it's true. I am so crazy about you I can hardly stand it. I think about you all day long. I control myself by remembering that Jesus is between us for the time being, right here in your womb. With him around, the animal in me chooses to be a gentleman."

"I wish every man thought like you," pondered Mary out loud. "I've talked with women who say their romance died the day after they got married. They are intimate with their husbands, but the courting is over, if you know what I mean. I want to satisfy you in every way, Joseph, but it feels good to be wanted."

Midway through Mary's eighth month, the occasional cloudy days and cooler temperatures reminded Joseph that it was time to discuss their departure from Caesarea.

"Mary, in a couple of weeks, let's take advantage of a transportation service to Tiberias so you can have a more comfortable ride up the Via Maris into Galilee. If we stop at Japtha, we could have a private visit with your parents before traveling to Bethlehem. I'll be alongside on Zephyrus."

Two weeks later, they began their journey. In Japtha, Joseph rented a room and hired a runner to carry a message to Mary's parents, urging them to come secretly for a short visit. Fortunately, Heli was in town and the next day, he and Rebekah appeared at the door. It was an ecstatic reunion of mother and daughter. Rebekah tried to persuade Mary to come home and have a comfortable delivery in Nazareth.

"It will be so much easier to travel to Bethlehem after your baby is born," she argued.

"If it were just about us, Mother, of course I would come home. But this is God's child that I am carrying, and I can't be having a baby in Nazareth six months after our wedding! You know that."

"My goodness, Mary, everyone knows that Joseph took you to Beth Hakkerem nine months ago. These things happen to a lot of really wonderful people, believe me. Do you have to insist that yours is a miracle child?"

"Of course I do, Mother. This is God's story, not ours. We are sure that he wants me to give birth in Bethlehem."

Heli managed to pull Rebekah away from a final embrace of her daughter at the edge of town, reminding her of the steep climb up to Nazareth and the need to arrive before dark.

It was late September, and a change of seasons was in the air as Joseph and Mary began their trip to Bethlehem. Joseph tried to rent a wagon and driver but they were all committed to the fall harvest. He had no choice but to start their trip with her riding on Zephyrus, or just walking slowly, when she preferred.

Village by village they followed the same route they had taken nine months earlier. Near Bethel, the first light rains of the wet season slowed their progress but, by the afternoon of the fifth day, they approached Jerusalem.

Joseph found a room and left Zephyrus at the Roman stable for two days. The next day was the Sabbath, so they got up at daybreak, attended the morning sacrifice at the temple, and rested the entire day. As they left Jerusalem the following morning, the roads began to fill up with hundreds of men carrying branches, poles, and roof thatch. They were arriving in Jerusalem to occupy small booths during the week-long Festival of Ingathering.

As Joseph and Mary approached Bethlehem, the traffic of foot travelers and riders increased noticeably. Tents and temporary shelters were scattered everywhere. After reaching the crowded village square, Joseph helped Mary off their horse. He knocked on a few doors and mentioned the names of some recent ancestors in hopes of locating a distant relative. One resident, a baker who was taking down his bread sign for the day, listened thoughtfully and replied,

"I think I've heard some of those names mentioned by a family that lives near the birthing stable. Why don't you check out there. But, if it's a guest room you are looking for, I'm afraid you will find them all occupied."

When Joseph returned to Mary, he found her in obvious pain, leaning heavily on Zephyrus and biting her lower lip.

"Joseph, I didn't want to say anything because I wanted to be sure it was more than the discomfort of riding, but I've been feeling a lot of back pain these last few hours. It doesn't seem to be going away either. Wherever we spend the night, we should probably find a midwife, just in case."

"I was counting on another week or more," countered Joseph. "Some of the villagers here are our distant relatives and I was hoping to locate some of our kin who could offer us a room."

With one hand on Zephyrus and the other around Mary, he held her tight and prayed into her head covering,

"God, here we are in Bethlehem. We are looking for a birth place for your son and need your help. My plan isn't working and we don't know who to turn to."

The residents of the town all knew about the birthing stable, and pointed them toward some homes on the outskirts of Bethlehem. Again, Joseph inquired about the availability of a guest room but the answers were the same. Nothing was available. One elderly man suggested that they spend their first night at the birthing stable and try again the following day to find an available room. As he led them to the stable, he explained,

"The shepherds raise their sheep in the fields. When the ewes are ready to give birth, they turn them over to priests here at the stable. Priests from Jerusalem are responsible for the selection of unblemished male lambs. After being weaned, the selected ones are transported to Jerusalem. The normal birthing season provides hundreds of lambs and goats just before Passover. That's when they are needed the most."

"So at this time of the year would the stable be empty?" questioned Joseph.

"Not quite. The shepherds have altered the breeding season for some of the ewes. That way they can provide newborn lambs all year round. A couple of full-term ewes were dropped off today. The priests are in Jerusalem this week for the Festival of Ingathering but one of their helpers is on hand. Here is the stable."

The birthing stable was a large circle of covered stalls, each separated from the other by a low wall of rock. Most of them were the right size for a single ewe and her offspring, but a few were large enough for a mare or a donkey. Two stalls provided access into hillside caves where clean straw and rolls of cheap burlap cloth were stored. Inside the circle was a large limestone rock hollowed out on top and draped over with strips of the coarse cloth.

"That's the manger," explained the elderly man. "After the newborn male has begun nursing and is able to stand up, he is carried to the manger for examination. If chosen, he is wrapped with the burlap cloth as a protection from dirt or blemishes. As you can see, there are a few ewes here waiting to give birth while others are nursing their newborns. Onan, the stable boy, can help you with lamps and water. The best midwife in the village is Judith, and she lives close by."

Joseph turned to Mary and started to apologize but she interrupted him,

"I know what you are going to say," as she patted on his chest. "But no apologies are necessary. First of all, I don't have the strength to take another step. Secondly, we prayed and God brought us here. He has something in mind that we will eventually understand. Maybe he doesn't want us in some relative's guest room where we will have to answer a lot of questions. If you would fix me a place to lie down and contact the midwife, I will be very happy to stay right here tonight."

Joseph quickly raked a mound of straw around the manger, unloaded Zephyrus, and spread out their wool blanket on the straw. When Mary was comfortable, he rode off and located Judith, the midwife. She asked a couple of questions and promised to look in on Mary shortly.

Joseph proceeded to the village well and filled his pouch with fresh water. After purchasing some bread and fruit, he returned to find Judith examining Mary.

"Your wife's labor is progressing normally," she said to Joseph. "According to her description of the contractions, it will be a few hours before the baby is born. But it could be sooner. Will you be waiting somewhere until the child is born?"

"Absolutely not," replied Joseph. "Mary and I are in this together. I want to see the baby as soon as she does. Is there anything I can do to help right now?"

"I have no idea where the birthing chair is tonight," answered Judith. "Why don't you hang a couple of leather straps from that beam over the manger. Mary can use them to hold herself up and push. I've delivered babies in worse conditions than this, but I've never had a father who wanted to help. Be sure you have extra oil for these lamps and a large clay pot of clean water."

"I'll get right on it," responded Joseph.

"Where did you find this guy?" Judith inquired of Mary. "Is he always like this?"

"He is," laughed Mary. "Actually, I didn't find him. He found me. And I know he won't let our little boy out of his sight."

"Oh, it's a boy, is it? And how do you know that?" queried Judith.

Mary smiled wryly and passed her predicament on to Joseph, "How do we know that, Joseph?"

"Well," he reflected, "we think we have some divine assistance on that question. So you'll just have to take our word for it. If we are wrong, I'll bring you a roasted lamb. Is that a fair answer?"

"Fair enough, young man," laughed Judith. "Now, call me when Mary's pains are about sixty heartbeats apart and barely tolerable."

Joseph obtained the water and extra oil. He then sat down beside Mary and together they pondered the drama that was steadily enveloping them.

"Mary, can you grasp all of this? We are stumbling into history's greatest event. Our future king, the Son of God, is about to arrive in a stable in Bethlehem, and no one knows except us. Is this a dream or a nightmare?"

"We don't have a choice anymore," she answered. "We have to believe. Jesus is coming, and I can't stop him. Listen to me, Joseph. I may act a little crazy and scream at you or something. Just stay steady and keep talking to me, okay? God got us into this, and I know he will get us through it. I believe He wants us here."

"Whatever you say, my bride," he answered.

"In case you haven't noticed," Mary added. "This place is spotlessly clean. Onan explained that the priests are under a rabbinical mandate to keep themselves, the birthing stalls, the limestone manger, and the newborn lambs ceremonially clean. As soon as Jesus is born, I will be considered unclean for seven days so we will need to get out of here quickly tomorrow."

"And take our straw with us," speculated Joseph. "Here, let me hold your wrist. I want to count your heartbeats between contractions. Hmmm, that was two hundred heartbeats. I guess Jesus is not quite ready to make his appearance," observed Joseph.

By midnight, Mary's contractions had become stronger and more frequent. Joseph rode back to the residential area and knocked on Judith's door. After some brief questions, she promised to be there shortly. When Joseph returned, Mary asked him to retrieve a small blanket of soft cotton from her things. They were ready.

Judith arrived with a friend and a pail of warm water just as Mary let out her first uncontrolled cry of pain. About ten paces away, Zephyrus snorted, stamped his feet, and reared up. When the next contraction came, Judith instructed Mary to grab ahold of the leather straps and push. Mary's face was hot and damp as she lay back and waited for the next contraction. The two midwives chatted excitedly, encouraging her and, before long, little Jesus appeared.

"Well, you two were right. It's a boy and a healthy one at that," chimed in Judith. "Mary, you did beautifully. You cried out some but never lost your focus."

Shortly thereafter, they had Jesus washed and wrapped in the cotton sheet. "Here you are, Mary. What a perfect little baby. Already looks like his father."

Mary was eager to take Jesus into her arms. With a sense of compassion and wonder greater than she had ever known, she looked into his face. Completely engulfed in the moment, she was not even aware of Joseph's scruffy beard on her cheek. In the flickering light, they gazed intently upon the most sacred revelation of all time.

"Immanuel," Mary whispered. Then she spoke out loud, "Hello Jesus. Welcome to your world! We barely made it on time, but here we are in Bethlehem, just like you wanted."

"Now wait a minute," interjected Judith. "First you tell me it's a boy. Then, you call him Jesus. Now, you welcome him to Bethlehem like it was his decision. Am I missing something here?"

"Oh, Joseph can explain," Mary replied, not the least bit distracted.

Joseph stood up and pulled some more hay together for Mary to lean against.

"Just a moment," he said and stepped out from under the thatched covering over the manger to take a few deep breaths. He was still feeling light-headed from seeing the raw realities of childbirth up so close.

Joseph looked back and saw Mary's priceless expression as she gazed intently into Jesus' face and kissed him repeatedly. She was deep inside her private new world of mother and child. She was welcoming Jesus to earth with the warm words and gentle touch of an adoring mother, no matter who was listening.

As Joseph approached the women again, Mary glanced up and mouthed the word,

"Sorry."

"To put it simply, Judith," said Joseph, "I guess it's more of a God thing." Having no clear idea what to say next, he just continued talking.

"Each of us brings to our family story some strong convictions. Mary was convinced she would have a son. We were both convinced that we should name him Jesus. We had to register here for the census because both of our families are descendants of King David. So, it made a lot of sense for Jesus to be born in Bethlehem. When we barely made it in time, it gave us peace that this was what God wanted and that he helped us get here."

Judith stood quietly, pondering what Joseph had said. She then stared at Mary and Jesus. Finally, she reached down, pushed Mary's damp hair out of her eyes, and said,

"Honey, there is more going on with you two and your baby than I can figure out. But that's okay. Now, let me show you how to wrap Jesus, as you call him. Your cotton cloth is good for a start but you need something more substantial."

"Joseph, would you cut me a strip of that coarse burlap cloth? No, wait! A strip is already draped over the manger. Watch, Mary, and I will show you what this manger is good for."

As she picked up Jesus and laid him down in the carved out surface of the manger, Judith commented affectionately,

"All right, you little lamb of God, let me wrap you up tight."

When she had finished, she placed Jesus back in Mary's arms.

"Now you two get some rest. I'll come back in the morning and see how you and Jesus are doing."

Joseph slid down beside Mary and asked her what she was seeing.

"I think I see contentment and pleasure when his face is touched."

Cupping the infant's head ever so gently, Mary whispered,

"Jesus, did your Father say something to you just now, like 'You are my Son, today I have caused you to be born of a woman?' Perhaps he said it as you were leaving heaven, if that makes any sense. Anyway, I am that woman, your mother."

In the stillness of the moment, Jesus' eyes stirred and his lips parted, or so Mary thought. Over the years, she wondered what might have been his response to her question, if he could have spoken.

"And this is Joseph, your earthly father. I think you know his voice."

Joseph placed his rough, calloused hand on Jesus' forehead.

"Hello, Jesus. Welcome to Bethlehem. I'm sorry for not finding a better birthplace, but your Heavenly Father picked out the most wonderful woman in the whole world to be your mother. She'll take good care of you and I'll be around to keep you safe."

Mary looked up.

"Joseph, please don't punish yourself any more. This place is perfect. Do you remember that song we sang as kids about where God lives?"

"Heaven is my throne, the earth a mere stool.
Will you build me a house, a place for me to rule?
It's with people I have made that I want to stay,
With the meek and the humble who care what I say."

"I think God chose this stable because here we have nothing to offer him. Here we can only receive. It's like we are the stable, Joseph. The stable is us. So, here, open your arms and receive what God has given to you."

Joseph took Jesus in his hands and quietly thought about Mary's comment.

"I'm not sure I really get it yet, Mary, but if what you are saying is true, about us being the stable, that changes everything."

He then looked up and prayed,

"Almighty God, it pains me that I have nothing to offer you, but I really don't. I can't even offer you a good attitude. So, yes! I do receive your gift to me as undeserving as I am. Mary was the first and I'll be the second to embrace your son and receive him into the stable of my self-centered life."

Emotions welled up inside Mary as she took Jesus back into her arms. After Joseph tossed some clean straw into the manger, Mary unwrapped Jesus, laid him on the straw, and checked him over carefully.

"Just perfect," she whispered.

Joy and amazement filled their hearts as they gazed into his little face. Mary quietly sang a song of adoration and played with Jesus' little hands.   It was a precious moment they would never forget.

An hour had passed and two of the lamps flickered out. A wave of exhaustion came over Mary and so she asked

Joseph to hold Jesus. He took the child and stood up to make sure that that he would stay alert. And as he paced back and forth, she curled up in the hay and fell asleep. Joseph wrapped Jesus up again in the cotton cloth and coarse outer strip. While cradling him in the crook of his arm, he relit the lamps that had flickered out.

Mary had been asleep for a while when a commotion outside the stable area caught Joseph's attention. Several men were talking excitedly. Not wanting to needlessly wake up Mary, he carefully laid Jesus down in the manger and retrieved his sword from the bottom of his travel bag.

As he buckled on his sword belt he heard the men approaching. They had lanterns and were disturbing the ewes. Zephyrus became particularly agitated as they approached the entrance. At that moment, Joseph faced the age old question of warriors and guardians.

"When faced with danger, does one advance or retreat? Should I step out and challenge the intruders or blow out the lamps and hide?"

Joseph chose to advance.

SEVENTH MIRACLE

The Angels' Celebration

Shortly after Joseph and Mary entered Bethlehem and began their search for a place to stay, a middle-aged man named Joash prepared to leave on the same road.

"Pray that the weather clears up this afternoon," called out his wife as she wiped her eyes in the smoke-filled cooking area of their home.

"What good will prayer do?" muttered Joash to himself, not wanting to offend the women who were working feverishly to prepare a hot meal for his herdsmen.

Half an hour later, he left the main road to Jerusalem and headed in the direction of an ancient stone structure called Migdal Eder, meaning "tower of the flock." The old stronghold had been rebuilt many times over the centuries and was once again in considerable disrepair. At one time, the ground floor served as a birthing room for lambs to be selected and sent to the temple in Jerusalem.

Climbing to the highest window he could safely reach, Joash gazed intently across the rolling hills. His eyes were searching for a flag that would identify a flock of sheep belonging to his brother James. "Late again." mumbled Joash when a small banner finally appeared on a distant rise. He and James had agreed to bring their two dozen herdsmen together at the end of the day to enjoy a hot meal sent to them from their wives in Bethlehem. When he finally reached the flocks, Joash located his brother and announced,

"Hey James, the priests in Jerusalem are sending your lambs back because they were all underweight."

"Sure they were," retorted James. "It's because you switched your pathetic little critters for my enviable lot."

Eventually the bantering wore down and the news that roasted chickens, potatoes, vegetables, and a few skins of Galilean wine were scheduled to arrive before sundown, spread quickly from shepherd to shepherd. As Joash departed to inform his own herdsmen, he reminded James of another matter to be resolved.

"Tonight let's decide what to do with the folks' old homestead. Mother has been with us for a year now and doesn't want to go back out there. I recently saw that another rafter has fallen down and it's going to take some serious work to make the house livable again."

Joash and James were the owners of the flocks. Each of them had a home and a family in Bethlehem, but they took turns spending nights in the open country with their herdsmen. Their combined flocks now numbered over seven hundred sheep and were divided into smaller bands of sixty to eighty. Each band was led by two shepherds and a sheep dog. A good herder knew every sheep in his flock and named each one. It was solitary, time-consuming work. Baths were rare and food was sparse. During the long, cold winters, the shepherds had to endure rain and snow with their makeshift tents and occasional camp fires.

The hot food was a big success that night, largely due to the unexpected baskets of fresh bread that Joash's wife, Hannah, sent out to them. It was James' turn to head back to town, taking the wagon of empty baskets with him. After a full meal and some entertaining conversation, he decided to stay until morning. At midnight, the final shift of herdsmen took their place, and everyone else laid out their bedrolls around the campfire. All would be quiet until daybreak.

Without warning, an intense light spread throughout the encampment and surrounding hills. Every shepherd was jarred awake and sat up. Right there, in the middle of their camp, positioned above the embers of their fire pit, appeared an angel.

The power and brilliance of this heavenly being drove every shepherd to his knees. The sheep were undisturbed. When the angel spoke his voice was heard everywhere, like a strong wind, and his words were clear as a bell.

"Do not be afraid. I bring you good news of great joy that will be for all the people. Today in the town of David, a Savior has been born to you; he is Christ the Lord. This will be a sign to you: You will find a baby wrapped in cloths and lying in a manger."

Suddenly, the light intensified and every shepherd flattened himself on the ground. Peeking out above the palms of their hands, they witnessed the indescribable sight of thousands upon thousands of shining angels above them, around them, and as far as they could see.

A chorus of resounding praise enveloped them from every direction as if they had been plunged into a sea of sound and light. Some remembered it as singing, others as shouts of victory and joy, but audible words were branded on their memories,

"Glory to God in the highest, and on earth, peace to men on whom his favor rests."

The shepherds lay motionless until the light had faded and the cool, dark night enveloped them once again. The angels were gone. First one shepherd, then another, raised his head, looked around, and stood up. Joash was the first to speak.

"Men, I have no idea what to say. I never really took God seriously. Obviously, I was wrong. When I first saw the angel, I was sure he was going to rebuke me. Instead, he gave us some news about a child being born in Bethlehem that he called Christ, the Lord. That would be the Messiah. I didn't know that so many angels even existed and have no idea why we were allowed to see their celebration."

One by one, each shepherd admitted his indifferent attitude toward God. They were amazed that they had even survived such close contact with heavenly beings. As they talked among themselves, their curiosity grew stronger. The angel's explanation of the newborn child's location seemed like a compelling invitation to go into Bethlehem and search for him.

"Let's go to town and check it out," proposed James. "If God wanted his angels to tell us about it, then it sounds like we are supposed to go and find him. If he is a newborn wrapped in strips of cloth and lying in a manger, where else could he be except at the birthing stable?"

"We can't abandon the sheep," added Joash. "So half can go now and the other half need to assume the night watch. When we return, I'll take the rest of you back into town so that everyone can see what's going on."

Excitedly comparing memories of the angels and their messages, fourteen of the shepherds hurried to the main road and on into Bethlehem. Their freshly lit lamps swung haphazardly as they headed for the birthing stable.

From the entrance to the stable they could see a few small lamps flickering inside. They paused a moment out of respect for the newborn baby and his mother. At the same time, a horse stirred and snorted its awareness of their presence. The moment they took a step into the stable area, a confident, male voice spoke to them from the shadows.

"What is your business, men?"

Lifting up their lanterns, they found themselves face to face with an imposing, young man holding a drawn sword.

"This may be difficult to believe," stuttered Joash. "We are shepherds from the hills to the west and tonight we were surrounded by a sky full of angels. They were singing and praising God about the birth of a Savior they called Christ the Lord. One of them told us where to find the newborn. The child should be right here somewhere."

A broad smile settled across Joseph's face and he put away his sword.

"Your story is hard to believe, but we are getting used to that. Actually, a couple of hours ago, the child's mother said that there should have been a celebration somewhere. We had no idea that it occurred in the hills outside of town. Wait here until I wake her. She will want to hear what you have to say and you can see the baby you were told about. His name is Jesus."

Joseph could see that Mary was completely exhausted since she'd slept right through all of the commotion. He knelt beside her, pushed some hair out of her face, and kissed her forehead.

"Mary, a celebration really did take place tonight just as you imagined. Apparently, a myriad of angels appeared on the hills outside of town. They sang and praised God and announced Jesus' birth. Some shepherds saw it all and one of the angels told them where to find us."

"Oh my!" blurted out Mary. "Where is Jesus?"

"He is right there, sound asleep in the manger," said Joseph as he pushed some hay behind Mary's back.

By then, the shepherds' lanterns were beginning to illuminate the entire stable. Mary smoothed her skirt and adjusted her headdress as the approaching circle of light reached her. One by one, the faces multiplied until all fourteen stood gazing at her and Joseph and the limestone manger. What the shepherds saw at that moment was fixed in their hearts and memories for the rest of their lives.

There in the flickering light of a few clay lamps was a mound of hay stacked up in front of one of the larger stalls. Leaning back against the hay, sat a young woman wrapped in a blue mantle and a white headdress. With her youthful face and striking black hair, she didn't seem old enough to match the wisdom and confidence in her eyes.

Mary warmly welcomed them with a smile as she said, "Hello there. Please come closer."

Joseph was kneeling to one side, his dark hair tightly bound behind his head. Still wearing a sword belt over his knee-length tunic, he portrayed the relaxed confidence of a well-trained soldier, ready to protect his family at a moment's notice.

Next to the hay was the large, limestone manger where a newborn appeared to be sleeping on a bed of hay. He was tightly wrapped in the strips of cloth mentioned by the angel. The baby's black hair was quite visible against the folds of a soft, white blanket that protruded from the external wrapping. With everyone watching, Joseph picked up Jesus and gently placed him in Mary's arms.

"Men, my name is Joseph and this is my wife, Mary. We are from Nazareth and, through our own contact with angels, we are very much aware of the nature of the child you now see. We cannot explain why God's Anointed One should be born in a stable. But frankly, there was nothing we could do to prevent it. Please tell us who you are and what you have seen tonight."

"Please sit down on the straw and make yourselves comfortable," added Mary. "We have only known Jesus for a few hours. I am not sure yet whether he is aware of what is happening around him, but I want him to hear what you have to say."

"We've never seen angels before, ma'am!" burst out Joash. "But one appeared at our campsite with frightening brilliance. He said that a Savior had just been born to us in Bethlehem and that he is Christ the Lord. He then told us where to find you. Your highness, can you explain this to me? Why is the LORD of heaven here among us as a baby?"

Joseph wanted to step in and deflect the question. He knew that Mary needed rest, not to try to explain God. On the other hand, he had learned to trust her spontaneous insight. Joseph could never predict what she would say and many times it was priceless. So he held his tongue.

"First of all," Mary laughed. "I am no highness. In fact, I am only eighteen years old. Just call me Mary."

She looked up from touching Jesus' hair and fixed her eyes directly on the questioner, "What is your name?"

"Joash, Mary...I am Joash."

"Well, Joash," Mary continued. "As far as the LORD visiting us, I don't understand it either but I believe it's true. Seven hundred years ago, one of our prophets wrote,

'But you, Bethlehem Ephrathah, though you are small among the clans of Judah, out of you will come for me one who will be ruler over Israel, whose origins are from of old, from ancient times.'"

"Joseph and I grew up hearing that God's Messiah would be a heroic warrior, a descendant of King David who would deliver us from our enemies. The angels told us to call him Yeshua, or Jesus, if you prefer Greek. One of them said that he is going to save us from our sins. He is the Anointed One who has been with God forever. We may never understand that, Joash, but we can accept him and love him with all of our hearts. He is also called Immanuel by the prophet Isaiah, because he really is 'God with us.'"

Mary became distracted by the baby in her arms and stopped to hug and kiss her little newborn. Joseph then asked Joash to introduce his friends.

"This is my brother, James. He and I have been shepherding all our lives. We have a contract with the priests at the temple to deliver lambs every week for the daily sacrifices. Our herdsmen were all together last night for a hot meal. Around midnight, we were jolted from our bedrolls by light that lit up the sky as far as we could see in every direction. James, tell them what you saw."

"I don't talk as good as Joash, ma'am, but I can see pretty good," began James. "Right there in the middle of our camp was this blinding, angelic figure. I was scared stiff and when he spoke, I fell to my knees. We all did! His voice was strong and commanding, like a roll of thunder. He told us to look for the newborn Savior in town and said that he would be wrapped in strips of cloth and lying in a manger. We all knew where to look. Adin, tell them what you saw."

Adin happily joined the conversation and said,

"I was watching the farthest flock out there when the light came. It just turned night into day. The angel was a long way off but I could hear him speak like he was right in front of me. As I knelt down, we were suddenly engulfed in waves of supernatural beings. They were everywhere…as far as I could see. And the noise, it was indescribable. They sang and shouted, *'Glory to God in the highest, and on earth peace to men on whom his favor rests.'* I wanted to stay out of their way so I just flattened myself on the ground and covered my face."

"That's exactly the way it was ma'am," blurted out another young herder. "My flock was next to Adin's and when I finally opened my eyes, the angels were gone. I went over and pulled Adin to his feet. We then ran all the way to the campsite. Our sheep never even stirred and we have no idea why."

"This is amazing," Joseph pondered out loud. "It seems like the celebration of Jesus' birth took place in heaven and, apparently heaven is not that far away. God picked you to see the angels' jubilation and tell us about it. You have magnified the wonder of Jesus' arrival beyond anything we had ever imagined. Thank you for coming and telling us about your experience tonight."

The shepherds all grinned and felt really important.

"I have a question for you," continued Joseph. "Do you think that people are going to believe you when you tell them about this?"

The shepherds looked at each other and thought about how their relatives and friends might react to the news. They suddenly realized that some people might think that they made up the story or accuse them of drinking too much.

"You know," concluded one of the younger herders, "I wouldn't believe it if I hadn't been there. But, I was there and I saw everything with my own eyes. I have to tell them."

Joash had been quiet for a while. He finally spoke up again and asked,

"Joseph and Mary, what are you going to do now? Will you take Jesus to the temple in Jerusalem and announce that the Messiah has arrived?"

This time Mary responded.

"So far we have not received any instructions about that. We will go to Jerusalem in forty days for the consecration of our firstborn, but we are not planning to make any public announcements on his behalf. Up to now, God has taken extraordinary measures to keep Jesus' arrival a secret. If he wants to make a public announcement, we will certainly cooperate, but that is his decision not ours."

"I agree," added Joseph. "I think our part is to keep Jesus safe, healthy, and out of sight. We want to welcome you into a very small circle of people who know that Jesus is God's Messiah. We came here to register for the census and then we will look for a place to live here in Bethlehem. Hopefully, I can find some work in carpentry or construction."

Joash paused thoughtfully and then started to get up.

"Listen, we have to get back out to our flocks and let the other half of our crew come in for a short visit. Will that be okay with you?"

Mary answered, "Yes, of course, we want to hear their stories too. But before you go, Joash, tell me how the appearance of the angels has affected you personally?"

Joash sat back down and slowly let out a chest full of air. A tear coursed down his leathery face.

"Mary, we hardly know you, but you have a way of reaching into someone's heart and touching the core issue.

As soon as the angels left us, I confessed to my workers that I had held God at arm's length most of my life. I just pray at mealtimes and figure that God will help those who help themselves, if you know what I mean."

"Surrounded by his angels and allowed, for a moment, to see into heaven itself, I was ashamed of my pride and self-centeredness. Now I know that God wants me to live like he is really here. Maybe you and Joseph can teach us how to do that."

After the shepherds said goodbye and hurried off, Joseph sat down beside Mary and exclaimed, "This story just keeps getting bigger and bigger; how do you suppose it will end? Since it really is Jesus' story, maybe it never does end."

Joseph slipped one arm behind Mary's head and kissed her hair. She snuggled in close and tucked her head under his chin. Jesus squirmed a bit, partially opened his eyes, and let out a really good cry.

"Oh, oh," chuckled Mary. "I think we are talking hunger here and I'm not sure whether I have any milk yet."

There was little that an eighteen year-old, working-class girl from Nazareth had not seen or heard about mothering. So, with a little persistence, she and Jesus made enough progress to satisfy him for the time being. She then sat back and took a deep breath.

"What a night! We arrived in Bethlehem, I went into labor, we moved into a stable, you found a midwife, I gave birth to Jesus, we missed a celebration of angels, we received fourteen visitors, and now twelve more are coming. Did we miss anything? Like maybe some sleep?"

"Sleep?" inquired Joseph. "And lose out on all this excitement? I think it's time to celebrate Jesus' birth with a song. How about the one you did in Nazareth on the day I first saw you?"

"Yes! Singing is what Miriam did on the day that our nation was born out of the Red Sea. And that song you like really is Jesus' birth song, isn't it?"

As they sang together, both of them were sure that Jesus made an effort to open his eyes. And when they had finished, he received even more tender kisses. A faint glow of first light touched the sky to the east as Mary looked up, and said,

"Before the shepherds arrive, would you talk to God for us? I feel like we are very close."

"Almighty God in heaven," began Joseph hesitantly. "Your son, Jesus, is here with us. Of course, you already knew that. But thank you for letting us hear about the celebration last night. We can't even begin to comprehend that Jesus birth was watched by the angels in heaven. We want to join them now in saying, *'Glory to God in heaven and peace to men on earth who receive your favor.'* You have granted to us the favor of being Jesus' human parents, and we are absolutely humbled. It is a gift beyond price or description. Please keep us from making any big mistakes and help us to find a place to live."

"Mary...Joseph...Judith, here!"

The prayerful moment ended abruptly as Judith rounded the corner with a pail of water and a basket of food.

"Well, you two look like you survived the night. My goodness, Mary, you need to get up and start moving around. Have you bathed yourself yet? And let me see little Jesus. Hmmm, now doesn't he look content. Did you try to nurse him yet?"

Judith asked Joseph to cut a curtain from the big role of burlap cloth and hang it in front of the stall behind them. She then sent him off to freshen up elsewhere while she helped Mary bathe herself and change her clothes. Jesus lay quietly in the manger until it was his turn. Eventually, Joseph returned with a bench and they all sat down to enjoy the fruit, cheese, and bread that Judith brought with her.

The two thanked Judith profusely for her help and agreed to come to her house sometime. When Judith asked where they were going next, Joseph explained,

"We have some visitors coming shortly and after that we will see about housing and registering for the census."

"Visitors?" questioned Judith. "I thought you didn't know anybody here."

"Actually, Judith, we had fourteen visitors last night and twelve more are coming this morning. None of them are family as far as we know."

Judith stood there shaking her head.

"Like I said last night, there are things about you three that I just can't figure out. But I like you a lot. That son of yours, he is a sweetheart. You take good care of him, Mary." And off she went.

As they began to gather their clothes and belongings, a familiar voice came booming from the street. It was Joash. He had another twelve herders in tow and couldn't wait to introduce them to Joseph, Mary, and Jesus.

"Here they are, men, just like I told you. And this is the baby the angels told us about. He was born at the same time that we saw all those angels last night."

"Come in, come in," beckoned Joseph. "Here is the palace where God's Anointed One arrived. From what the other herdsmen told us, it would have been too small to accommodate the celebration you attended."

They laughed at the reference to a palace and all started talking at once. The conversation was even more animated than before since the sun was up, the town was stirring, and there was no need to be quiet. Their stories matched up perfectly with the others and Mary asked them to repeat everything until she knew exactly what the angels had said. She later wrote it all down in her scroll.

Before departing, Joash extended an invitation.

"Joseph, we know that guestrooms in town are full. I have spoken with my wife, Hannah, and we would like you to stay at our house here in Bethlehem. Hannah has a lot of questions about last night. Perhaps Mary could explain it to her. James and I have a proposal to make since you are looking for work. It might even turn into a long term housing situation for you."

"That would be amazing, Joash, and we accept your hospitality. By the way, we have another good friend traveling with us. We need to decide whether to leave him here or take him with us to your house."

When Joseph whistled, Zephyrus snorted, stomped the ground with his front hoofs, and stared at the shepherds. The herders approached him admiringly as Mary and Joseph spoke with Joash about the move to his home.

The herders soon headed back to their flocks, although some took detours on the way to inform their friends and family members about the night's events. People listened with amazement but didn't immediately embrace their story.

Joash promised to return shortly, so Joseph tied their belongings onto Zephyrus' saddle and sat down beside Mary.

"Are you still sure that we were supposed to be in this stable last night?" he asked.

"Oh, definitely," laughed Mary. "It makes perfect sense now. The angels in heaven knew exactly where we were and told the shepherds how to find us. They made no apologies for Jesus' birthplace. Plus, it was the best place to welcome fourteen visitors in the middle of the night. They probably hadn't bathed or changed their clothes in days and we weren't looking that great either."

"Hmmm, I guess you're right," responded Joseph. "If we had been in someone's guestroom, I suppose the host family would have felt obligated to turn away the shepherds. They would have blamed us for all of the commotion and gossiped all over town about the fact that we think our baby is the Messiah. That wouldn't have worked out too well. So, are you saying that God is letting us discover what he has already planned out?"

"I am sure of it, Joseph. When the circumstances we encounter are different than what we planned, we need to trust God and live that moment expectantly. Look at what is happening now. We never planned to stay in a home full of shepherds' families. But what are God's intentions for us, or for them? We are going to be surrounded by a whole community of people, some of whom have heard about Jesus from angels. The angel told them that the Savior was born for them, too. I have this feeling that God is sending us there to help them understand why Jesus has come."

Soon, Joash and Hannah arrived and lost no time in reaffirming the invitation to come and stay in their home.

"Hello, Mary," exclaimed Hannah. "I'm Joash's wife. Something happened to him and his herdsmen last night that I don't understand. He's been talking about angels and your baby and changing his ways. I don't know anything about angels, but I've had ten babies. If you are the newborn's mother, then I know that you need some rest, nourishment, and time to heal. So come, let's walk along together to our home on the edge of town."

By the next day, Mary was feeling stronger, but slowly realized that Hannah's home was a communal arrangement. Two of her married daughters and their children lived with her while their husbands worked for Joash herding sheep. All the women and children slept in one room while the men slept in another. Some of the single shepherds cycled through the home on their day off to wash their clothes, get a good night's sleep and hopefully, eat a big meal.

Mary could hear Hannah turning away other shepherd's wives who were stopping by to see the mother and baby at the center of all the circulating rumors. They wanted a firsthand look at the two. After hearing some of their questions, Mary suggested that Hannah let them all come back the following afternoon. She would do her best to explain what had happened two nights earlier.

Joseph spent the day in a long line, waiting to register for the census with Jewish officials from Jerusalem. He was also required to pay a head tax of one Tyrian shekel to a representative of the Roman emperor for each male member of his family. Arriving back at Joash's home, he was met by Mary who urgently wanted to speak with him.

"The shepherds' wives are coming tomorrow and want to hear an explanation of the angels' appearance to their husbands. Should I tell them that this is our baby or should we explain that he was miraculously conceived and I am still a virgin?"

Joseph started to answer and then paused. He then started again,

"You know, this is not an easy question, is it? Everyone in Nazareth knows we were married in April, just before Passover. But the angel appeared to you in January, and you conceived shortly after, right? I think we need to drop the matter of you being a virgin and speak of Jesus as our son. When Jesus is of age, of course, he can tell the story any way he wants."

The next afternoon, Hannah's home was packed with women. Mary sat on a padded chair in the middle, holding Jesus. She began with a question of her own,

"When the angels appeared to your husbands, what did the sheep do?"

Everyone sat quietly, looking at each other. Finally a young girl spoke up,

"Adin told me that his sheep were not disturbed at all."

"Well, the same thing happened at my house in Nazareth one night when an angel appeared and talked to me in the outer room," explained Mary. "My whole family slept right through and never moved. The angel was the one called Gabriel in Scripture, and he told me that I would give birth to a son who should be given the name Jesus. He is to become a great king and will occupy the throne of his forefather, David. The kingdom he is going to reign over will never end. An angel also appeared to my fiancé, Joseph, in a dream and told him that we should get married."

"Don't be surprised that your husbands have seen angels," Mary continued. "They are very much a part of this baby's story. My uncle, Zechariah, is a priest and an angel met him in the temple in Jerusalem. The angel promised that his elderly wife would have a baby. I visited them in Beth Hakkerem and Zechariah brought me scrolls of the prophets who wrote about the Messiah. I know how to read and write and copied down some of God's promises in this small scroll. Let me read something the LORD said about the LORD Almighty."

"'Shout and be glad, O Daughter of Zion. For I am coming and I will live among you,' declares the LORD. 'Many nations will be joined with the LORD in that day and will become my people. I will live among you and you will know that the LORD Almighty has sent me to you.'"

"I slowly began to understand that this baby is not just a man, he is the LORD, he is Immanuel. Apparently God values us enough to come and live among us. He wants to deliver us from the bad behavior and brokenness that is ruining the human race. I don't know how he will do that, and I don't understand how he can be here with us and also in Heaven."

"One day, I read in the Psalms of King David that the Anointed One is going to make a proclamation of something that God had decreed about him. The decree was that God Almighty said to the Messiah, 'Now you are my Son because today I enabled you to be born of a woman.'"

"Proclamations are big announcements, right? If the Messiah announced God's decree as he left heaven and arrived on the earth, how do you think the angels would have responded? Probably with amazement and celebration because at that moment heaven reconnected with the earth."

"I think that celebration was what your husbands witnessed two nights ago. No one in town noticed and neither did the sheep. God gave your husbands the ability to see into heaven and to hear from angels.

Jesus' birth in the stable was pretty simple. Joseph and I had a few lamps, two midwives, and a basin of warm water. For some reason, the angel thought that your husbands should attend both events, so he gave them directions to the stable. We were overjoyed to hear what happened out in the fields and it all came together to make perfect sense. That was a very special night. God and his Anointed One added something new to their relationship; they became Father and Son."

"Why God would choose a poor, country girl like me to be Jesus' mother, I cannot say. And why God included your husbands in this event, I have no idea. Your husbands told me that thousands of angels were singing,

'Glory to God in the highest and on earth peace to men on whom his favor rests. '"

"All that excitement was foreseen by the prophets as they looked forward to this day. Let me read to you something that Isaiah wrote,

"You who bring good tidings to Zion, go up on a high mountain. You who bring good tidings to Jerusalem, lift up your voice with a shout, lift it up, do not be afraid; say to the towns of Judah, 'Here is your God!'"

"Okay, Mary," interrupted Hannah. "You make me feel like I am watching a beautiful sunrise for the first time. You are telling us that your baby is God's Anointed One and that he has come to live among us. Will he set us free from Rome and from Herod? Do we have to wait for him to grow up before this happens?"

"Hannah, I don't know. When I think about all that God has shown me in the last nine months, I have no more doubts. I love Jesus, I trust him, and when he grows up, I will follow him. The more we learn about him from the

Scriptures, the better we can understand what he will do for us. Listen to what Jeremiah wrote,

'The days are coming,' declares the LORD, *'when I will raise up to David a righteous Branch, a King who will reign wisely and do what is just and right in the land...This is the name by which he will be called: the* LORD *Our Righteousness.'"*

"How many of you feel like you are good enough to be in God's presence?" asked Mary.

After a long silence, Hannah responded, "Mary, you know us. We are shepherds' wives. We are good souls, but we don't even know all of the commandments that God wants us to obey. I wouldn't dare go into the temple in Jerusalem, much less into God's presence."

"I know exactly how you feel," returned Mary, "but one day, this child will give us the right to be in God's presence. He will be the righteousness that we don't have. I don't know how he will accomplish it, but we can begin to trust him right now and believe that he will do it for us. The angels promised peace to those who receive God's favor. Jesus is God's favor. You can hold him and believe in him if you want to."

EIGHTH MIRACLE

Simeon and Anna

"There it is, Joseph," exclaimed James with an air of wistfulness and pride. "That's where we grew up."

Joseph stepped forward and glanced over the picturesque valley where a small lake and natural stone house caught his attention. He paused thoughtfully and then responded,

"What an idyllic setting. How could Mary and I not be interested?"

As he and his new friends approached the abandoned structure, he could see that two ceiling beams had collapsed, leaving a rubble of roof material and weeds scattered across the floor.

"If you would like to renovate this house and occupy it with Mary and Jesus, we will do our best to provide you with the building materials," proposed Joash. "You can stay here as long as you want."

"Don't get us wrong, Joseph," observed James. "It seems like you, Mary, and Jesus should be housed in a palace somewhere. But, then again, we found you in a stable and you didn't seem to have a problem with that."

"Honestly, I had a big problem with it. But Mary wouldn't let me get away with it. She was sure that God wanted us in that stable. She believed that God didn't send his Son to receive anything special from us but rather to do something special for us. That's quite a thought, isn't it?"

After discussing the project of renovating the shepherd's childhood home with Mary, Joseph agreed to do it. They sensed that God had dramatically chosen this community to care for them and to learn from them about God's simple and long-awaited plan to revive mankind.

On the eighth day of his life, Jesus was circumcised in a brief ceremony at the home of Joash and Hannah. Members of the families of James and Joash families, along with some off-duty herdsmen, filled the home to overflowing. The women prepared a substantial noon meal that drew Joseph, Mary, and Jesus even more tightly into what they were now calling their adopted family.

Hannah managed the household with remarkable efficiency and warmth and constantly involved the younger women in meal preparation and cleaning. Mary was well-prepared to help in the home but the constant flow of questions from family members and visitors distracted her from her tasks. Sensing the dilemma, Hannah stepped in with some advice,

"Mary, I want you to leave the chores to us. We know you have a very special baby and we want to learn all that we can about him. Right now, you are his mouthpiece, so when the women have questions, you need to stop and talk with them. We are all stuck on the same question. Was it a dream the men had? Was it the wine they drank? Or is heaven really all around us if God would allow us to see it?"

"After our gathering with the women," responded Mary, "I remembered something else that I read from the scroll of Isaiah when I was at my aunt's home in Beth Hakkerem. Isaiah wrote four songs about the Lord's servant. When I learned that Jesus is going to be that special servant, I copied them into my scroll."

"This will stretch your imagination, Hannah, but in these short ballads, God and his servant are talking to each other. It takes some getting used to, but Jesus has been around for a long time and maybe time doesn't even matter to him. Here, I'll read you a few lines from the second song."

"And now the LORD says –
  he who formed me in the womb to be his servant
  to bring Jacob back to him
  and gather Israel to himself...

  It is too small a thing for you to be my servant
  to restore the tribes of Jacob
  and bring back those of Israel I have kept.
  I will also make you a light for the Gentiles,
  that you may bring my salvation to the ends of the earth...

  Shout for joy, O heavens; rejoice, O earth;
  burst into song, O mountains!
  For the Lord comforts his people
  And will have compassion on his afflicted ones."

"Hundreds of years ago, God revealed to Isaiah the conversations that he and Jesus were having about his mission on earth. He then tells the hosts of heaven to shout for joy. I think that's what your husband saw happening."

"But, Mary, why did God pick Joash and the herders? Why didn't he pick the Sanhedrin or some priests in the temple? No one is going to believe shepherds!"

"I don't know, Hannah. Maybe it was to prove that everyone is special to God. Or maybe it was to keep Jesus safe. I'm not sure that God wants the Sanhedrin to know about Jesus right now. Do you think Jesus would even survive if he had been born in Jerusalem? Herod kills anyone who might replace him, even his sons and wife. Let me share a song with you that I wrote after the angel told me I was going to be Jesus' mother."

Mary quietly sang her song about magnifying the Lord. When she finished, Hannah leaned forward and gave her a warm embrace.

"Mary, it's getting easier to believe in your son. Will you teach me your song? I want to sing it, too."

Forty days after childbirth, Joseph and Mary needed to appear at the temple in Jerusalem, just as Zechariah and Elizabeth did. The three departed on foot for Jerusalem, intending to find lodging and appear at the temple the following morning. As they walked along, Jesus wrapped in Mary's mantle or nestled in Joseph's arms, fresh questions arose about the nature of their son.

"Do you sense anything about Jesus that is different from other babies?" inquired Joseph.

"He seems to be completely normal. He smiles, he cries, he stretches, he looks into my eyes when he is nursing and I can hardly look away. All of that is typical of newborns. Most women I know feel the same way."

"There is one thing, maybe. When I took him to the Bet Midrash the other day and read out loud from the prophets, he became very still and just looked at me. I'm probably imagining things but he seems to have a special connection with the words of Scripture."

"When I think of all the prophecies I have read about Jesus," Mary continued, "it's more than I can grasp. The angels called him Son of God, Heir of David's Throne, Savior, Christ, LORD, and Jesus. Add to those names the ones given him by the prophets, like Anointed One, Immanuel, the LORD's Servant, Wonderful Counselor, Mighty God, Everlasting Father, and Prince of Peace. How can we ever distinguish between Jesus and his Father?"

"I don't know. I really don't know," responded Joseph. "Maybe Moses gave us the Shema to remind us of their oneness.

When the city came into view, Mary wished to walk up the Kidron Valley and enter the city through the Eastern Gate.

"I have a song that I want to sing to Jesus, and I've been thinking about it for a long time," she said.

When the gate came into view, Mary moved to the edge of the road, lifted Jesus up, and turned his face toward the city. She then sang softly into his ear,

> "*Lift up your heads, O you gates;*
> *be lifted up, you ancient doors,*
> *that the King of glory may come in.*
>
> *Who is he this King of glory?*
> *The* LORD *strong and mighty,*
> *the* LORD *mighty in battle.*
>
> *Lift up your heads, O you gates;*
> *lift them up, you ancient doors,*
> *that the King of glory may come in.*
>
> *Who is he, this King of Glory?*
> *The* LORD *Almighty –*
> *he is the King of glory."*

Joseph took Jesus into his arms, lifted him up to his face, and whispered,

"Our timing may be a little off, Jesus, so let's just call this a dress rehearsal. Someday, we will follow you into Jerusalem by the thousands, and I can hardly wait."

Smiling proudly and quietly humming her song, Mary grabbed ahold of Joseph's arm as they stepped back into the crowd flowing through the gate that afternoon. Their course took them past the temple mount and into the lower city where they found a room for the night.

Elsewhere in the city lived an aging, senior resident of Jerusalem by the name of Simeon. As a rabbi, Simeon had taught for many years in one of Jerusalem's academies of learning. His devotion to God and careful observance of the Law of Moses were an inspiration to all who knew him.

Simeon was well-versed in all of the Scriptures that addressed the arrival of Israel's coming deliverer. For years, he had given himself to praying earnestly that God would fulfill his promises and send the Messiah. One day in the temple, Simeon was overwhelmed by a sense of peace that God had heard his prayers; that he would allow him to personally see the Messiah before his life ended.

Simeon was not the only senior citizen in Jerusalem to live out his years with these expectations. A widow named Anna from the Hebrew tribe of Asher spent all of her waking hours in the temple. In spite of her eighty-four years, she was among the first to enter and the last to leave each day through the southern doors. As a passionate worshiper of God, it was Anna's delight to attend the morning and evening sacrifices and pray constantly for the promised Messiah to appear.

It was a cold, wintry morning when Joseph, Mary and baby Jesus left their room and walked briskly through the quiet streets of Jerusalem toward the temple. A three-fold blast of silver trumpets echoed across the city and announced the opening of the temple gates. Hearing this, their pace quickened. It was Jesus' first visit to what, in the minds of his parents, already belonged to him.

Most of the worshipers were wrapped in wool shawls and mantles. Mary had made tiny stockings for Jesus' feet and wrapped him in a new wool blanket. With the comfort of a full tummy, he was wide awake and his bright eyes watched expectantly for anything that came into view.

They crossed the enormous Court of the Nations and entered the women's court together. Joseph took Jesus into his arms and made his way across the courtyard to a chamber near the back of the temple. He spotted a priest standing beside an offering box and approached him. A line of young fathers began to form in front of the priest. When Joseph's turn came, the two exchanged greetings and Joseph presented his son. As the priest held Jesus and greeted him as a firstborn son of Israel, Joseph deposited five shekels in the coffer. The priest offered a prayer of praise to God, returned the child, and gave a final blessing.

At the same time, Mary was beginning her ceremony of purification. A sacrifice was required and she chose to offer two doves that she had purchased in the Court of the Nations.

The low crescendo of the temple bellows marked the placing of spices on the altar of incense. Mary and other mothers present for purification were called to ascend the fifteen steps at the front of their court, to prostrate themselves and offer their prayers together with those of the men and priests who filled the Court of Israel before them. They observed their sacrifices being laid on the altar of burnt offerings and heard the benediction that brought God's response to the worshipers. A final hymn, led by a chorus of trained singers, filled the temple courts and marked the end of the morning celebration.

Joseph and Mary reunited in the women's court and waited as the majority of worshipers hurried off to their homes and work sites. Mary was holding Jesus up to her face and telling him about the temple when a short, elderly man reached out and lightly grasped each of the parents by the arm. They looked into his face and were immediately captured by the kindness of his eyes and the expectation in his voice.

"God's blessing on you and on your child. Do you know the true nature of this little one in your arms?"

"We do," responded Joseph. "And has God sent you here to meet his Anointed One? We are never sure who is going to be next."

"My name is Simeon," offered the kindly man. "And for many years I have prayed diligently for the consolation of Israel. Recently, the Spirit of God gave me assurance that I would not die until I had seen the Lord's Christ. I heard nothing of his birth. Was it in Bethlehem, the city of David? Did he receive a royal welcome?"

"He did," smiled Mary. "But, actually, all three of us missed the welcome. The celebration took place on the hills outside of Bethlehem. A host of angels, apparently beyond number, sang and shouted praises to God. About two dozen shepherds saw it all and were sent to tell us all about it. That was the night of Jesus' birth."

"Here," continued Mary, "Since you have prayed so diligently for Jesus to come, then you certainly should hold him, just as we do."

Simeon struggled to hold back his tears but carefully took Jesus into his arms. So great was his respect for the child that he could hardly look into his face. As he raised his eyes to heaven, the tears broke free and ran down his weathered face.

"Sovereign Lord, as you have promised, you now dismiss your servant in peace. For my eyes have seen your salvation, which you have prepared in the sight of all people, a light for revelation to the Gentiles and for glory to your people, Israel."

Mary placed one hand under Jesus, sliding him gently into the crook of her arm. With the other, she reached out to blot Simeon's eyes with a folded cloth. She and Joseph were moved at the scope of his prophecy. Jesus' light would reach out to all nations, not merely the Jews. But Simeon was not finished. Strangely, he turned to Mary with words of warning.

"This child is destined to cause the falling and rising of many in Israel, and to be a sign that will be spoken against, so that the thoughts of many hearts will be revealed. And a sword will pierce your own soul too."

Mary was startled. It was the first time that the messages contained anything other than joy, peace, and blessing for her. Simeon's words briefly awakened the dread she had felt reading Isaiah's fourth song about the LORD's servant. The horrible suffering foreseen by the prophet was locked in her heart and she had never even mentioned it to Joseph.

Yes, there was a dark shadow on Jesus' mission, and now Simeon was predicting that it would touch her life, too. She might have pursued the matter with him, but just then, another person approached.

She was an elderly woman whose back was curved and face wrinkled. A few wisps of thin gray hair escaped her tightly clasped headdress. Her eyes and her voice, however, told another story. She knew who it was that stood before her and her excitement was palpable. She quietly whispered,

"Thank you, Holy God, thank you. Our Redeemer and King has come."

"Dear ones, I am Anna of the tribe of Asher. I never leave this place, so strong is my desire to worship God and await his Anointed One. When I saw you enter the women's court this morning, I felt an inner peace, as if my deepest longings had been met. I know Simeon, and when I saw him approach and take your child in his arms, I knew that our Savior had arrived.

"What a wonderful surprise, Anna. I am Mary, this is my husband, Joseph, and this is Jesus."

She pulled Anna close and let Jesus' face press into Anna's as they embraced.

"Anna," Mary continued, "we know that Jesus is the Redeemer who is to come. How wonderful that you are among those to whom God has revealed his arrival. We tried to keep it a secret but from the moment he was born, God himself has been choosing people to meet his Son. We never know who might be next."

The four lingered in a quiet corner of the women's court as Mary shared some of the miraculous events that had occurred in previous months. Anna and Simeon stood motionless, their eyes fixed on Mary and Jesus. Mary's warmth and animated words captured their souls like an adventure story being told to two small, wide-eyed children. Finally Joseph broke in with a word of caution.

"We know that Jesus' arrival in Bethlehem is an event of such significance that words escape us to describe it. But there are reasons to believe that we should not make any public announcements. So, please use some caution in mentioning this matter to others."

Anna had many friends who were earnestly looking for some sign of God's Anointed One and asked if she could tell them the news privately. Mary was entirely supportive and even invited Anna to come and visit her at Hannah's home.

On the way back to Bethlehem later that afternoon, Mary brought up Simeon's foreboding comments.

"Do you think he was speaking with divine insight or sharing a private reflection of his own?"

'I don't know," returned Joseph. "How could you be subjected to something so painful that it would be like a sword passing through your heart? And why won't I be there to protect you or, at least, to share it with you? It doesn't make any sense."

Mary continued, thinking aloud.

"Simeon described Jesus as a signpost that will force people to make a decision. What do you suppose he meant by people rising or falling?"

"Hmmm," thought Joseph for a moment. "Maybe people have a natural inclination to trust God and love him or to distrust God and reject him. What if Jesus' presence among us will compel our inclinations to become choices, like a signpost compels us to choose one road or another? Look at Joash and Hannah. They weren't particularly interested in the spiritual dimension of life until the angels told them about Jesus. The then chose to believe in him, like we do."

"I think you are right, Joseph. Simeon also said Jesus would be a light for all nations. How will Jesus extend his kingdom to the nations? And why will he become a sign that will be spoken against?"

"I really don't know," said Joseph. "Why would anyone speak against Jesus? Is it because he is going to become our king? I have heard you quote the psalm that says that kings and rulers will gather together against the LORD and against his Anointed One. I just can't see why God would ever let them get away with it."

"Joseph, could we visit Zechariah and Elizabeth sometime? I want to see if his speech has returned and ask him some more questions. I'm dying to see Elizabeth again, and I would love to meet their little son, John. He might even be taking his first steps now."

Back in Bethlehem, Joseph's and Mary's lives were immediately filled with more people and activities than they could manage. Joseph cleaned out the rubble and weeds from the old homestead but decided to wait until the rainy season was over to replace the roof. Once the weather cleared for a couple of days, he and Mary left town to visit Zechariah and Elizabeth.

It was midafternoon when they approached Zechariah and Elizabeth's small home. Joseph dismounted and knocked on the door while Mary pushed her shawl back, held Jesus upright, and sat erect on Zephyrus' back.

The door opened slowly and a sizeable, eight-month-old boy with a head of dark, curly hair appeared first, followed by the woman whose hip he was seated on. Elizabeth, slightly detained by something she was placing behind the door, finally stepped into view. She paused hesitantly, not recognizing Joseph, and then glanced at the horse and its riders.

"Mary, it's you!" she cried out.

"Zechariah, come quickly," Elizabeth shouted as she gently set John down on the doorstep. Joseph moved quickly to take Jesus and help Mary slide to the ground as Elizabeth ran up. The two embraced fervently.

"Here you are, Mary," Elizabeth exclaimed a second time. "And this must be Joseph. If I dare ask, young man, is the baby in your arms the Holy One for whom we are all waiting? What a glorious moment! Please, come and meet our son, John."

By now Zechariah had appeared in the doorway and scooped up his son.

"Yes, here he is!" announced Zechariah proudly. And I am the talking father! Welcome back, Mary, and hello to you, Joseph."

Still holding his son, Zechariah knelt down in front of Joseph, bowed his head and said,

"May all the blessings and promises of Almighty God be on the one you are holding, Joseph. By what name do you address him?"

"His name is Jesus," answered Joseph. That's what the angel told me to call him when Mary returned to Nazareth."

"So you saw an angel, too?" inquired Zechariah as he struggled to his feet.

"Yes," replied Joseph, as they filed into Zechariah's home. "I was about to make the wrong decision about Mary's pregnancy so God sent an angel to stop me."

It took a couple of days for the four of them to relate all of the excitement of the last eight months. Rarely have two couples of such diverse age hung on to one another's words and feelings with such wonderment. When Elizabeth heard that Mary gave birth to Jesus in a stable, she could not contain her surprise.

"How did that happen, Mary? Did you think that God had abandoned you?"

"Honestly, Elizabeth, the labor pains were so strong that I didn't care where I gave birth. Joseph had higher expectations than I did, but in the end, we concluded that God wanted us in that stable. I remembered Isaiah's scroll where he quotes God who said, 'I live in a high and holy place, but also with the person who is contrite and lowly in spirit.'"

"There is another reason God wanted us in the stable," added Joseph, "and it proves that God knows everything before it even happens."

He went on to explain how the shepherds outside of Bethlehem were pulled into an angelic celebration of Jesus' birth that was truly beyond description.

"The angels told the shepherds how to find us," interjected Mary. "They knew what kind of cloth the midwife was using to wrap up Jesus and the fact that our baby would be lying in a manger when they arrived. Can you believe that, Auntie?"

"Oh, my," gasped Elizabeth. "It means that all of heaven was watching you give birth to Jesus. They must love him deeply and had to be astounded by his transition into our world. They are probably watching him right now."

On their last day in Beth Hakkerem, Mary was anxious for an opportunity to talk with Zechariah alone. Eventually, Joseph took John outside to sit on Zephyrus and Elizabeth went along with Jesus in her arms. Mary saw the opportunity, took a deep breath, and plunged in.

"Uncle Zechariah, I need to ask you about something that is troubling me. It came to my attention when I was reading Benjamin's scroll but was too disturbing to show you. The last of Isaiah's four songs about the LORD's servant clearly describes suffering that ends in death. It was so shocking and horrible that I couldn't even write it down in my scroll. Zechariah, Isaiah envisioned the LORD's servant suffering like a lamb being offered as a sacrifice."

"Even your scroll of the prophet, Zechariah, says that the inhabitants of Jerusalem will look on the one they have pierced and mourn bitterly. What is that all about? I don't understand. Will Jesus have to suffer someday? Can you explain this to me?"

To have finally put her deeply guarded fears into words brought tears to Mary's eyes. Simeon's grave predictions had only added to her inner distress, but now her voice was so choked with emotion that she couldn't even bring herself to mention his warning.

"Yes, Mary, I believe I can," replied Zechariah. "And I know that your role as the Messiah's mother makes the thought of suffering even worse. So please listen carefully."

"Sometimes Isaiah's servant refers to the Messiah and sometimes the servant refers to the nation of Israel. In his scroll, Isaiah writes about 'Jacob, my servant' and 'Israel, my servant'. Those are references to our nation."

"We have suffered terribly, Mary. Our people are suffering today. Because of our disobedience as a nation, we have been led to the altar and sacrificed. If you read Isaiah's fourth song with that in mind, it will explain everything. I agree with you that it makes no sense for God's Anointed One to suffer. We have lambs for that as required by the Law. Mary, your Jesus is going to reign forever. His kingdom will never end."

"Oh, thank you, Uncle Zechariah...you don't know how much that relieves me. This matter has grieved me terribly. I have not even dared to look at the fourth servant song recently. Your answer sounds right. I need to let it sink in and hopefully it will set me free. Thank you so much."

The next day, Joseph and Mary pulled themselves away from Beth Hakkerem. Mary and Elizabeth could hardly let go of each other as tears of affection dampened their faces. The rich, meaningful conversations, the transparency of shared prayers, and the preciousness of their two sons was unforgettable.

Arriving back in Bethlehem, Mary was once again engulfed by the unpredictable demands of life in Joash's home. She worked alongside Hannah who served the shepherds tirelessly with food, lodging, and personal attention to their families.

Joseph focused on gathering the materials he would need to rebuild the old homestead. Occasionally he joined the shepherds in the fields when they were shorthanded. One day he volunteered to spend another night watching the sheep with his new friends. Mary caught a frown on his face and quietly pulled him aside.

"Joseph, I honor you for putting yourself on the same level as the shepherds. It reminds me of our son. If all those angels were his adoring subjects in heaven, then he has stepped down a lot further than we will ever have to."

"Yes, I know you're right, Mary, but do you really know what it's like shivering all night in the rain?"

"I don't. I really don't. But, yesterday it was my turn to throw dirt in the hole out back. Unfortunately, the hole was so full that I had to shovel out several clay pots of human waste and carry them to the edge of town. Hannah offered to do it for me, but I knew that wouldn't be right. I held a cloth to my nose, but poor little Jesus had to breathe it since he was wrapped up on my back."

"Oh how disgusting!" exclaimed Joseph. "Joash told us to take care of that and dig a new hole, but we all forgot about it. And who did it come down on? You and Jesus! Mary, I am so sorry for complaining!"

The wet season eventually passed and, along with blue skies and green fields, a fresh sense of enthusiasm emerged in the shepherding community. Every morning, Joseph rode off to work on the restoration of his and Mary's future home. One day, as the almond trees were beginning to bud, he appeared unexpectedly to take Mary and Jesus out to see the progress. To her surprise, Mary discovered a sign over the door that read, "Happy Anniversary!"

"This is a secret celebration so don't tell Hannah or anyone about this," he cautioned Mary. "They all think we were married in January, not April. And we have never even brought up the matter up."

"It's a good thing you said something," responded Mary. "I was just thinking about how fun it was going to be to tell her about our anniversary picnic."

As they sat out on a blanket beside the lake, Joseph candidly posed a question.

"Mary, living with the shepherds and their families has pretty much eliminated any opportunity for us to enjoy any intimacy in our relationship. Have you been thinking that our new home might change that?"

"Joseph, I am so sorry. With us sleeping in separate rooms and getting caught up in answering everyone's questions about Jesus, I couldn't think of a solution. I do believe that God wants us to be intimate and I want it to be really special. I just couldn't imagine how to make it happen."

"So you think that our commitment to abstinence has been fulfilled?"

"Oh yes, absolutely! The angel told you to take me home to be your wife, didn't he? Not your sister, not your maid, but your wife! This home will be a wonderful place for us to finally be alone together."

"It's hard to admit it," Mary added, "but I have been caught up in this role of being a prophetess and have enjoyed the admiration of the shepherds and their wives. Joseph, I am ready to have my own home and to be your wife."

"Thank you, Mary. I don't want to be selfish while you are living so selflessly. Just remember that I love you and long for you all the time. Now I am more motivated than ever to get this house finished."

NINTH MIRACLE

The Magi

The arrival of the dry season brought fresh inspiration to the gardeners, herders, and carpenters of Bethlehem and set in motion a wave of commercial trade across the lands east of the Great Sea. Caravans from Mesopotamia took up their annual journey into Syria, Galilee, Judea, and Egypt. These multilingual merchants sold tea, spices, jewelry, linen, silk, Persian rugs, and articles of silver, bronze, and copper in the major cities along their route. In Egypt, they replenished their loads with goods from Africa and Arabia and made their way back through the same crescent of populous markets to their cities of origin.

In late summer, as Joseph was finishing his renovation project, a caravan appeared in Judea that was different from the rest. In the lead were a dozen mounted soldiers whose square-cut beards, braided cloth headbands, and powerful-looking bows easily identified them as Parthian. Ten camels followed. The first five each bore a sun-shaded seat occupied by a person of distinction. Five more camels bearing loads and sixteen mounted servants made up the rest of the company.

The dignitaries were Parthian scholars from the Royal Academy of Learning in Susa, an ancient city of imperial status during the Assyrian, Babylonian, and Persian Empires. These dignitaries were known as wise men or Magi in the East. Wearied from fifty-seven days of travel, the Magi found themselves energized by the rich display of gardens, trees, and fruit laden vineyards in the beautiful Jordan River Valley. Late in the afternoon, the caravan chose a campsite near Jericho. Servants and soldiers launched into a disciplined sequence of tasks to care for the horses, camels, and travelers.

Before retiring, the Magi gathered with the trip marshal, Marshach, to discuss their arrival in Jerusalem. The natural leader among the five was Mithridath, chancellor of the Royal Academy in Susa. His colleagues were Oristides, Arsames, Phrates, and Tobiah. They decided that Marshach should go ahead to request an audience with King Herod. The caravan would rest a day by the river and prepare for an early departure on the second morning. Marshach and his guards would wait for them on the main road into Jerusalem.

The next day, Mithridath and Tobiah, the latter a devout Hebrew by both religion and parentage, visited city officials in Jericho. They learned about King Herod's failing health and ruthless murders of family members whom he suspected of disloyalty.

"What a dilemma," observed Mithridath upon their return to the caravan. "It appears that the very thing we are searching for is Herod's greatest fear. How is he going to respond to our quest of finding the Messianic heir to David's throne?"

"It doesn't sound good at all," agreed Tobiah. "On the other hand, to enter his kingdom in search of the Messiah without permission would be suicidal. I think it's a test of our faith. If the founder of our order, Daniel, prayed openly to God at the risk of being thrown into a den of lions, why should we desist?"

"Well, I can think of a few reasons," sighed Mithridath. "But one thing I'm learning about faith in God is that we shouldn't give up at the first sign of trouble. We should pray and wait for the Almighty to work things out as he wishes, right?"

That evening, the Magi enjoyed a marvelous meal together. Reflecting on their anticipated audience with King Herod, Mithridath asked Tobiah to explain again the prophecy of Daniel regarding the Messiah's arrival.

"Daniel's prophetical scroll is highly respected by scholars of our tradition and regarded by most Jewish rabbis as inspired Scripture," began Tobiah. "He describes a vision of the angel, Gabriel, who told him that four hundred and eighty three years after a decree for deported Jews in Persia to return to Judea, the 'Anointed One' would appear."

"Rare as it may be for conquering kings to decree that the people they have defeated should be allowed to return to their native lands, this actually happened during the reigns of three Persian emperors - Cyrus, Darius, and Artaxerxes. The early decrees envisioned the rebuilding of the temple in Jerusalem, but those of King Artaxerxes, in the sixth and twentieth years of his reign, envisioned the teaching of the Jewish faith and the rebuilding of the city itself."

"Since the angel told Daniel that this exact number of years would begin with a decree to restore and build Jerusalem, we examined closely the two decrees of Artaxerxes. Believe it or not, we were amazed to discover that by following a solar calendar from the earlier date or a lunar calendar from the latter, we could actually arrive at the same year for the coming of God's Anointed One. That year, you will be happy to know, is twenty-nine years from now. Unfortunately, in twenty-nine years, we will all be dead."

The four chuckled at Tobiah's humor and repositioned themselves in their chairs. Mithridath commented, "I'm sure Herod will enjoy that piece of critical information."

"A little more scripture and cultural background can resolve this dilemma," added Tobiah. "The Jewish prophet, Isaiah, predicted the Messiah's arrival as a newborn, whereas the prophet, Malachi, wrote that he would come to his temple suddenly as an adult. What we have here may well be the difference between a private appearance and a public appearance. Jewish law requires that a spiritual leader, like a priest, must be at least thirty years old. If we subtract thirty years from his public appearance, the child we are seeking may have been born a year ago."

"And when did you first see the star, Oristides?" questioned Phrates.

"Just short of eleven months ago," he replied.

At that moment, a guard stepped into the Magi's tent and indcated that the head cook wished to speak with them. After being ushered in, the chef explained,

"Your honors, we discovered today that two of the cooks we hired in Susa are actually women in disguise. They shaved their heads and wrapped their bodies in such a way that we believed they were men. They are excellent cooks and, in fact, prepared all of the meals that you have eaten on this journey. In Marshach's absence, I wasn't sure what to do and so I requested an audience with all of you."

Mithridath ordered that the two women be brought in. They entered and immediately fell to their knees. Dressed in typical male servant clothing, heads shaved, tanned, and covered by cooks' caps, they immediately begged for forgiveness. And as they did, tears of remorse began to stream down their faces.

"My goodness!" exclaimed Mithridath. "Your meals are remarkable, but you deceived us. Why have you done this?"

"Please forgive us, your honor," exclaimed one of them. "We are single Jewish women from Susa and have always dreamed of being the mother of the Messiah. When we heard that a caravan was going to Judea to look for the child, we knew that this was the only chance we would ever have to meet the chosen woman and her son."

"Well, colleagues, what do you think we should do?" asked Mithridath.

"I say that it's a good thing this matter was discovered today," offered Arsames. "If Marshach were here, he would have them on the slave block in Jericho tomorrow morning. I, for one, hope we can find another solution. The meals these two are preparing are better than anything I get at home." The others readily agreed.

Tobiah knew how passionate Jewish women were about the prophecy of a virgin conceiving the Messianic child and decided to do what he could to rescue them.

"Why don't we simply tell them to drop their disguises and be the women and cooks that they are. We can issue an order that no one is to bother them in any way."

"I like that very much," responded Mithridath. Turning to the cooks he said, "Early tomorrow, you two will be escorted into Jericho. Buy some appropriate clothing for yourselves and rejoin the caravan as soon as you can. We will speak to Marshach on your behalf."

The young women were amazed at this unexpected ruling. They bowed repeatedly and voiced their profound gratitude.

The next afternoon, the caravan crested the Mount of Olives and there before them lay the famed city of Jerusalem. Immediately to their front and rising spectacularly above the Kidron Valley was the gleaming, white stone of the Jewish temple. Rising fifteen stories above a massive open court, it held all of its viewers spellbound. To the right, at the corner of the temple mount, was the easily identified Antonia Fortress. This was the headquarters of the Roman forces in Judea. Across the city, on the western side, King Herod's Royal Palace could not be missed.

Hebrew rabbis were so proud of their city and temple that they boasted, "Eight measures of beauty were given to the world. Seven were taken by Jerusalem and one was left for the rest."

That night, Mithridath asked Oristides to review the sighting of the star that launched their journey but had not been seen since leaving Parthia. "I want to prepare myself for any questions that might arise in the audience with King Herod," he said. "We don't even know if the star has been seen in Judea."

"An excellent question," began Oristides. "When we determined last year that the full number of years of Daniel's prophecy had arrived, we chose to follow his example and implored the Lord God to fulfill his promise. In those days, I observed a new star in the direction of Jerusalem. It was low in the sky but glowed with unusual intensity."

"Tobiah showed me an oracle in the writings of Moses where God compels a prophet named Balaam to tell the truth about Israel's future. Balaam said, '*I see him, but not now; I behold him, but not near. A star will come out of Jacob; a scepter will rise out of Israel.*' Make of it what you will, but a future king accompanied by a star is an extraordinary prediction. We took this celestial light to be a God-given sign that our interpretation of Daniel's prophecy was correct."

The Magi rested that night and shortly after the city gates opened the next day, a portion of the caravan entered. Marshach and ten mounted soldiers in full Parthian military dress led the way. Next came the Magi on camels, each one outfitted with festive harnessing. In the rear, ten servants rode in brightly colored, Persian garments. The crowds stopped and stared, while a few approached the servants to inquire about their city of origin and mission in Jerusalem.

Passing through the royal gates, Marshach and the Magi dismounted and entered the palace. Escorts guided them to a formal hall where Herod's staff and a number of officials were waiting. Shortly after the Magi were seated, Herod appeared and took his place on a gold-covered throne in front of them. The Magi rose and bowed until Herod granted them leave to be seated again.

The King's secretary made a brief presentation of the visitors based on Marshach's earlier description and the King invited them to explain the purpose of their trip to

Jerusalem. Mithridath stood and addressed the king and his court in Aramaic.

I am Mithridath, chancellor of the Academy of Learning in Susa of Parthia, your honor. My colleagues are Oristides, Arsames, Phrates, and Tobiah. We are most grateful to the King for granting us this audience today."

"Our arrival in Jerusalem owes itself to the presence in our land of the great Hebrew prophet, Daniel, a wise and noble counselor to Babylonian and Persian kings. Daniel brought to our land the knowledge of the Most High God of heaven and earth. We, too, are worshippers of the God of Daniel and students of the Hebrew Scriptures. The Spirit of the One True God resided in Daniel. That was proven to us beyond all doubt by the visions he was given over five hundred years ago about the rise and fall of four great empires; Babylon, Medo-Persia, Greece, and Rome."

Immediately Herod interjected, "Are you telling me that the prophet Daniel spoke of the fall of Rome?"

Unbaffled, Mithridath continued, "Yes he did, your honor, but it is apparent that the fall of Rome is nowhere in sight, nor is it the subject of our journey. Daniel predicted that during this fourth great empire, God himself would set up a kingdom unlike all others, a kingdom that would endure forever."

"Even more striking, your honor, is Daniel's revelation of the exact number of days to pass before God's Anointed One, also called the Messiah, would appear. It is our understanding that the days of the Messiah are upon us. I confess that we have waited nearly a year for news from Jerusalem of the birth of the heir to David's throne."

"About this time, our colleague, Oristides, brought to our attention that in the western night skies, as one would look toward Jerusalem, a burning light, a new star if you will, had appeared."

"Another of our colleagues, Tobiah, himself a descendant of the Hebrews, showed us an oracle recorded by Moses.

This oracle predicts that when a star comes out of Jacob, a scepter will rise out of Israel. We felt in our spirits that this burning light was beckoning us to journey to Judea and seek God's Anointed One. Not wishing to trouble your honor any more than is necessary, our question is simply this, *'Where is the one who has been born king of the Jews? We saw his star in the east and have come to worship him.'"*

Utter silence fell over the room. No one dared to move. Herod appeared as if someone had just informed him that Jerusalem was surrounded by a foreign army. A minute passed. Finally, Herod stirred himself to give an answer.

"My advisors have failed to inform me of the matters you speak about so eloquently. If you will return tomorrow at this time, I will tell you what I can. In the meantime, my staff will provide you with some refreshment and guidance to the temple, which I understand you wish to visit."

After the Magi departed, Herod summoned the high priest with urgency. He was irate.

"How is it that Parthian Magi know more about the predictions of Jewish prophets than you do?" he fumed. "Did Daniel actually give a date for the arrival of this Anointed One? And where is he supposed to be born? Why have you been keeping me in the dark about all this? I built you the greatest temple in existence today. Are any of you actually reading the scrolls you so zealously guard?"

The high priest, having been appointed by Herod, began his defense by casting serious doubt on the idea that astrologers of the Persian tradition would know prophecy better than the priests in Jerusalem. He then deferred to his senior biblical scholar to answer the matter of Daniel's prophecy.

"Your honor, there are many possible interpretations of Daniel's sixty-nine weeks. None of them actually indicate the current year. As far as the place of birth, the prophet, Micah, identified Bethlehem as the site of the coming Messianic ruler. Bethlehem is the birth city of King David, that is true. His descendants, however, are scattered everywhere in Judea and Galilee. The recent census ordered by the emperor clearly confirmed this. Bethlehem is a humble village, your honor, and none of its leading families is harboring a child of Messianic aspirations. We are quite sure of that."

Meanwhile, the five Magi had dismounted a short distance from the southern entrance of the temple. To their left, the retaining wall of the temple square rose nearly one hundred feet before reaching the main floor. They ascended the steps of the entrance and entered an enormous, open courtyard that surrounded the temple itself.

"This is the Court of the Gentiles," explained Tobiah. "It is intended to facilitate the worship of God by visitors from foreign nations."

As the Magi stood there, the presence of cattle, goats, sheep, and caged birds for arriving supplicants to purchase and offer as sacrifices was distracting. Hoping to find a quiet spot for contemplation and prayer, the visitors were gradually jostled into a corner of the plaza where the smell of animals and the din of bargaining gave them the impression that they were in a street market, not a house of worship.

"I'm not sure what to say, Tobiah," uttered Mithridath. "The temple over there is awe-inspiring but the entrances to it are all marked 'For Jews Only.' I think I would rather pray to God from my rooftop in Susa than kneel here in this courtyard. Is this what God had in mind when he told Isaiah to write, "*my house will be called a house of prayer for all nations?*' Is this really it?"

The next morning, the Magi met with Herod again. Herod had with him a few senior staff members and a couple of military officers. He questioned the Magi at length about when they first saw the star and how old they thought the royal child might be. He then informed them that the high priest and members of the Jewish Sanhedrin were all in agreement that the likely birthplace of the coming ruler was the village of Bethlehem, just a half-day trip to the south.

"My honored guests, I am humbled that you have come such a great distance to worship the future king of the Jews. I want you to proceed quietly with your search. As soon as you have found the child, come back and tell me personally where he is. I want to be among the first to kneel and worship the new king myself."

Totally surprised byt this radical change in Herod's demeanor, the Magi took their leave and returned to their campsite. A sense of elation and urgency settled over them.

They decided to leave their camp at daybreak and circle Jerusalem at some distance before pursuing the main road south to Bethlehem. Marshach's guides were dispatched ahead to locate a campsite out of sight of the small village. Mithridath wanted them to project the image of a passing caravan totally disinterested in the life of Bethlehem's residents.

The next evening, after dusk had settled over the hills around Bethlehem, the Magi were dining in their tent. Suddenly, Oristides burst in with an exuberant announcement.

"The light is back and burning brighter than ever before."

They all dropped their plates and dashed out to see. Sure enough, there it was, low and bright in the direction of the village. Soon, the whole caravan was staring at the light and chattering in amazement. Marshach and a few soldiers walked with the Magi to a hilltop north of Bethlehem. The majority of houses occupied a valley filled with trees and gardens and the residents seemed quietly unaware of the phenomenon taking place overhead. Oristides observed,

"The burning light is so low over the hills to the west that its light may not even be visible in the village."

Everyone's excitement was palpable and Mithridath suggested that they return to the caravan and plan a course of action. Back inside their tent, the five knelt and poured out their wonder and gratefulness to God. The growing realization that the Anointed One was hidden to most, if not all of the very nation he was coming to save, left them with a feeling that they should tread very lightly on the newborn's surroundings. Stepping outside, they discovered that the star had disappeared again.

Phrates proposed that they stay in their camp the following day and send some innocent-looking foot travelers into the village to ask about newborns and possible residences in the hills to the west.

"And who might that be?" questioned Arsames. "I'm afraid that our entire delegation looks and talks like Parthians." A long pause ensued until Tobiah spoke up,

"Wait a moment, our two female cooks speak Hebrew flawlessly and are even wearing locally made garments. They would be perfect."

"Wouldn't you know it," muttered Marshach under his breath.

The two were immediately summoned and the task explained to them. They responded enthusiastically. The possibility of redeeming themselves and having a strategic role in discovering the whereabouts of the royal child was beyond their wildest dreams.

The next morning, the women worked with Tobiah and Phrates on a plausible explanation for entering Bethlehem and the two set out just before noon. Two other servants were sent on foot to circle the village, looking for roads and residences in the hills to the west.

In the late afternoon the two cooks reappeared and were immediately surrounded. The news was obviously good because their eyes were dancing and they were out of breath. Nervously entering the Magi's tent, they bowed and knelt beside the pillows they were offered.

"We talked with the women who were washing clothes at a public pool and explained our interest in meeting families with newborns who might need maids to cook and help with children. The fact that we had come from Jerusalem made perfect sense to them."

"The women counted up all of the newborns they could think of and told us there were seventeen births during the last twelve months. One of the babies belongs to a carpenter who is rebuilding a house in the hills to the west."

"On our way back, a young woman caught up with us and said she overheard our conversation at the pool. She is married to a sheep herder in Bethlehem. She told us that on the night that the carpenter's son was born, a lot of angels had a celebration in the fields where her husband was. When people in town began to make fun of the shepherds' report, they stopped talking about it openly. She said the name of the carpenter is Joseph, his wife is Mary, and the baby is…"

The cook who was speaking became choked with emotion and embraced her companion. The other took a deep breath and continued, "The baby's name is Yehoshua. It seems like this might be the child you are looking for."

Mithridath stepped forward, lifted the two to their feet and embraced them both at once.

"My dear daughters, you have done an invaluable service. If the star leads us tonight to this child and his mother, I promise that you will be there to meet them."

As the cooks left the tent, the Magi were moved with excitement. Tobiah couldn't resist unfolding another pearl of wisdom.

"The boy's name is Jesus to those who speak Greek. Yehoshua is Hebrew and means 'the LORD is Salvation.' It is often shortened to Yeshua. This is too good to be true."

At dusk, a small caravan of five camels, ten soldiers, and a few servants prepared to depart. The Magi paced nervously back and forth and glanced into the darkening sky. They then gathered in a small circle while Mithridath prayed.

"Our Great and Holy God, we have followed your star to this place…"

Suddenly, Oristides interrupted.

"Look behind you, there it is! And brighter than ever!"

They all glanced to the west and gasped in amazement. "What are we waiting for?" someone blurted out.

Off they hurried to their camels. Before being helped to mount, Mithridath called one of the remaining guards.

"Tell everyone that our mission will soon be accomplished. I will personally explain its meaning to all who wait up for our return. Check and see that the two female cooks are mounted and in our company."

The caravan followed Marshach and the two servants who had confirmed the location of a simple stone house to the west of the village. As they slowly progressed in the moonlight, the burning light seemed to be closer than ever.

An hour later, the light was as much over them as ahead of them. Marshach stopped and sent some servants to assist the Magi dismount and come forward.

There in a shallow valley, was a small stone house. The roof was extended to the back over an animal stall and light could be seen through an open door and single shutter.

Mithridath choose to send Marshach ahead with Tobiah, in case the Hebrew language was preferred. The two lit a lamp and walked down a path toward the house. As Tobiah and Marshach neared the door, a mature, young man stepped confidently outside as he finished buckling a sword belt around his waist. Tobiah spoke in Hebrew.

"Forgive us for appearing at night, but are you the carpenter they call Joseph?" When Joseph answered affirmatively, Tobiah continued.

"I am Tobiah, a descendant of the tribe of Benjamin and a resident of Parthia. This is Marshach, a Parthian of Persian descent. We have traveled here with other companions who are worshipers of the One True God. It was revealed to us in recent days that God's Anointed One had arrived in Judea. We were guided to your home by the burning light that is now above us."

Joseph looked up and gasped.

"For the sake of my companion, may I continue speaking Aramaic?" added Tobiah.

"Yes, of course," responded Joseph in Aramaic, still looking up.

"Before I signal my companions to approach, may I inquire with profound humility, do you have a son whom you know to be the Messiah, God's Anointed One, and future King of the Jews?"

Joseph paused and looked into the doorway where Mary stood holding Jesus. Turning back to Tobiah, he answered,

"As far as I know, aside from my wife and myself, there are only six elderly Jews and a few shepherds in all of Israel who know of what you speak. Why God would reveal this matter to worshipers in Parthia, I do not know. If you intend any harm to the child or his mother, I will give my life in their defense and some of you will lose your lives as well. But the answer to your question is yes. God has shown us from before the child's conception that he is the Anointed One, the Messiah, and the Son of the Living God."

Tobiah and Marshack both knelt.

"Praise be to the LORD our God, who has sent salvation to his people and to the nations," offered Tobiah.

"Marshach, signal to the others that they may approach."

More lamps were lit as the four Magi made their way down the hill to the house, followed by a column of horsemen and camels. Marshach guided the caravan into a semicircle in front of the house and ordered everyone to dismount. Mary stared from the doorway in disbelief. Among the miraculous events surrounding Jesus' birth that she had witnessed, none was more unexpected than this.

Tobiah introduced Joseph to the others. Mithridath took a step forward and tried to soften the magnitude of their intrusion.

"Joseph, we are no less surprised than you at the circumstances of our meeting. We have for many years studied the Hebrew Scriptures and discovered that the time had come for Israel's Anointed One to appear. The burning light you now see convinced us some months ago that he had arrived."

"We made the journey to Jerusalem and requested an audience with King Herod. He knew nothing about a recently born King of the Jews. After consulting with the chief priest, he told us that Bethlehem was predicted to be the birthplace of the coming Ruler."

"As far as we know, none from Jerusalem are following us tonight. We will not tarry long but our deepest desire is that we might meet and worship the child that God has placed in your keeping."

Mithridath kneeled and continued, "We give you our pledge before the God of heaven and earth that we will not harm or frighten the boy and his mother."

The others also knelt in agreement, so Joseph stepped into the doorway and asked Mary if she had overheard everything.

"I think I did, Joseph. This is beyond anything I have ever imagined. But this is God's story and our safety comes from Him. If you wish, Jesus and I are ready to receive them."

Joseph stepped back to the Magi and bowed.

"We honor you for coming so far to meet our son. Mary and I welcome you into our simple home. Jesus meets people easily, so do not fear that you will disturb him. Please come in."

The Magi carefully filed into the outer room followed by Marshach. They could barely fit inside. Mary hastily pulled a headdress over her hair while Jesus, sitting erect in her arms, watched them comfortably with one arm resting around his mother's neck. As the six knelt again, Joseph spoke first.

"Honored guests, this is my wife, Mary, and our son, Jesus. We accept your respect and devotion to Jesus, but please stand."

"Mary, would you sit on this stool and make yourself comfortable? This is Tobiah. He is a member of the tribe of Benjamin and his home is in Parthia."

Joseph continued, "Tobiah, please introduce your companions to Mary and tell us of your activities in the land that so readily defeats the Roman legions."

At Joseph's compliment, the travelers smiled, nodded in appreciation, and relaxed a little.

Tobiah introduced each of the Magi. One by one they stepped forward to acknowledge their names and bowed again. Joseph continued to facilitate the conversation.

"Gentlemen, we are as much surprised at the dignity and honor you bring to us as you must be at the simplicity we offer to you as Jesus' family. We make no apologies, however, since the story of our son is of God's design. It is our immense joy and privilege to serve as Jesus' human parents. Please ask your questions and we will do our best to answer them."

Standing in her lap now, Jesus looked at his mother, pushed her headdress off and hugged her head tightly. He then shifted to one side, turned and, once more, fixed his eyes on the Magi.

Their gaze was momentarily captured by Mary's loose black hair and fresh, youthful face. As she attempted to reposition her headdress, Joseph intervened.

"Tobiah, would you please show Mary the star that led you to our home? She must see it, too. I will stay here with the others and show them around the palace."

The Magi chuckled and shifted to make room for Mary. When she stepped out of the door, Jesus became instantly agitated. He tried to climb up her face, pulling on her hair by the fistfuls. She couldn't see a thing and tried to guess what was disturbing him.

"Oh my, I think he is frightened by the camels."

Tobiah watched with fascination and called out,

"Joseph, we need some help out here."

As Joseph stepped out and took the squirming child in his arms, Tobiah provided Mary with the answer.

"I don't think it's the camels, Mary. It's the burning light that he wants. He saw it immediately and began reaching up to it."

Mary looked up and gasped. Tobiah continued,

"That's the star we saw from Parthia and tonight it led us to your home. It's rising higher now. Perhaps its mission is complete."

Irrepressibly excited, Mary exclaimed, "Can you believe this, Joseph? The miracles with which God is surrounding his son's arrival are beyond anything I could have ever imagined. What is going to happen next?"

As they reentered the house, Jesus' agitation was hard to control. He grabbed Joseph's face and beard with both hands, turned to look out the door, and launched into a series of unintelligible syllables.

The formality of the Magi's visit was quite dispelled as Mary sat down and took Jesus into her lap again.

"There's no charge for the theatrical performance tonight," Joseph quipped. "It's on the house."

Everyone chuckled. Mithridath knew that their time was short and asked a routine question. The answer was one that would turn over in his mind for years to come.

"Mary," he asked, somewhat condescendingly,

"How old is the child?"

Mary was enjoying the lighter mood, and without a second thought, responded,

"Oh, yes, Joseph and I have talked a lot about that. We think that he participated in that conversation in the opening lines of the Hebrew Scriptures where God says, '*Let us make man in our image.*' In that case, Jesus has been around for a very long time."

"Of course, Herod probably missed it," Mary continued. "But the prophecy about Bethlehem actually gives Jesus' age. His origins are from of old, from days of eternity."

With a twinkle in her eye, Mary looked directly at Mithridath and added,

"But you probably want to know how long he has been with us, right? I gave birth to Jesus here in Bethlehem eleven months ago. What a night that was. If you have the time, I could tell you some things you would never forget."

The Magi were speechless. Joseph had his head down, shaking with suppressed laughter. This was vintage Mary - the wisdom of the gods and the spontaneity of a teenager. He loved her for it. Mithridath was trying to remember another of his questions when Mary spoke up candidly.

"May I ask something? The night that Jesus was born, angels appeared to shepherds near here and told them that Jesus would be *'great joy for all the people.'* When we presented him to the Lord in the temple, an elderly priest called him a light for revelation to the nations. You have come from Parthia to worship him as king, so after tonight, will you also be part of his kingdom?"

Mary's question was simple, yet so profound that the Magi hesitated to answer. They looked awkwardly at one another until finally Arsames broke the silence.

"Well, I want to be...that is, if Jesus will accept my faith and allegiance."

The others enthusiastically agreed, sensing it was the right answer but realizing that they had not yet fully contemplated the question. Mary glanced nervously at Joseph who understood her predicament of not knowing what to say next.

"Honored guests," he inserted, "if you will allow me to speak for Jesus, I would like to welcome you into his kingdom. Mary and I, and a number of shepherds in Bethlehem, have pledged our allegiance to him. According to Isaiah, he will be a *'light for the nations and bring God's salvation to the ends of the earth.'* Tonight, it appears that Parthians are also among his followers."

By now, Mithridath had regained his composure and spoke up.

"Joseph, we would like to give the child some small tokens of our allegiance and worship."

One by one, the Magi knelt down, each holding a small, richly-decorated canister. The containers held incense, myrrh, perfume, precious stones, and gold coins.

Mary slid Jesus to the floor where he was able to stand as he rested against her knees. She reached out to receive each gift and held it briefly for him to touch. Jesus listened as Mary thanked them for each gift. Following the last gift, she paused. Jesus looked at her and then back at the Magi. He then quietly whispered "thank you" all by himself.

An embroidered coin bag seemed of greatest interest to Jesus, so Mary retrieved a single gold coin and gave it to him. He looked at it closely and then lifted it up to Joseph. Joseph couldn't resist saying,

"You can see that we have trained him well. Gold coins are for papa."

The Magi chuckled as Joseph continued,

"These gifts are priceless and we hardly know what to say. We promise you that your devotion and generosity will be invested in the child's well-being as best we know how. God alone knows the path by which his Son will fully embrace his humanity and your assistance may be more important than any of us know. We humbly thank you."

"Well said," returned Mithridath. "And we couldn't be more enthusiastic about God's choice of a mother and father for his Anointed One. Before we take our leave, however, may I call two young women in our caravan to meet the child and his mother?"

Joseph and Mary nodded affirmatively as Marshach stepped out to call them. Mithridath gave a brief introduction before the two entered the room, hurried to Mary, and knelt down on either side.

An excited three-way conversation in Hebrew broke out immediately. The exchange dashed through names, families, dreams of meeting Mary, the Magi's trip, and hiding their identity as male cooks. Mary pushed their hoods back to caress the first signs of new hair.

Jesus was seated in Mary's lap, but turned attentively to whichever girl was speaking. Each girl held one of his hands in her own. Looking into Mary's face, the love and admiration they exhibited was indescribable. She was every Jewish girl's dream.

One of them paused as Jesus' eyes fixed on hers. His little hand reached up and touched her face. Mary whispered, "He loves you." The Magi were riveted to this moving scene until Joseph broke in.

"Gentlemen, I think this is the high point of the evening. Wouldn't we all rather be cooks?"

They all chuckled in agreement. Phrates couldn't resist adding, "Mithridath, if you have any more questions for Mary, you can just stop by the cooks' tent when we get back."

"Mary, I think we should let them go now," interjected Joseph.

The conversation between the three spilled out more rapidly than before. Tears were running down the young women's faces and Mary's sleeves could barely contain them. Mary finally stood up and placed Jesus into the arms of one while she embraced and kissed the other. Jesus seemed to catch the spirit of the moment and, with each of the women, he repeated his parents' response to his occasional hurts, "No cry. No cry."

At last, the two girls tore themselves free and hurried out to their place at the end of the caravan. After several more embraces and kind farewells, the visitors mounted their camels again. As the caravan circled and passed in front of the simple stone house, the Magi's final memory of Jesus was the image of him sitting on Joseph's shoulders, Mary standing at their side, and all three waving goodbye.

Back at the camp site, Mithridath gathered the remaining soldiers and servants around a torch and told them the evening's story. He even used Mary's observations from Scripture to explain the eternal nature of the child. He then added how honored they all were to have been summoned from Parthia to meet God's newborn Messiah. Finally, Mithridath lay down to rest in his tent. He was elated, exhausted, but worried about King Herod.

Just before dawn, Oristides entered Mithridath's chamber and shook him awake. Startled, Mithridath sat up and listened.

"I went to sleep last night thinking about the burning light," said Oristides. A short time ago, I dreamed of a light that grew so bright I was nearly blinded. A figure appeared in the light and spoke to me. He said, 'Oristides, tell the others that they must not return to Herod. He will seek to kill the child if you tell him where Joseph and Mary can be found.' Mithridath, I know that I have seen an angel from God. We cannot return to Jerusalem."

"Well, let's awaken the others and decide what to do."

Everyone agreed that the dream was a divine intervention and that they should leave Judea immediately by another route. At first, they considered heading for the Great Sea and traveling north through Joppa, Caesarea, Tyre, and Sidon. Herod's informants would be everywhere, however, and it would be impossible to hide along that route.

Then, Phrates mentioned the Nabataean trade route from Egypt that ran straight across the Arabian desert to Babylon. A three-day ride to the south would put them on the road. They all cringed at the thought of the burning desert sun and asked Marshach if the route was feasible. Marshach observed that with only a dozen soldiers, it would be easier to survive the desert sun than Herod's army.

"It is late summer now," he added. "The desert is starting to cool off and will become more tolerable with each day. For the sake of the Messiah, I don't believe we have any other choice."

After informing the caravan to prepare for a hasty departure, Marshach sent one of his riders back to Joseph and Mary with the angel's message. He was instructed to inform them that, if they chose to, they could join the caravan and raise their son in Parthia. Hours later, the rider caught up with the caravan and reported that he found the house empty, the door ajar, and the family's personal belongings gone.

"We must believe," concluded Mithridath, "that if God intervened to save us, he has undoubtedly intervened to save Jesus and his family."

"God Almighty," he prayed, "wherever they are, please give them speed and safety."

TENTH MIRACLE

Escape to Egypt

"Did all that really happen?" exclaimed Mary, as the last Parthian disappeared into the darkness. "Wake me up and tell me it was a dream."

Joseph swung Jesus down to the ground and the astonished couple collapsed on the grass beside him.

"I'm as stunned as you are. Out of nowhere, Parthians arrived on our doorstep to worship the king! They said that they had been traveling for two months following a star that led them to our house. But we just moved here today! How can that be explained? Was it a conscious, thinking star? Was it the glory of the Lord that the prophet Ezekiel saw abandoning the temple in Jerusalem?"

Jesus steadied himself on his mother, squatted, and stood up. Wide-eyed, he listened to his parents' animated description of the Magi, the camels, and a star in the sky. They finally went inside where Joseph pushed two stools next to the wall. Mary readied Jesus for the night and nursed him to sleep as they relaxed together.

"I still can't believe it," Mary reminisced. "Camels and mounted soldiers all over our yard. Five educated Magi from Parthia in our little house, worshipers of God and scholars of the Scriptures. And those two cooks? How precious were they? Maybe we should go and raise Jesus in Parthia."

"That might be an option, my love. The gifts the Magi brought to Jesus could support us for a year or two. It troubles me that they were with Herod just two days ago. He will be waiting for them to return and tell him where we are."

Mary nestled close to Joseph and laid her head on his shoulder. "Please pray, Joseph. I want you to find out what we should do next."

"'Let the morning bring us news of your unfailing love,' began Joseph, almost without thinking, 'With all our hearts, We're trusting your control. Show us now the steps that we should take, for to you, our LORD, we're lifting up our souls.'"

"We are your servants, God, and can't thank you enough for the privilege of caring for your son. Soon our worst enemy will know where we are. Please show us what to do."

"You remembered my song," smiled Mary, as she tucked Jesus into his small bed. After blowing out the lamps the two embraced one another under their wool blanket.

"You really got them thinking when you asked if they would be part of Jesus' kingdom after tonight," recalled Joseph with amusement.

"Why didn't you stop me?" whispered Mary. "I was just babbling on, saying whatever crossed my mind."

"Stop you?" questioned Joseph. "Never! Just keep saying whatever crosses your mind, Mary. You were perfect tonight. Your spontaneous comments are one of the things I cherish the most about you. And you uncovered the biggest question of all. How will people in every nation respond to Jesus when they hear about him? Will he go to every city and talk to them? Will he speak in every language? Will the whole world come to him in Jerusalem? I don't think we will ever see the Magi again, but I believe they will be in his kingdom, whatever that looks like. And you helped them reach that decision!"

"Joseph, this was supposed to be our special night, but I wasn't expecting to have visitors from Parthia. Can we wait until tomorrow? I'm too tired to even think any more and just want to go to sleep."

Within a couple of hours, Joseph was dreaming. Typically, when danger threatened, his dreams dragged him into a frustrating struggle with armed adversaries. This time, a bright light flooded the scene in his mind and an angelic figure approached him.

"Get up," the angel said, *"take the child and his mother and escape to Egypt. Stay there until I tell you, for Herod is going to search for the child to kill him."*

Joseph bolted upright and realized that his dream was really a vision from God. The angel reminded him of the one who spoke to him in Nazareth and the message called for an immediate response.

"Mary, wake up!"

She sat up wondering if it was morning already and saw Joseph in the other room lighting a lamp.

"An angel just appeared to me while I was dreaming," said Joseph, "and he told me that we should escape to Egypt. Herod wants to kill Jesus and we don't know how much time we have left. We must leave now."

"Oh my! We prayed to God for guidance and he certainly gave it to us. What should we do next?"

"Let's get dressed and begin to gather some items on the table. We'll need extra clothes, sandals, Jesus' outfits and his blanket. Our wool blanket will serve as your saddle. Bring your scroll, parchments, personal things, and any food that is ready to eat. Here is my sword and the gifts from the Magi. I'll go out and saddle Zephyrus."

They soon had everything packed into a single bag. Joseph wrapped the gold, incense, and myrrh into a backpack for himself. It was still dark as he helped Mary up onto Zephyrus where she sat on the folded blanket. They each wore a cape to protect themselves from the cold and Jesus sat quietly in Mary's lap wrapped in his own mini-cape. After attaching the bag of clothes and things to the rear of the saddle, Joseph blew out the lamps in the house, left the door ajar, and swung up into the saddle.

Zephyrus carefully followed the well-worn path to the main road coming from Jerusalem, then headed south toward Hebron. As they passed the entrance into Bethlehem, Joseph breathed a sigh of relief and whispered to Mary that he felt like they were safe now. After another hour of steady travel, Mary reached forward and rubbed Zephyrus' neck affectionately. She then congratulated Jesus for riding so well. A hint of light to the east suggested that the night would soon end.

Zephyrus' ears flickered slightly and his head turned. Joseph caught the movement and flipped his head around, listening carefully. A faint echo of hoof beats came from behind them. Mary sensed the tension, held Jesus securely, and whispered,

"Anything wrong?"

"Hoof beats behind us. Two horses, I think," Joseph responded briskly. "Hang on!"

His arms encircled Mary and Jesus as he loosened the reins and buried his hands in Zepyrus' thick, black mane. Mary had just enough time to grab two handfuls of the long, course hair herself before Joseph's heels touched Zephyrus' sides. The powerful front legs and noble head shot forward as a ripple of muscles passed beneath the riders. In three powerful strides, Zephyrus had surged into a full gallop.

A word of caution from Joseph brought the horse back into a careful balance of raw speed and controlled strides. Several minutes passed at a steady gallop before Joseph pulled Zephyrus to a canter and alerted Mary,

"We can't outrun them. I need to pull off the road and get down."

Spotting some dark bushes to the right, Joseph reined his horse in behind them and dismounted in a flash. He quickly lifted Mary and Jesus to the ground and handed her the reins.

"If I tell Zephyrus to run, drop the reins and hide in the bushes. They will follow the horse."

With sword drawn, Joseph stepped to the edge of the road and crouched to catch a glimpse of the riders against the pre-dawn sky. Two armed horsemen passed by at full gallop, unaware of the kneeling figure hidden in the vegetation. Steadily, the hoof beats faded into the distance without a pause. Joseph stood up, listened a moment longer, and then began to chuckle.

"You won't believe this, Mary. I could see their square cut beards, helmets, and bows silhouetted against the sky. They were Parthians, probably an advanced guard for the Magi. And that means that their caravan isn't going back to Jerusalem at all. That is great news, for the moment, at least."

"Oh, my!" Mary gasped. "Are you sure? Here, hold Jesus for a few minutes and give him some assurance. I could use some, too, while you are at it."

By late afternoon, they reached Hebron and skirted the city to the west. Joseph slipped inside the western gate on foot to purchase a few loaves of bread, some fruit, and a small sack of grain for Zephyrus. They then headed west toward Gaza. With the extra supplies tied down behind the saddle, Joseph walked while his family rode. As the sense of immediate danger lessened, Mary found herself increasingly disturbed by the underlying enigma of their flight to Egypt.

"Why does God's Anointed One have to face a murderous plot by Herod?" Mary argued out loud. "Is the side of evil so strong that it can actually threaten the life of God's Messiah? I don't understand. What is going on, Joseph?"

"That's a hard question. Do the prophets say anything about the Messiah having enemies?"

Mary was silent for a while. She then replied, "Actually, they say more than I want to hear. Do you remember the opening columns of the Torah where God rebuked Satan? He said that he would put hostility between Satan and Eve and between his offspring and her offspring. The woman's offspring is going to crush Satan's head but Satan will strike back and bite his heel. Benjamin's scroll identified the offspring of the woman as the Messiah. If Jesus has come to destroy Satan, will he get wounded in the process?"

"We know whose offspring Herod is," muttered Joseph. "He is definitely on Satan's side."

Mary pulled back on the reins and Zephyrus came to a stop. Joseph sensed that something was wrong and reached up, taking Jesus into his arms.

"I have to get down, Joseph." Mary's voice quivered as tears formed in her eyes. Joseph helped her dismount and walk toward a small tree where they both sat down.

Mary began to cry. It was a deep, painful emotion that had been under the surface for far too long. Her sobs were heavy as she leaned on Joseph's chest. Joseph held her with one arm and embraced Jesus with the other. Slowly, she regained control.

"I try not to think about it, but ever since I conceived Jesus there has been this conflict in my mind. On one side are all the Scriptures about the Messiah who reigns but on the other side are the Scriptures about the Messiah who suffers. I don't want Jesus to suffer."

The very words were too much to bear and Mary began weeping again. Amidst tears, she continued,

"I talked with Uncle Zechariah about this when we stopped by their home. He said that the suffering Messiah was the nation of Israel. While that was helpful, it just doesn't explain everything."

"Then there was Simeon in the temple. He said that Jesus is destined to be a sign that will be spoken against and that a sword will pierce my soul. I can't bear to have anything happen to Jesus, Joseph, I just can't bear it. And, now, God wants us to run off to Egypt and hide. I want to escape, of course, but why does it have to be this way? Can't God protect us?"

"Mary, I don't understand either," responded Joseph. "I feel the same way that you do, although I'm not sure that anyone can feel it as much as you."

In his mind, Joseph quickly prayed, "God please give me some words for Mary." He then continued aloud,

"One time you shared God's promise to Moses with me, *'My Presence will go with you, and I will give you rest.'* If that worked for our people when they left Egypt, I'm sure it will work for us going back to Egypt. God is right here, right now, and we can trust him."

Just then the sun dropped out of sight to the west and that's when Joseph realized that it would soon be dark. He spotted another tree a little farther away and out of sight of the road.

"Let's settle under that tree over there for the night, and when dawn comes, we can get a fresh start."

It took another nine days for the three to reach the Nile River. As each day passed, the temperature rose higher. Eventually, the dry, arid wasteland between Judea and Egypt turned into shrubs and vegetation. Occasional herds of goats and sheep bordered small villages with vegetable gardens and fields of wheat, corn, and flax. As their route approached the river basin, they found themselves engulfed in Egyptian language and culture. The people dressed in tightly woven linen skirts, knee-length for men, full-length for women. Workers and slaves wore only a loin cloth.

In contrast to the Jewish homeland, Egyptian culture displayed a certain level of sensuality. Water was in abundance everywhere. The people bathed frequently and perfumed themselves after. Women's attire was straight, usually sleeveless, and often topless. Small children played comfortably with no clothes at all. Strangely, wigs were popular with men and women.

The main road into Egypt followed one of the delta waterways upstream to where it came out of the mighty Nile River below Memphis. An ancient, mysterious waterway, the Nile originated deep in the heart of Africa. It passed through countless miles of trackless desert until it fed into the rich river valley of lower Egypt.

Cliffs marked the boundaries of this sanctuary of black fertile soil. Gardens flourished with onions, garlic, leeks, lettuce, radishes, cabbage, asparagus, cucumbers, legumes of all sorts, and many spices. An abundance of fruit trees, nut trees, olive trees, and date palms surrounded the towns and villages.

Joseph's intent was to cross the Nile at Memphis and then make their way to Alexandria. Not only was he familiar with Alexandria from a previous trip there with Tribune Tavius, but the Nile River seemed like a natural barrier beyond which they could relax. Joseph wanted to travel far enough into Egypt that they would never be found.

After reaching the Nile, the young family had to wait for several hours before a boat appeared that was large enough to carry Zephyrus and transport them to Memphis on the other side. Arrangements were made in Greek, which both Mary and Joseph were comfortable with. Crossing the Nile symbolized for Joseph a successful escape into Egypt. As the three relaxed on board, Joseph took Mary's hand and quietly prayed in Hebrew.

"Dear LORD our God, thank you for the strength and safety you have given us on our journey into Egypt. Your provisions are amazing, gathered in Parthia, and delivered to us by wealthy Magi. If you brought us here for something more than hiding from Herod's soldiers, please let us know. We are your servants. Our eyes are fixed on you every hour of every day."

"Shall we turn in our wool clothing again for some linen outfits?" asked Mary, thinking about their experience in Caesarea.

"Well, we don't want to represent our homeland this time," laughed Joseph. "Whatever we can do to melt into the Egyptian population is the right thing to do. Let's find a room in Memphis for a few days. We need to get some local currency and find out what the Magi's incense and myrrh are worth."

The next day the two began a metamorphosis from being traditional Jewish separatists to being adaptive, friendly, foreign residents. Joseph shaved off his beard and Mary stepped up a class level to find some linen dresses she was comfortable wearing. She also bought a couple of small linen tunics for Jesus and shortened them enough to facilitate his first steps. After another day or two, she began to entertain the thought of him dressing "Egyptian" like the other children. It certainly made sense with the warm temperatures and pools of water to play in.

Memphis was an exotic city. It was the commercial crossroad for trade between Asia, Africa, and the nations bordering the Great Sea. The presence of boats, caravans, warehouses, palaces, and temples in this historic capital of ancient Egypt left Joseph and Mary nearly speechless. They were astonished at the enormous statue of Ramses, the huge alabaster Sphinx, and the pyramids up on the desert plateau. They found themselves wondering how Jesus would ever bring his light and offer his salvation to a nation like Egypt.

"I grew up thinking that the Messiah would subjugate the nations to Israel and to Moses' Law," observed Joseph. "But, if he is going to be *'good news of great joy for all people,'* why would he want to subjugate them or suppress their cultures?"

"I don't think it's the culture that needs to be changed," responded Mary. "I'm beginning to like the Egyptian way of life. It fits the weather and physical features perfectly. One day, I believe Jesus will provide an answer that we don't yet understand yet. Maybe his kingdom will somehow embrace all this diversity. The Parthian Magi showed us that it can happen. Look, there is a shallow pool for small children. Let's put Jesus in the water."

"Without swim wear?" questioned Joseph.

"Of course not," laughed Mary, "with Egyptian swim wear."

It wasn't long before Jesus was gleefully crawling through the water with other little bathers. He loved to sit and splash or reach out and touch the other children. Mary and Joseph sat on the edge of the pool with their feet in the water.

A few days later, they reached the outskirts of Alexandria. The principle route into the city was lined by five kilometers of colonnades. The nearest delta waterway teemed with shallow-draft, cargo vessels, fishing boats, and even shaded tourist craft for visitors from Rome and Greece. Five excellent harbors served as transfer points for food and merchandise on the river boats to be loaded onto the larger ships that plied the Great Sea.

Founded by Alexander the Great and built by his successors, the Ptolomies, Alexandria was a showcase of palaces, the most magnificent of which had recently been occupied by Anthony and Cleopatra. The city was a center of education, wealth, and Greek culture that was unmatched, except by Rome itself. Native Egyptians spoke Coptic, but Greek was the dominant language of the city.

Having accompanied Tribune Tavius to Alexandria three years earlier, Joseph was eager to show Mary the gardens, libraries, bazaars, and markets that lined the city streets. Mary was amazed at his ability to navigate this labyrinth of sights and sounds.

The travelers headed for the Jewish quarter and realized that it was larger and more affluent than they had previously imagined. For centuries, Jews had been migrating into Egypt from Palestine and had prospered in the international economy of the Roman Empire. Three hundred years earlier, their leading elders had funded the translation of the Jewish Scriptures into Greek, a project that was completed on an island in the harbor of Alexandria.

Synagogues were numerous and beautifully landscaped. The central synagogue was the most impressive of all and even maintained a hall for seventy priests that constituted a national Sanhedrin. This body of elders looked after the religious affairs of more than a million Jewish inhabitants.

After inquiring into the distinctiveness of the various synagogues, Joseph discovered that one was frequented by immigrants from Galilee. He and Mary hoped that this would further distance them from Bethlehem and Judea, should any inquirers of Herod appear.

The next day, they visited the synagogue. One of the priests, Rabbi Gershom, received them warmly. As Joseph was explaining his professional experience and interest in serving the Jewish community, the rabbi interrupted him with the question, "Do you have a place to stay?"

"Well, actually, not yet," replied Joseph.

"Some years ago," the rabbi explained, "the elders in our synagogue built a series of cottages for the use of our regular members at a fishing village on the coast. We encourage families to periodically leave the city and spend a week or two there for emotional and spiritual benefit. One of the units will be available for ten days starting tomorrow. Would you be interested in staying there?"

Joseph started to decline the offer when he felt the weight of Mary's foot on his own. She pretended to adjust Jesus' position in her arms but was quietly looking for a way to get eye contact with Joseph. Her foot pressed harder. When Joseph glanced her way, she mouthed the Hebrew word for "yes."

"Well, actually," continued Joseph, "thinking a bit more, I believe we would like to take you up on your offer. Is there a charge for the unit or something I can do to repay your generosity?"

"No, not at all. Why don't you come to my home this afternoon and share the evening meal with my family. I'm sure that my wife, Sarah, will enjoy meeting Mary and she can explain some details about the cottage and tell you who to contact in the fishing village for food, water, and other supplies."

The rabbi's home was large and tastefully decorated. Apparently, the members of this synagogue were far more affluent than typical villagers in Bethlehem or Nazareth, and they generously supported the rabbi and his family of four. Jesus was an immediate hit with the rabbi's two young daughters, who kept him busy investigating their house and garden.

Suddenly, Jesus seemed to be on a whole new pace of learning. The girls played games with him and got him laughing so hard that Mary couldn't believe it was really him. She had to go and see for herself. Finally, one of the girls ran into the kitchen and said,

"Mother, Jesus is amazing! I think he understands us but he doesn't talk yet. He learns games really fast though. Can he stay with us tonight?"

"It's fine with me," replied Sarah. "How about it, Mary? We have everything he needs and you can pick him up to-morrow morning on your way to the beach."

Mary was still processing the whole situation and sud-denly realized that, in her fear and protectiveness of Jesus, she rarely let him out of her sight. She suddenly saw all that he had been missing: the fun of games, physical activities, language skills, social interaction, and everything that older kids could teach him.

But to let go of Jesus to a family she had only met that very day, and in a foreign country, could she do that? She knew that she wouldn't sleep a wink the whole night.

"Sarah, you don't know what a blessing you are. I love your girls and your family and want Jesus to play with them. He loves it here, but he can't stay tonight. I can't explain it in detail, but I have to work through some things. Maybe our time at the beach will help me to do that. There is something else that you might be able to help me with before we leave tomorrow."

The two talked privately and Sarah responded, "Mary, I think I can get it for you in the morning. You are so creative. I think Gershom is going to be very happy to have someone like you in my life."

The next morning, the three stopped by the rabbi's home. Sarah had a long, round package with her for Mary.

"Just something for the cottage," Mary explained to Joseph as she slipped it into their clothing bag.

The thought of an extended break was so novel that all three mounted Zephyrus in anticipation of the fun and excitement ahead on their small adventure. Along the way, Joseph bought a string of colorful flowers for Mary to wear around her neck. They laughed and waved to perfect strangers as they passed; any silly thing they could think of was cause for laughter. The murderous threats of Herod seemed so far from their exotic new world that they barely crossed their minds.

The cottages were beyond their expectations, with tile floors and arched, barred windows facing the sea. When the wooden shutters were removed, beautiful, full-length curtains waved gracefully in the ocean breeze. Together, they rode to a small market in the fishing village and purchased bread, fruit, wine, vegetables, fresh fish, and grain for Zephyrus. Large jars of water were already waiting for them in the cottage.

The next morning, the three doused themselves with vegetable oil and spent the morning playing with Jesus in the sand and surf. Mary and Joseph took turns galloping through the water on Zephyrus. Then, with one on each side, they held Jesus upright in the saddle as Zephyrus walked through the shallow waves.

By late morning, they were ready to escape the sun. Jesus was alert through his bath of soap and cool water in a large clay basin, but after eating some crushed fruit and nursing, he fell into a deep sleep. Joseph washed down Zephyrus with fresh water outside while Mary showered herself with a pitcher inside. Gathering up some grapes, bread, and wine, the two sat on a patio facing the sea and searched for words to describe what their life-threatening escape to Egypt had turned into.

"I have a serious, theological question for you, Mary," said Joseph playfully. "Are you sure that we are supposed to stay in the cottage tonight?"

Mary burst out laughing, recalling their conversation when they left the stable. "To answer that, I need to read to you," she said. "Bring the grapes and we'll rest on the bed."

As Joseph stretched out, Mary unrolled her package from Sarah. It was a small scroll and Joseph just caught a glimpse of the title, "Song of Songs."

"You are going to like this," Mary said as she sat up straight and began to comb out her freshly washed and toweled hair. "It's in Greek, not as romantic as Hebrew, but it will do."

She then added, with a hint of fabrication,

"It's a conversation that the parents of the Messiah will have one day in a very romantic place. I don't know how we missed it all this time."

Joseph knew that something was up but he was so distracted by Mary's captivating appearance that he replied,

"Read to me, my love, read to me."

With a whimsical glance into Joseph's eyes, she began to read.

"Beloved
 I am a rose of Sharon,
  a lily of the valleys.
Lover
 Like a lily among thorns
  is my darling among the maidens.

Beloved
Like an apple tree among the trees of the forest
 is my lover among the young men.
I delight to sit in his shade,
 and his fruit is sweet to my taste.
He has taken me to the banquet hall,
 and the banner over me is love.
Strengthen me with raisins,
 refresh me with apples,
 for I am faint with love.
His left arm is under my head,
 and his right arm embraces me.
Daughters of Jerusalem, I charge you
 by the gazelles and by the does of the field:
Do not arouse or awaken love
 Until it so desires…"

Mary set the scroll aside and relaxed across Joseph's chest. She quietly whispered, "Take me to your banquet hall, O Lion of Judah. Love has been awakened and its desire is strong."

Ten days on the Mediterranean coast left Joseph and Mary with memories of intimacy, relaxation, and fun that neither had experienced to that point in their lives. Near the end of their trip, Joseph reminisced,

"I never felt healthier or happier to be alive than I do right now. I thought I knew what God was thinking when he said, '*It is not good for the man to be alone.*' Growing up, I thought that women were created to pick up the work load of fixing meals and raising kids, but I didn't understand the fulfillment of a man and a woman becoming one. Maybe two becoming one is what God's image is all about. And you, my beloved, led us into this garden with the 'Song of Songs.'"

"Wow!" responded Mary as she moved in close for a prolonged hug. "Words like those will get you so much more than the roar of a lion. But don't lose your fierceness. Without it, I wouldn't have survived. And on top of this romantic adventure, God has allowed us to take care of Jesus. That is beyond comprehension."

"Just today," she continued, "I was thinking while sitting on the beach, 'How will Jesus, so easily upended by a wave, sputtering from sand and salt water, ever turn into the King of Kings?' Right now he seems like a fragile little boy whose life could be snuffed out in a moment of carelessness or treachery."

"Maybe the real question is, 'How did the King of Kings turn into a baby boy?'" replied Joseph. "Do you suppose that he set aside all of his divine powers at conception and will take them up again as an adult?"

Arriving back in Alexandria, the sun-drenched family stopped by the Synagogue of the Galileans to thank Rabbi Gershom. He welcomed them eagerly.

"Well, look at you three tanned pilgrims from the homeland! If you were wearing wigs, you could easily pass for Egyptians. I wouldn't even have recognized you. Sarah and I we're hoping that you would stay with us for a few days until you get settled."

After Joseph and Mary enthusiastically accepted the invitation, Gersom continued, "By the way, there is a very special lecture this coming Sabbath after the synagogue service. One of Alexandria's favorite scholars of Messianic prophecy, Rabbi Theophanes, will talk about the song that terminates Moses' writings. I hope you can attend."

Mary was so anxious to hear the presentation on Moses' Song that she skipped the Sabbath morning service and let Jesus play near the synagogue, hoping he would get tired and sleep through the lecture. Joseph was sitting in front with the men as Mary slipped into a free seat behind the curtain that separated the women from the men's view. A woman next to her looked dubiously at Jesus sitting in her lap and whispered,

"How long do you think he can endure this lecture? Rabbi Theophanes is never brief."

"Just a little longer than his father up front," responded Mary with a smile.

The song, which described a story through a series of rhythmical stanzas, had already been read during the earlier service, so the rabbi entered directly into his observations.

"This song of Moses traces human history from its inception to the present. Moses calls heaven and earth to listen as he proclaims the greatness of God who rescued our people from slavery in Egypt. Sadly, he goes on to recount the calloused disinterest and outright abandonment of God by that generation."

"Brothers and sisters of Israel, let me call your attention to the purpose of this song as God explained it to Moses. All of the zeal and efforts with which we strive to obey God are put into a paradox from which we cannot escape. God told Moses to write this song as a witness against us."

"But that's not all. Moses told the keepers of the Torah to place it beside the Ark of the Covenant as a witness against us. An even greater paradox! The Law, which we cherish as our pathway to acceptance by God, is a reminder that we have failed to keep it. We have not obtained the right to stand before God; the covenant has been broken."

The Rabbi stood quietly as silence settled over the congregation. Jesus had been sleeping but the stillness woke him up. He sat up and looked into Mary's face, as she gently placed a finger over his lips.

"Now dear friends," said the rabbi warmly, "I have some words of encouragement. In the final few lines of his song, Moses provides us with a wave of hope that rises out of a sea of despair and washes across us with some good news of great joy for all people."

Mary could not hide the impact of the rabbi's words and drew in a deep breath. Jesus sensed her surprise and looked up. Even though he wouldn't understand, she whispered in his ear, "the rabbi just quoted the angels who sang at your birth."

"Let me read to you the final lines of Moses' song," continued Theophanes. "And let me tell you what I learned during a period of study at the School of the Consolation of Israel in Jerusalem."

> *'Rejoice O nations, with his people,*
> *for he will avenge the blood of his servants;*
> *he will take vengeance on his enemies*
> *and make atonement for his land and people.'*

"First, why should the nations rejoice? Because, according to Isaiah, the LORD's servant is coming to be a light to the nations and to bring God's salvation to the ends of the earth."

"Second, how will God take vengeance on his enemies? His greatest enemy is not Rome. It is Satan, the Great Deceiver, who tempted the human race to believe the lie that they could be independent and self-sustaining, like God is."

"Third, how will atonement for our land and our people be achieved? Again, Isaiah explains that God's Messianic servant will justify many people by his knowledge and he will bear their iniquities. Yes, atonement is the very heart of the Messiah's work. Somehow, he will achieve it for us!"

"But that's not all! The most popular Hebrew text of Moses' song has lost a critical line. This line is included in our Greek translation here in Alexandria. The end of Moses' song actually reads like this,

> *'Rejoice O nations, with his people,*
> ***and let all the angels worship him,***
> *for he will avenge the blood of his servants;*
> *he will take vengeance on his enemies*
> *and make atonement for his land and people.'*

"Of what value is this short line about angels worshiping the Messianic Deliverer? We get so caught up with what the Messiah will mean to us on his arrival that we completely forget what heaven will be feeling about his departure. Moses tells us that all of God's angels will be overwhelmed with amazement and will participate in a celebration of worship that we can't even begin to imagine."

In their separate seats, Mary and Joseph each felt a flush of heat and emotion rise up their necks and faces. Was it possible that the most dramatic miracle surrounding Jesus' birth was being addressed openly by this rabbi? Mary felt the urge to stand up, hold Jesus high, and shout,

"Here he is!"

She couldn't contain herself any longer. Embracing Jesus tightly to her chest, she slipped out of her seat and hurried to the door. Once outside, she went to the door where Joseph was most likely to exit the synagogue. With eagerness and excitement dancing in her eyes, she watched anxiously for him to appear.

They suddenly saw each other and ran to meet at the edge of the departing crowd. Mary lifted Jesus up to Joseph's free arm as he swept her in tight with the other.

"Could you believe that, Joseph?" Mary exclaimed. "I wanted to stand up, and lift Jesus as high as I could, and shout, 'Here he is! The night he was born, the angels came to worship him. I am his mother. It's all true everybody. It's all true!'"

"Yes, Mary, yes! I felt the same way. I'm glad we were sitting apart because if we had been together, I could easily have joined you in making a public announcement."

"In retrospect, I'm sure that it was best to contain ourselves. I think Jesus is going through a process like the development of a baby bird in its nest. There is a delicate human shell around him while he fully adapts to his human nature. You and I are sitting on the nest, providing warmth, protection and parenting. When the time is right, he will break out of his shell on his own, and what happens next will be up to him and his Father in heaven."

"Wow," responded Mary thoughtfully. The hint of a smile tugged at the corners of her mouth as she added,

"Is Joseph also among the prophets?"

Both of them broke out in uncontrollable laughter as they walked down the street together. Caught up in their excitement, Jesus vigorously rocked up and down on Joseph's shoulders, inducing his own toddler age giggles and reigniting the laughter of his parents.

ELEVENTH MIRACLE

Return to Nazareth

Mary pulled back the curtains that covered the garden view of their second-story guest room in the home of Joel, a prosperous Jewish businessman who exported grain and corn to major seaports around the Great Sea. While she and Joseph were at the seaside cottage, Rabbi Gershom spoke with a few storage facility managers about Joseph's experience in carpentry and construction. Joel, an in-law of the famous Nicanor family, showed interest in meeting Joseph. He needed to build an additional warehouse before spring and was looking for someone to oversee the construction.

Pausing to look out on the attractive palm grove and pool in the courtyard of Joel's spacious home, Mary's gaze was captured by the beautiful white lotus flowers floating along the borders of the pool. As the morning sun touched the uppermost branches of the palm trees, she sang one of her personal renditions of a favorite morning psalms.

> "Hear me, Oh my God, I belong to you alone,
> I wake up every morning searching for you.
> The thirst in my soul only you can satisfy,
> My body craves the strength that you alone supply.
> Life on earth is a dry and thirsty land,
> You are the water and I'm the burning sand."

Passing through the courtyard below, a maid paused to listen as Mary's song unfolded an intimacy with God beyond anything she had ever imagined.

"That was beautiful," commented Joseph from the edge of their bed. "Are you feeling better about Jesus spending another night at Sarah's? The first night he stayed there, I don't think you slept a wink."

"Yes, I did sleep better last night. Would you wait here a moment while I find us something to eat? There is a matter I need to discuss with you."

Mary had been gone only moments when she returned with a servant girl carrying a tray of bread, fruits, and juices.

"Can you believe it? This dear girl was waiting for us to wake up so that she could serve us a morning meal. Don't get accustomed to this. We typically do the serving, right?"

As the two sat on the floor with their backs to the bed, Mary explained,

"We need to decide when Jesus' birthday is going to be. Will it be this week or three months from now?"

"How's that?" inquired Joseph.

"Well, I told Sarah that his birthday was in a couple of days. That's true and would make sense to all our friends in Bethlehem. But people in Nazareth are assuming he was conceived at the time of our wedding and that would place his birthday nearly three months from now. So, we can celebrate his first birthday now to make sense in Bethlehem or wait three months to fit with expectations in Nazareth.

"How about this," said Joseph. "Let's celebrate his real birthday now. You can tell a man most anything about a baby's age and he'll believe you. But I don't think you can convince Sarah that Jesus is only nine months old. Depending on where we finally settle, we can decide at that time when to celebrate his birthday. The older he is, the less likely it will be for people to guess his exact age anyway."

"Yes, I think you are right," returned Mary. "But, the more we talk about him, the more I'm missing him. Hurry, let's get dressed. I can't wait any longer."

When they arrived at the rabbi's home, Mary called from the street. "Jesus, we are here!" When he appeared, she grabbed him in an emotional embrace and kissed him multiple times. Sarah looked on with amusement and questioned,

"Do we have a little setback here?"

"Every morning we have a little setback," confessed Joseph. "But you and your girls are getting us through it."

"By the way," continued Sarah. "Didn't you say that Jesus' birthday was the day after tomorrow? Why don't you all come over that afternoon and the girls will do some fun things with Jesus. Our neighbors have a shallow pool and let our daughters play in it whenever they want. At dusk we can eat the Sabbath meal together. Would you enjoy that?"

"That would be wonderful," said Mary. "You are so kind and I have no idea how to repay you."

Later that night back in Joel's guest room, Mary brought up Rabbi Theophanes again.

"Do you think we could have a private conversation with Rabbi Theophanes sometime? I have some questions about the last two songs of the servant in Isaiah. You need to lead the discussion because I could get emotionally involved. I'm sure Sarah would take care of Jesus for us."

A week later, Joseph returned from the construction site with the news that he was able to arrange a meeting with Rabbi Theophanes the following day. He then asked Mary to brief him on the questions she wished to discuss.

"Do remember the deep sadness I felt on our escape from Bethlehem? It never really goes away. It's those predictions that Isaiah made about the LORD's Servant having to suffer. Sometimes they feel very heavy inside me. Am I supposed to carry this fear in my heart that something horrible is going to happen to Jesus? Is that what Simeon meant in the temple?"

"Mary, I don't know the answer to that, but let's not rush to any conclusions. If all of the angels in heaven rejoiced at his coming, how could his story end in defeat? Those prophecies are not for casual readers, you know. Maybe we don't understand them yet."

The next day Joseph introduced Mary to the Rabbi and gave a very brief summary of their background, the trip to Bethlehem to register for the Roman census, and the impromptu decision to visit Egypt. To this he added,

"Mary and I share more than a casual interest in the Scriptures that speak about God's Messiah and enjoyed your lecture on Moses' song. We want to ask your opinion about some long-standing questions of our own."

"Well," interjected the rabbi, "I am surprised and intrigued to meet some working folk from Nazareth who wish to converse about Messianic prophecies. Had you ever heard of the School of the Consolation of Israel before my lecture?"

"Oh yes," interjected Mary enthusiastically, "I have been there."

"You have been there?" gasped Theophanes, momentarily startled.

"Yes, sir. I spoke with Rabbi Beniah on behalf of my uncle, a priest from Beth Hakkerem who was suffering from an impairment of speech and hearing. My uncle wished to borrow the scroll of Benjamin, a student from his village who died unexpectedly. Did you know Benjamin?"

"Well, this is all quite remarkable, Mary. Yes, I did know him. He arrived as I was finishing my course of study. He was a gifted young man and knew the Scriptures well. I was truly saddened by the news of his passing."

Unsure as to where Mary's spontaneity might lead the discussion, Joseph entered the conversation again.

"Mary grew up with a deep appreciation for the sacred scrolls and even taught herself how to read. Benjamin's scroll was a great inspiration to her and she has shared with me many of the prophecies about which he wrote. Our questions arise from the writings of the prophet Isaiah."

Joseph continued, "The last of Isaiah's four songs about the LORD's servant paints a disturbing picture of the Messiah suffering on our behalf. Most prophecies predict a reigning Messiah who will live forever. Mary's uncle told her that the fourth song refers to the suffering of God's people, Israel. Can you help us understand the dilemma between a reigning Messiah and a suffering Messiah? Is Israel the suffering Messiah?"

Rabbi Theophanes took considerable time to personally identify with their dilemma and to cite the different oral traditions about Isaiah's suffering servant. He explained that his personal preference was the tradition that held to the existence of two Messiahs, one who would suffer and one who would reign. Mary was relieved to hear Theophanes' conclusion, although she couldn't immediately dismiss the thought that Zechariah and Elizabeth's son, John, might be implicated in this scenario.

As they stood to thank Theophanes for his time, the rabbi made a routine inquiry into their Jewish tribal background.

"We are of the tribe of Judah," spoke up Mary, "and from the house of David."

"Why that's wonderful. And do you hope to start a family soon?" inquired Theophanes.

"I think we were a little nervous when we introduced ourselves," replied Joseph. "We neglected to mention that God has already blessed us with a wonderful son. He is staying with Rabbi Gershom's family today."

Joseph had the feeling that the rabbi's rising curiosity over a young Jewish couple with a profound interest in the Messiah might lead him to wonder if they could be Immanuel's parents. Inconspicuously he squeezed Mary's arm, hoping to put her on the alert.

"And did your son come with you from Nazareth to be registered in Bethlehem?" questioned Theophanes.

"Yes," answered Joseph directly. "I registered all three of us on the second day in town."

"Oh, I see…hmmm. Well, I wish you God's peace and prosperity during your stay in Egypt."

As soon as they were out of earshot, Joseph burst out,

"That was so close! I think he was trying to find out if Jesus was born in Nazareth or in Bethlehem. Tell me, Mary, if the rabbi had asked us directly, 'Are you the parents of the Messiah?' what would you have said?"

"I would have said yes," Mary answered. "That's what we told the shepherds and the Magi. What do you think would have happened?"

"Oh, my, I think that Theophanes would want to question us thoroughly and report the matter to the Egyptian Sanhedrin. The Sanhedrin would start an official inquiry and even send a delegation to Nazareth to question your parents. Jesus' life would never be the same. I am beginning to think that his story and all these miraculous interventions are secrets for us to keep to ourselves for now."

Joel and his wife had relatives in Jerusalem and occasionally someone would arrive with news about recent events there. One report instantly caught Joseph's attention.

"Herod is seventy years old and suffering from incurable diseases. He lives in constant suspicion of treachery and rebellion, so imprisonments and executions are common. Everyone in Jerusalem is relieved that he has moved to his palace near Jericho to enjoy the warmer temperatures during the wet season."

"A few months ago a delegation from Parthia arrived in Jerusalem. Their caravan got the whole city stirred up because they came with the expectation of meeting Israel's future King, the Messiah. Herod was very disturbed but decided to let the dignitaries search for the Messiah on their own. Then, the caravan disappeared. Herod's soldiers went everywhere, torturing people for information. But they never found the caravan or any sign of it anywhere."

Joseph dismissed himself and rushed back to Mary with the news. It was very sobering. Mary took Jesus into her lap and they prayed together for God's continued protection.

In late winter, another of Joel's associates came from Jerusalem with more horror stories about Herod. Assuming that Herod was close to death, two rabbis and forty Jewish zealots had pulled down a huge golden eagle that Herod had fixed above the main gate into the temple. Hoping this would inspire a general revolt against Herod, the zealots allowed themselves to be captured by Herod's guards. Unfortunately, they were marched to Jericho where Herod himself judged them and ordered that they be burned alive.

The dry season quietly enveloped Egypt with a fragrance and beauty all its own. There was a noticeable warming of the temperature, a calming of the seas, and a breathtaking emergence of flowers, shrubs, and budding trees.

As the grain harvest from Ethiopia began to arrive on boats descending the Nile River, Joseph entered the final phase of construction of the new warehouse. He wanted to complete the project before the Jewish festivals of Passover and Unleavened Bread.

Rabbi Gersom invited Joseph and Mary to celebrate the Passover meal with his family. When all were seated, the rabbi recited an initial prayer that included the words, "…in remembrance of the departure from Egypt. Blessed are you, O LORD our God, who has kept us alive, sustained us, and enabled us to enjoy this season." Mary's hand searched quietly for Joseph's and squeezed his palm. During the week-long Festival of Unleavened Bread, they reflected on the angel's message to stay in Egypt until he told them to return to their homeland.

One night, Joseph slept restlessly. Shortly before dawn, he fell into a deep sleep. In a dream, the scene was suddenly dominated by a growing light. A bright, angelic figure approached him, and Joseph knew immediately who he was.

"Get up," said the angel. *"Take the child and his mother and go to the land of Israel, for those who were trying to take the child's life are dead."* The figure disappeared, the light faded, and Joseph awoke.

Raising his head, Joseph perceived that the morning light was beginning to fill the eastern sky. He rolled over and kissed Mary who was sleeping soundly. She raised her head, checked on Jesus, and turned to Joseph.

"Mary, I just had a dream and the angel who told us to escape to Egypt appeared again. Do you want to know what he said to me?" Mary instantly sat up.

"Yes, yes, tell me. I'm awake!"

"Herod is dead!"

"Oh, thank you, God," she exclaimed, falling back on the bed with overwhelming relief. Quickly gathering her strength, she sat up again.

"What else did he say? Is that all?"

"This is what he said, *'Get up, take the child and his mother and go to the land of Israel, for those who were trying to take the child's life are dead.'* I don't think he meant that we should leave Alexandria today. I think he meant that we should start our preparations and leave as soon as possible."

"Joseph, this is the eleventh time that God has miraculously intervened in our lives for the sake of his son, Jesus. It gives me a lot of peace to know that he is watching us. "

The day before their departure, an acquaintance of Joel returned from celebrating the Passover in Jerusalem. Joel asked him to give whatever news he could to Joseph and Mary. This was his report.

"When we arrived in Jerusalem, we learned that Herod had died a few days earlier. Most of his officials, along with a delegation of priests, were at the fortress of Herodium for a burial ceremony. Three hundred heads of families from all over Galilee and Judea had been imprisoned and taken to the Hippodrome for execution, just to make sure that the nation was mourning at the time of Herod's death. In the end, however, they were all released."

"Herod had another son killed just days before his own death. The remaining two, Archelaus and Antipas, are disputing which of Herod's wills is legitimate. It is not yet known who will be the next king. Things are really tense, so we left Jerusalem as soon as we could following Passover."

The next morning, Mary was not feeling well and suspected it was something she had eaten the night before. After a couple of hours, she felt better and asked to see Sarah one more time. Joseph thought it would be better to delay their departure another day to be sure that Mary was well enough to travel. Mary and Sarah visited a physician the next morning and, by afternoon, declared that she was fine and cleared for travel.

Mary asked Joseph if the two of them could walk along the beautiful, shaded banks of the canal to Canobus that evening. That was where the most luxurious inns and villas of the city were to be found. She arranged for them to stay at the rabbi's home that night and leave in the morning.

Guessing that Mary might be feeling a certain emotional loss about saying goodbye to an unexpectedly pleasant time in Egypt, Joseph purchased a necklace of colored glass beads for which the Egyptian artisans were famous. As the two sat under the palm trees and reminisced over their most memorable experiences, Joseph pulled out his present for Mary. She was delighted.

To Joseph's surprise, she, too, had a present for him. It was a small ebony carving of a couple with a child in hand and a baby in arms. Joseph was puzzled until Mary whispered,

"You are going to be a father. I'm carrying your baby!"

Nostalgia quickly turned into laughter and embraces.

Rabbi Gershom and Sarah were waiting for them to return and had food, wine, and songs prepared. It was a special night that they would always remember.

The next morning they loaded Zephyrus with their most important possessions. There was only room for Mary and Jesus on the horse this time, and after many tearful embraces, they departed for Memphis.

The trip back to Palestine took considerably longer than their escape into Egypt. They were in no rush and Mary's morning sickness delayed each morning's departure. With the earnings from Joseph's professional activity in Egypt and the Magi's gifts exchanged for gold coins, they turned some secret compartments in the leather saddle into a virtual treasure chest. There was nothing to do but surrender themselves and their savings into God's safekeeping.

Two weeks later, they reached Gaza and took a room at an inn so that they could pick up more information about the political situation in their homeland. They were not comfortable with the thought of living in Bethlehem, but since it was the city of David, they thought they might be destined to live there. Joseph spoke with some traveling merchants in order to pick up the most recent news.

The reports were quite unsettling. Two weeks earlier, a rebellion of the Jews occurred in Jerusalem. In retaliation, Archelaus ordered Herod's army to slaughter three thousand Jews in and around the temple. Then, he and his brother, Antipas, left for Rome where Emperor Augustus would settle the dispute over Herod's throne.

One itinerant trader mentioned that Bethlehem was one of his frequent stops so Joseph inquired into any activities of Herod's soldiers seven months earlier.

"You don't know about that?" questioned the trader. "Herod had this hallucination that a Jewish Messiah had recently been born in Bethlehem, so he sent his soldiers there to kill every baby boy under two years of age. The soldiers arrived at night with torches, gathered up the babies, and speared them to death. Then they tortured a couple of midwives for more information on recent births. One refused to cooperate, so they chopped off her hands and left her to bleed to death."

Joseph was shocked and completely at a loss about what to do. If he told Mary, she would be horrified. But how could he hide it from her? He returned to their room at the inn unable to speak or even look her in the eye. She immediately sensed that something was terribly wrong and insisted on more information.

"There is some dreadful news from Bethlehem and I don't want you to hear it. I know you will be devastated."

Mary agreed that she didn't want to know, but the silence between them became so awkward and disturbing that, by the end of the day, she changed her mind.

"Maybe this is the sword that Simeon said would pierce my heart. I think you better tell me, Joseph. We can't function with you holding it in."

As soon as Mary heard the news, she burst into tears. A deep wrenching sadness tore through her soul. She fell into Joseph's arms and sobbed uncontrollably. When she did attempt to speak, more emotions welled up inside and no words came out. The two sat down on the floor where Jesus quietly watched them grieving. As Mary continued to weep, Jesus walked over, sat in her lap, and leaned up against her. Finally, Mary managed to express herself.

"Somehow I feel responsible for the grief of all of those families. It's not Jesus' fault. It's Herod's fault. But could we have done something to avoid it? Why did the Magi have to consult with Herod anyway?"

"I can't say, Mary. God's angel told us to leave town immediately that night. He didn't say anything about other children being in danger. Then Joseph broke down. He grimaced, trying to hold back his tears. Mary had never seen him so grief-stricken. Setting aside her own distress, she got up on her knees and held his head in her arms. He finally admitted his own distress.

"I'm just afraid that the midwife they killed was Judith. She knew where we were and would never have told them."

"Dear God," Mary prayed. "Please comfort that dear woman and grant her joy in your presence. When she understood that Jesus was your Son, she believed in him and loved him just like we do."

The next day, the two began to cautiously unveil their deepest questions about this terrible tragedy. Joseph listened for a while and then admitted,

"I keep wondering why God allows evil in the world at all. I know he has given us the freedom to behave well or badly, even if it destroys us. But some people are completely out of control. Why doesn't he stop them? Why do innocent children have to suffer the brutality of depraved adults?"

"Here is God's Anointed One who has come to save us from our sins," he continued. "But how can he be as fragile, as innocent, and as precious as he is and deal with something as awful as sin? What can we do to help?"

"We've talked about this before, Joseph. I don't think we can help except to give him a normal childhood and keep him out of sight until he is ready to begin his work. Then it's up to him and his Father. I can't imagine Jesus having a normal life in Bethlehem, and I could never face those mothers who lost their sons. What should we do?"

"Honestly, I don't know."

Unsure about where to go, they continued to mourn the death of Bethlehem's baby boys and the likely death of Judith, whose love for Jesus may have cost her own life.

Finally, another merchant from Jerusalem brought the news that Archelaus had been appointed the provincial ruler over Judea, Idumea, and Samaria. Joseph was warned in a dream not to settle anywhere in Archelaus' jurisdiction, so he concluded that they should return to Galilee. He woke up Mary, told her about the dream, and explained,

"This latest nudge of divine guidance gives me peace about living in Nazareth. I am sure that Jesus will be fully accepted as our natural, firstborn son. We know who he really is but I can't imagine telling this whole story to others or even writing it down. Perhaps one day it will be told, but for now, it's sealed. Do you agree?"

"Yes, I agree completely."

Traveling along the coast to Caesarea and then inland toward Galilee on the Via Maris occasioned more thoughtful conversations. At one point, Mary asked Joseph,

"When did you first believe in Jesus like you do now?"

"Hmmm. Do you mean to believe in Jesus like the shepherds and the Magi came to believe in him?"

"Yes," Mary replied. "And I think that yes is the word I am searching for. When did you first say yes in your heart to Jesus as your Messiah?"

"I think I began to say yes to Jesus when you handed him to me in the stable. I was depressed about you having to give birth there and felt guilty for not finding a better place. Maybe it's a male thing. Until then, my self-confidence was high and I thought that God could count on me to take care of you and your baby."

Looking back, I can see that I was only believing in myself. Then I failed. Holding Jesus for the first time, I let go of my failure and said yes to him as God's gift to me. Jesus, of course, is just getting started, so I think my yes to him will need to grow. When did you first say yes to him, Mary?"

"When the angel appeared in Nazareth, I said yes without really understanding to what I was agreeing. Now I can see that a deeper yes to Jesus developed when I was with Elizabeth and Zechariah. There wasn't really any particular moment that I can point to and say, 'That's when I believed.' Reading and copying down all of those prophecies was a big part of it. Discussing them with Elizabeth was important, too. I came back to Nazareth a changed person."

"Yes, you did, Mary. I could sense a new strength and faith in God as the rest of us reacted to your pregnancy."

"I like what you said about our yes to Jesus continuing to grow,' Mary added. "Everything in me says yes right now. I would die for him. Most mothers would say that, however, so in time, I think my yes will need to grow, too."

The next day, as Joseph was carrying Jesus on his shoulders, he thought about Jesus' consistently cooperative behavior and asked Mary,

"Has Jesus ever disobeyed you or misbehaved in some obvious way?"

"That's a profound question, Joseph. I've avoided commenting on it because I didn't want to ruin his record, if you know what I mean. I'm a biased mother, but truthfully, I have never seen one sign of disobedience in him."

"Does that make any difference?" questioned Joseph. "We tolerate small imperfections in our own lives. Why should it be different for him?"

"I think it depends on why Jesus is here. Is he here to please God or to please us? Reading the scrolls at the Bet Midrash in Alexandria, I discovered some conversations between God and his Messiah and added them to my scroll. Let me read one to you. The Messiah says to God Almighty,

"Sacrifice and offering you did not desire, but a body you have prepared for me, burnt offerings and sin offerings you did not require. Then I said, 'Here I am, I have come – it is written about me in the scroll. I desire to do your will, O my God: your law is within my heart.'"

"I don't know when Jesus said that or if he is saying it right now. But, I do believe that he has come to do everything that God wants with his entire heart and soul."

"Look," interrupted Joseph. "There is a shade tree over there. Let's stop and give Jesus a chance to run around a bit. I don't want to be the one to push him over the line, expecting him to act like an adult."

While Mary lay down and rested, Joseph helped Jesus climb up the tree and sit in the branches. They then played in a nearby stream. After an hour or so they mounted up again with Jesus sitting in Mary's lap and Joseph walking.

"Did you finish your thought about Jesus choosing to do God's will perfectly?" inquired Joseph.

"Not really," responded Mary. "There is something about Jesus that is so extraordinary that I'm not sure if I can even put it into words. Jeremiah wrote that the offspring of David, the righteous Branch and coming King, will be called *'The LORD Our Righteousness.'*"

"Righteousness is a profound thought. Elizabeth told me to think of it as 'the right to be in God's presence.' I asked the shepherds wives if they felt worthy to enter God's presence and they all kept quiet. Tell me, what can we offer to God that will earn us the right to be in his presence?"

"I know the answer that we learned in Hebrew school. *'If we are careful to obey all this law before the LORD our God, as he has commanded us, that will be our righteousness.'*"

"So how is that working out for you?" Mary asked.

"Not too well. I can't even keep the first commandment to love God with all my heart, soul, and strength. The rabbis say there are six hundred and twenty-two more laws in the Torah beside that one. I can't even remember them all. Honestly, I don't have any right to be in God's presence."

"I feel the same way, Joseph. But what if Jesus leads a perfect life and then takes our place before God? What if he really is the LORD Our Righteousness and he takes us into God's presence based on his performance instead of ours? How would you feel about that?"

"I would be overwhelmed, humbled, and grateful at the very thought of something like that. If he did that, I would love and follow him forever. Are you really suggesting that this is why he has come? What will he do with the long list of my sins and moral failures?"

"I don't know yet," answered Mary. "But I do know that Jesus is going to be my righteousness. That's like a rope for someone who is drowning, and I'm not letting go of it."

The next day was their last one on the road. Mary could hardly wait to present Jesus to her family and friends and tell them that another child was on the way. As they left the Via Maris and started up the steep hill into Nazareth, she suddenly remembered the matter about which they needed to have precise agreement between the two of them.

"Joseph, remind me again. How old is Jesus going to be in Nazareth?"

"Well," he replied. "We have to celebrate his birthday nine months after our wedding. We can tell everyone when we are going to celebrate his birthday and avoid mentioning his age for a period of two and a half months beforehand. Today he is still one and his birthday will be the twenty-fifth of December." In October and November we will only talk about his coming birthday and not about his age."

It was late afternoon when they walked up the old familiar street and stopped in front of Mary's home. She clapped her hands and called to her mother, waiting just a moment to see Rebekah's expression when the door was opened.

"Mary!" shrieked Rebekah. Screams of delight were followed by long, emotional embraces. Heli and Levi were both at home and the joy of reunion was shared by the whole family. Word of their arrival spread like wildfire and, for the rest of the day, bits and pieces of their story were interspersed with the arrival and greetings of more family and friends.

CLOSING SCENE

The Stable Revisited

On their second day in Nazareth, Mary pulled Joseph aside and whispered, "We need to talk."

Shouldering one of the empty water pots, Joseph proposed a walk to the village well. As soon as they were beyond hearing of her family, Mary blurted out,

"How can we explain the last two and a half years without telling people that Jesus is God's Messiah?"

"I know exactly what you mean. We're like fish that have been given wings. We know about air, sunlight, trees, and flowers. Now we're back in the water, where water is all that people know. Maybe this is the dilemma of Jesus' kingdom. To accept him for who he is changes everything."

"It reminds me of my pregnancy again. Instead of joyfully announcing the greatest event of human history, we were faced with the challenge of keeping it a secret. It's all backwards. I can't wait to be alone with my parents and find out what they are really thinking."

Not long after arriving in Nazareth, Joseph explained to Heli his interest in building or purchasing a larger home. He mentioned that God had provided them with some unexpected financial resources during their journey and asked if

Heli and Rebekah would be interested in joining them in the search for a new home.

"I want to build a sizeable carpentry shop and I know that you and Levi need space for your trading business, too. A central gated courtyard would give us the privacy and protection we need. Walls of rock and mortar would allow us to add a second floor with family rooms and some open roof space. The kitchen, pantry, carpentry shop, warehouse, and stable would all surround the courtyard downstairs. Meals would be served upstairs in a dining area at the top of the stairway. As you and Rebekah get older, you would never have to move again."

"That would be a dream come true, Joseph. You know that we are just barely surviving. On top of that the owner of the house is always threatening to evict us. Your idea is what every Jewish grandparent hopes for."

"I am just thinking out loud, Heli. We need to pray and ask God for guidance. Hopefully we can find a lot nearer to Nazareth's well, too. Perhaps a house like this already exists and could be purchased. Let's talk about it with Rebekah and Mary and be ready to act if the opportunity presents itself."

A few days later, Heli and Rebekah needed to visit a relative in Cana and invited Joseph and Mary to join them on the overnight journey. They quickly agreed, knowing it would give them a chance to discuss the events of their long absence and address the question of who could be told about Jesus' origins. While Joseph carried Jesus, Mary brought up a delicate question.

"Mother, did you manage to keep my pregnancy a secret?"

"I believe I did, Mary. After we met you in Jafta, we said you were expecting and that seemed perfectly normal. I wondered how you would handle Jesus' age when you arrived. When you said his birthday would be in late December, even your Aunt Joanna whispered to me, 'They didn't waste any time did they?' Now tell me about Jesus' birth."

After recounting the details of her delivery in the birthing stable, Mary described the arrival of the shepherds.

"I always imagined that the Messiah would be welcomed into our world with a magnificent reception," Mary reflected. "But with all of the secrecy that surrounded my conception of Jesus, I eventually realized that God wished to bring his son into the world very discreetly. Then, he made one big exception."

"You won't believe this, Mother, but there was a celebration for Jesus on the hills outside of Bethlehem. It was more of a heavenly event so we only heard about it later. As I was giving birth to Jesus in the stable, tens of thousands of angels were commemorating his arrival. They sang and praised God and wished peace to all of us on earth. Some shepherds witnessed the event and were completely awestruck. One of the angels told them where to find us."

"Think about this," added Joseph. "The angel told the shepherds that the baby would be wrapped in strips of cloth and lying in a manger. At the birthing stable, the priests cut strips of cheap burlap cloth and wrap them around the best lambs to keep them clean and unblemished until they arrive at the temple.

Mary had a small, cotton blanket for Jesus but the midwife used a strip of this cheap cloth to bundle him up tighter. When I heard the noise of the shepherds, I laid Jesus down in the manger to see who was coming. So there we were in the exact position that the angels described to the shepherds. Only God could have foreseen those details and told the angels what to say to the shepherds."

The two went on to relate four more amazing miracles that occurred after the angel's celebration. Joseph finally concluded,

"God swept us up into this adventure of Jesus' departure from heaven and arrival on the earth. As normal as he appears, we can never doubt his divine origin and mission."

"Joseph, I know that you and Mary believe that Jesus is God's Messiah," responded Heli. "Rebecca and I have a hard time believing it but we will support you in any way we can. If Jesus turns out like you and Mary, we will be very happy. With Rome's iron-fisted dominion over our land, I don't see much hope for a Jewish prince to regain the throne of Israel."

"You two were gone so long," said Rebekah, "that we began to think the angels' messages to you and Joseph were dreams or something. I want to believe you, I really do. But, it's not easy to believe that something is from God when our priests don't even know about it. And Jesus seems like a pretty normal kid to me."

"Well, now you have the whole story, Mother. We hope you will embrace it and believe in Jesus like we do. In the meantime, you can help us raise him. We have concluded that it's best to not even tell people about his Messianic mission, so you don't have to worry about that. When the time is right, Jesus and his Heavenly Father will reveal his true identity. Our part is to protect him from public exposure and let him experience normal life."

A few weeks later, Heli arrived with the news that a relative of Joanna was interested in selling the very home where Joseph and Mary held their wedding reception. This was exciting news! Joseph and Mary concluded that this was the open door for which they had been praying. Mary was exuberant and burst into her song about magnifying the Lord. Afterward she said to Joseph,

"The song that God put in my heart on the road to Beth Hakkerem is the story of our lives. *'His strong arm has worked wonders of all kinds...The humble he lifts up and gives to them a crown...The hungry he fills up with a sumptuous feast.'*"

Moving into the new home was a watershed moment for Mary and Joseph. For two years, they had been caught up in a wave of supernatural interventions that played across every emotion they possessed. It was high adventure. Unexpectedly, moving into their new home was where the adventure came to an abrupt halt.

Accustomed to being in charge of her home, Rebekah found herself in occasional conflicts with Mary. Joseph worked long hours and traveled frequently to find tools, wood, hardware, and customers. Mary's younger siblings, Aaron and Teresa, resented the lack of attention they had enjoyed in their previous home and criticized Mary for making everyone's life revolve around her. Worst of all, Jesus seemed to be barely noticed in all the confusion. Finally, Mary got Joseph's attention and poured out her frustrations.

"Please listen, Joseph. I can't seem to find my way through all the demands I'm faced with each day. It didn't occur to me that I would have to carry our second child up and down those stairs all day long. I'm exhausted. And what about Jesus? He is so sweet and uncomplaining, but isn't there something we should be doing for him?"

"Mary, I've been caught up with the challenges of building a new business and haven't been thinking about our real mission, or about your work load in managing the household. Forgive me."

Together they prayed and reflected on their goal of giving Jesus the skills he would need to communicate with their nation. They concluded that Mary should continue reading the Scriptures to him at the Bet Midrash until he was old enough to start Hebrew school. Two afternoons a week were selected and Joseph agreed not to travel on those days. Finally, he shared some thoughts about their future.

"Mary, here is what I see ahead. We do have a mission from God and this house should be part of that. I want you to be free to fulfill the special role God has given you of guiding Jesus through childhood. You also have a gift for encouraging other women to love God extravagantly, like you do. Maybe you could read and discuss the Scriptures to a group of them."

"Jesus is our top priority, but he needs to be surrounded by family and normal life experiences. If you are okay with being a mother to our children, a student of the Scriptures, a song writer, counselor, and manager of our home, my suggestion is that we hire a couple of younger women for cooking, cleaning, and sewing. You can do those tasks well, but I believe your personal mission is something else."

Just days before Jesus' birthday, Mary gave birth to a second son whom they named James. Rebekah was thrilled and wanted extra time to hold him since she had completely missed out on cradling Jesus as a baby.

Mary continued to watch Jesus carefully as he moved into the third year of his life. There was none of the usual testing and rebelling that most other children exhibited. She couldn't remember him ever telling a lie or hiding the truth. A transparent spirit seemed to facilitate his memory and disposition to learn.

"Upon arrival in Nazareth, Jesus was hesitant to speak. In Alexandria, the Jewish community had spoken Greek, Coptic, and some Hebrew but here in Galilee, the common language was Aramaic Mary knew that Jesus' comprehension of Hebrew was remarkable for his age. When she asked him about something she had read to him, he could always give a brief but thoughtful answer.

At three, the hesitation ended and Jesus began to speak Aramaic, Hebrew, and Greek with equal proficiency. It seemed like he had stored up everything he was hearing, sorted it all out, and was now able to respond to each person in his or her primary language.

Something else caught Mary's attention. The men normally led in prayer at meals and special occasions but one day when the men were all away, Mary asked Jesus if he would thank God for his food. Without hesitation or even closing his eyes, Jesus said, "Thank you, my Father, for the food you have provided."

"Mary," whispered Rebekah, "You should rebuke him. We never address the LORD Almighty as 'My Father.' What if he did that in public?"

Mary glanced at Jesus and sensed that he understood Rebekah's disapproval. She immediately responded,

"Jesus, that was a wonderful prayer. Thank you."

Then to Rebekah, she added,

"Mother, I am still discovering new passages about the Messiah in Scripture and recently copied one down from the scroll of Psalms. God is talking about the supernatural off-spring of King David and says this,

'He will call out to me, 'You are my Father, my God, the Rock, my Savior.' I will also appoint him my firstborn, the most exalted of the kings of the earth...'

That's about Jesus, Mother, and Almighty God says that he will call him 'my Father'. We just saw it happen!"

Mary thought of this as a moment of "Messianic emergence". When new ones occurred, she could hardly wait to tell Joseph about them. After explaining this one, she added with a sparkle in her eye,

"Speaking of emergence, O Lion of Judah, there is something else emerging in our lives."

She paused and waited for a response. Joseph seemed perplexed.

"I think I am expecting again."

"Mary, that's wonderful!" burst out Joseph as he leaped to his feet and scooped her up in a passionate embrace. They immediately called Jesus to gave him the news. They also explained that when the baby arrived, he would be able to start Hebrew school at the synagogue.

The synagogue in Nazareth was an active center for the Jewish population. Boys from ages five to twelve met every morning at the synagogue to learn Hebrew and study the Torah.

More advanced programs in the Scriptures and oral in-terpretations of the Torah took place at the Bet Midrash.

There the senior rabbi and other circulating teachers of the Mosaic Law led students from ages twelve to eighteen in individual study and group discussions. Rabbi Sherebiah set aside a room in the Bet Midrash for fathers to have access to the scrolls, and periodically, reserved time for his wife, Judith, and for Mary, to read the scriptures too.

In her twenty-second year, Mary gave birth to a baby girl. They named her Salome and she quickly became the delight of their household. That same year, Jesus started Hebrew school at the synagogue. Mary's habit of reading the scrolls to him from infancy placed Jesus in a class all his own. After a few months, the young priest who taught the first-year students spoke with Joseph and Mary.

"What impresses me the most is not that Jesus' reading skills are so advanced but that he seems so free of arrogance, shame, and fear, wherever I place him. He knows the answers but politely waits for the others to have a turn and he never ridicules them for being wrong."

"Do you think we have pushed him too hard?" asked Joseph.

"If you had I think it would have shown up in his attitude," replied the priest. "But I've seen nothing wrong. He is a delight to have in our school. I like to think of him as a magnificent young horse. Loosen the reins, give him affirmation, and see how fast he can run. His gifts are from God. Why should we stand in the way?"

When Jesus was six, Joseph and Mary agreed that they could begin to converse with him about who he really was. Mary was sure he knew more than they realized, so one afternoon she opened up the subject.

"Jesus, how much do you know about who you are and why your Father sent you to live with us? Do you know what I am talking about?"

"Yes, Mother. I've heard you and father talking about it as long as I can remember. I know you named me Jesus because salvation is what I am. When my Father speaks with me, he calls me by my name. He wakes me up every morning and teaches me about being his son. We were always together, you know."

"Of course," thought Mary to herself. "The songs of the Servant again. He is saying exactly what Isaiah predicted he would say. *'He wakens me morning by morning, wakens my ear to listen like one being taught...'* It's right there in my scroll and I just didn't notice it."

That was the dawning of a new day for Mary. She felt a deep satisfying peace that even though her work was not done, the outcome was guaranteed. The burden was lifted. Jesus was under the tutelage of his Father. She went to the rooftop the next morning and poured out her thankfulness and praise to God Almighty.

The following year, Mary began to speak with Jesus about the miraculous events that preceded and followed his birth. She took Jesus' left hand and raised it up beside his face, fingers extended. Starting with his little finger, she recounted five events, one for each finger. Jesus listened intently as Mary explained.

"First, the angel Gabriel appeared to your great uncle Zechariah in the temple and told him that his wife Elizabeth would have a baby. When Zechariah doubted the angel, God took away his speech and hearing. Second, Gabriel appeared to me at our old house here in Nazareth and told me that I would be your mother."

"Third, when I visited your great Aunt Elizabeth, the tiny little baby who is your cousin John, jumped up and down inside her and Elizabeth knew that I was your mother. Fourth, an angel appeared to your father and told him to marry me. Fifth, your great uncle Zechariah regained his lost speech and hearing on the day that cousin John was circumcised."

Then, Mary touched Jesus' nose.

"You are the sixth and greatest miracle of all because never before has a baby been conceived without a human father. Now, lift your right hand and I'll tell you the rest of the events. Seventh, the night you were born, all the angels in heaven celebrated your arrival in Bethlehem. They praised God and told some shepherds where to find you. Eighth, two elderly people in the temple recognized you as a newborn because God pointed you out to them."

"Ninth, five wealthy Magi came from Parthia to meet you and followed a star to our house outside of Bethlehem. Tenth, an angel told us to escape to Egypt because a wicked king wanted to kill you. Eleventh, an angel told us to return to Israel and guided us back into Galilee."

Mary held Jesus' two hands on either side of his face and counted across.

"One, two, three, four, five, six, seven, eight, nine, ten, eleven. Both hands beside your face can be our secret signal to remind each other that you are on your mission and that your Father sent you. Is that a good idea?"

"That's a good idea, Mother," replied Jesus. "Will you tell father?"

"Yes, of course, I will." With a sly look, Mary added, "And which one would that be, Jesus?"

Jesus looked into her eyes with just a hint of a smile, "Only one of them doesn't know yet, Mother."

Joseph and Mary's family continued to grow. Salome was followed by Joses and Joses by Elizabeth. By age ten, Jesus was released from the primary school and passed on to the course of study for senior students. After his twelfth birthday, Rabbi Sherebiah visited with Joseph and Mary and gave them some surprising advice,

"Listen, dear friends, Jesus knows the Scriptures as well as I do. He is fully conversant in the oral interpretations of the Torah and we only keep him in our advanced program because he has such a positive influence on the other students. I think you should consider enrolling him in one of the academies in Jerusalem. Hillel and Shammai are too elderly to teach personally, but their academies are both highly recommended. Joseph, on your next trip to Jerusalem, you should look into these schools."

Every year, Joseph attended three religious feasts in Jerusalem. Two of them were commonly attended by men only and he customarily made the trip with other devout fathers from Nazareth. The Passover Feast, held in the spring of the year, was an event that attracted whole families. It was the highlight of the Hebrew religious calendar.

When Jesus was twelve, Joseph and Mary were especially excited about celebrating the Passover in Jerusalem because Jesus would be receiving instruction about his induction into the congregation of Israel as an adult at age thirteen. Mary was pregnant again but felt healthy and ready for the excursion.

They traveled with several other families from Nazareth. Zephyrus carried a large load of food and camping equipment, which meant that everyone had to walk on foot, including three-year-old Elizabeth. It was a fun journey though. At night, the children ran from tent to tent, sharing in meals and even sleeping over with their friends. The youngsters would all participate in the Passover meal in the campground but not enter the temple.

Joanna and Ebron were unable to come this year, so Ebron's relatives in Jerusalem invited Mary and her family to share the Passover meal with them. The city was packed with worshipers who spent hours waiting in lines to enter the temple itself. Jesus questioned Joseph extensively about the priests, the sacrifices, and the rooms where the rabbis could be heard teaching the Law. He paused at the door of several rooms and listened with fascination.

On the final night, the Nazareth group packed up most of their things and prepared for an early departure the next morning. The permanent residents of Jerusalem observed the Feast of Unleavened Bread for an additional seven days.

As thousands of families broke camp and headed out on the main road to the Jordan River Valley, it was impossible for Joseph and Mary to stay in contact with all their friends. James, Salome, Joses, Elizabeth and Zephyrus were all they could keep track of. Jesus had helped pack things up but in the confusion of the departing crowds, he was nowhere in sight. No one was more trustworthy than Jesus, so Joseph and Mary assumed that he was helping some less agile member of their party. He would appear eventually with a gratifying story of assistance that made perfect sense. By noon, however, Mary became concerned about his absence.

"I can't understand why Jesus hasn't checked in with us by now. We haven't seen all of the families from Nazareth yet but he knows we like him to keep us informed of his whereabouts."

The Nazareth party had agreed on the first night's campsite before leaving Jerusalem. When Joseph and Mary arrived and accounted for the rest of their party, they were shocked to realize that Jesus was not among them. There was nothing to do but turn around and go back to Jerusalem.

Unwilling to part with their younger children and unable to travel at night, the entire family left their friends the next morning and arrived back at the home of Ebron's relatives that evening. The family gladly gave them a room and took care of the children as Joseph and Mary began their search for Jesus the next morning.

Contact with city officials, gatekeepers, medical centers, and temple guards all proved fruitless. When they reviewed Jesus' conversations during Passover, it occurred to them that, if his disappearance was totally his own choice, he might be in the temple, listening to the priests and teachers of the Law.

"We have to remember," pondered Joseph, "that this whole trip represents his acceptance as an adult member of God's congregation, a son of the Law. Could it be that, from his point of view, his mission has superseded his family ties?"

"It would be nice if he had told us that, don't you think?" countered Mary.

With this fresh idea, the two walked around the temple courts peering into every room and chamber where they could see a meeting taking place. Finally, Joseph stopped and stared.

"Mary!" he exclaimed. "Isn't that Jesus with his back to us, surrounded by doctors of the Law? Look at the borders on their mantles; some of them are members of the Sanhedrin. Let's slip into the back of the room and listen. It would really embarrass him if we disturbed the meeting."

"May I ask a question, your honors," Jesus was speaking. "Our fathers entered into a covenant with the LORD our God and Moses told them, *'If we are careful to obey all this Law, that will be our righteousness.'* Later, the LORD declared through Jeremiah that he would make a new covenant with Israel and send a righteous Branch from David's line who would be called *'The LORD our Righteousness'*. When the Anointed One comes will he give us his righteousness or must we continue to seek our own?"

Mary's fingers buried themselves into Joseph's arm as the religious dignitaries pondered his question. The silence was finally broken by the kindly priest who had taken Jesus into his home for the last two nights.

"Son, you speak with a clarity that is uncommon among those of us who are considered to be experts in the Law. And you have placed your finger on the great dilemma expressed by Isaiah, *'How then can we be saved...for our righteous acts are like filthy rags.'* How we wish that the righteous Branch would appear. But, until he does, the Law, the temple, and the sacrifices are what the LORD God has given us for the pursuit of righteousness."

"By the way, young man, it appears that someone may be waiting to see you. You have honored us with your questions and we hope to see you again."

When the meeting was dismissed, Jesus turned and saw his parents. In spite of the prestigious company, Mary hurried to him and knelt down.

"Son, why have you treated us like this? Your father and I have been anxiously searching for you."

Her eyes searched his for a response. There was compassion and understanding but no guilt or frustration.

"Why were you searching for me?" Jesus questioned. *"Didn't you know I had to be in my Father's house?"*

Later, Joseph expressed his feelings to Jesus in private. "Son, I was so proud of you when I overheard your dialogue with the teachers of the Law. I wish I could have heard all of it. Your mother and I have a deep sense of responsibility for you. When your time comes, you are free to leave us, but we had no idea that your time had come."

Impressed by Jesus' perspective and acceptance in the temple, Mary felt somewhat relieved. For that reason, perhaps, she surprised Joseph the next morning with an unexpected request.

"Since we have already delayed our departure, can we take another day and visit Bethlehem? I would like to see the stable one more time. I don't want to visit our old friends there, but I do miss the stable. I don't know when we will ever have another chance."

They decided to leave Jose and Elizabeth with Ebron's relatives for the day and make the four hour walk with Jesus, James, and Salome. It was a beautiful morning and brought back many memories. As they journeyed, Mary asked Jesus to fall back a few paces and walk with her.

"Jesus, how will you respond if, one day, I spontaneously ask you to solve a problem in public that might require you to reveal your true identity?"

Jesus walked along thoughtfully for a ways and then said,

"What would you suggest, Mother?"

"Well, I want you to be really firm with me. Why don't you just say, *'Woman, why do you involve me in this. My time has not yet come. '"*

"Okay, Mother. I'll remember that."

As they neared Bethlehem, Mary wished to take the eastern road toward Herodium and approach the village from a hill to the northeast.

As they walked down the slope and paused under an olive tree, Mary suddenly burst out, "It's gone!"

"What's gone?" said Joseph as he squinted toward the village.

"The stable is gone. It's an empty field now. I don't understand."

"I'll walk over and find out what happened. Do you want to come with me?"

"No, I can't do it. What if one of the women recognizes me? I'll just stay here with the children where you can see us. Here, Joseph, would you fill the water pouch at David's well? I have been waiting for a drink of that water."

They watched as Joseph crossed through the ravine and started up the other side into Bethlehem. Then James asked, "Mother, why can't you go?"

"Oh, it's a long story," Mary said. "A tragic thing happened to some mothers in Bethlehem and I feel partly responsible."

"What happened, Mother?"

"Never mind, James, maybe someday I'll explain. I just can't face those women."

Jesus had been listening thoughtfully to Mary's conversation with James. He then moved to her side and quietly took her hand.

"One day, you will, Mother."

Mary knew that Jesus never wasted words. He was telling her something new, something very important. Why would she be able to face these women one day? Suppressed Scriptures began to flood into Mary's mind. She thought about Simeon's prophecy of a sword piercing her own heart and Jesus' question for the teachers in Jerusalem. They all ended in one dreadful suggestion.

Mary knelt down in front of Jesus and looked into his dark brown eyes as earnestly as she had ever done. His look was calm, warm, and understanding.

"Jesus, what exactly is your Father's work?"

Jesus paused, contemplating something, and then he answered quietly,

"There is only one Messiah, mother. My Father's work is to gather his sheep, to suffer in their place, and to reign with them forever."

Mary's heart broke instantly. For twelve years she had feared this. She had done everything she could to protect Jesus from suffering. Was it not enough?

Mary held Jesus' head in her two hands and gently pressed his face to hers.

"No...no...no," she groaned as a word picture from Isaiah formed in her mind.

'But he was pierced for our transgressions, he was crushed for our iniquities. The punishment that brought us peace was upon him, and by his wounds we are healed.'

Then it struck her why she would be able to face the mothers who lost their sons. One day, she too would lose her son in an equally brutal way.

Tears poured down her face, her body began to shake, and she sobbed uncontrollably. Jesus pushed Mary's scarf back and wrapped his arms around her head, holding it close to his heart. He seemed to not only understand, but to have expected this. He was compassionate and deeply moved by his mother's agony.

James and Salome had no idea what was happening. They stood quietly on either side of Mary and rested their heads sympathetically on her shoulders.

It was some time before Mary could release her hold on Jesus. Her face was swollen from crying and her sleeves were soaked with tears.

"Oh, Jesus...Jesus...Jesus, I can't bear it. I don't understand, son. Why does it have to be this way?"

As Mary's emotions lessened slightly, Jesus placed one more hurdle before her.

"Mother?" he asked.

Mary pushed back to see him, but she couldn't. Her eyes were filled with tears and she could only make out a blurred image. Her hands continued to hold his face.

"Yes, Jesus?" she whispered.

He paused again, as if seeing something far away.

"I want you to be with me."

Mary tried briefly to imagine what moment that might be. Then Isaiah's description of a lamb being led to the slaughter came to mind and, once again, her heart was crushed. More tears poured out and once more,she collapsed into Jesus' arms, her heart throbbing. Jesus held her securely until the trembling stopped.

Mary's voice was no more than a hoarse whisper when she finally managed to speak.

"Yes, son, I'll be there."

There was a long pause and then, from some deep inner fountain of strength that had defined her life for years, Mary looked at Jesus through blurred eyes and carefully chose her words, pausing meaningfully between each of them.

"Jesus, I believe in you. You are my Shepherd...You are my Savior...You are my King!"

Another embrace ensued, lighter, gentler. Mary rubbed her eyes on her sleeve and looked into Jesus' eyes again. Warmth and wisdom affirmed her. As she struggled to her feet, Mary saw Joseph approaching.

She could read his demeanor, and she knew that he had something to say but didn't want to say it. When Joseph saw

Mary's face, he forgot his own dilemma and gathered her into his arms.

"Mary, what happened? You've had a worse time than I had."

"Maybe I did, Joseph. But it will take some time to explain what I went through while you were gone. Tell me. What happened to the stable?"

Joseph struggled for words but knew that he had to tell her the truth.

"The stable was where they found the baby boys after Herod's soldiers came through. They were all pierced with swords and spears. No one wanted to go there anymore, so they tore the stable down and moved it farther out of town. The old site is now a grave yard. I'm sorry, Mary, I didn't know how to tell you."

"It's okay," said Mary. "Our son actually gave me a new perspective on things. It was hard for me to believe at first, but now I'm beginning to understand."

"Well, how did he know what happened here?" reacted Joseph incredulously.

"I think we are going to be asking that question more often now," replied Mary. "At least, as long as he lives under our roof."

Jesus was looking intently at Bethlehem with James and Salome on either side. He seemed to be explaining something to them.

Joseph and Mary took one more long look at Bethlehem and, after a deep breath, Mary said, "Okay, Lion of Judah, please take me home?"

They walked along silently until they reached the crest of the hill. As their route joined the main road to Jerusalem, they quickened their steps. A short ways ahead, Joseph glanced around at the surrounding hills and suddenly stopped.

Sure enough, there on a distant hillside, perhaps a half mile away, was a flock of sheep grazing in a field of green grass. Two, three, yes, four shepherds could be seen around the edges.

"Shall we go over and see if they are our friends?" questioned Joseph.

"On any other day I would say yes," replied Mary. "But now, I just want to get to Jerusalem by nightfall."

Jesus had walked to a small knoll a short ways from the road. He looked thoughtfully at the shepherds for nearly a minute and then lifted his face to the sky. He finally turned and looked toward Mary.

He lifted his left hand to the side of his face with all five fingers extended. To the other side of his face, he lifted his right hand with only his thumb extended. With a beaming face, he smiled at Mary. Her heart warmed with affirmation and she whispered to Joseph, "Look, he knows!"

As they continued up the road, Mary told James and Salome about the shepherds they got to know when they lived in Bethlehem. Jesus was walking between Joseph and Mary, holding their hands. James hung on to Joseph's other hand, Salome to Mary's.

Without warning, Jesus broke into a run. "You can't catch me," he shouted over his shoulder. James and Salome instantly charged after Jesus, their legs and arms churning like geese on the run.

Mary glanced at Joseph, lifted her skirt, and broke into a run herself. Joseph was completely caught off guard, still trying to resolve all the weighty matters they had unearthed in Bethlehem. There was nothing to do but chase after his family.

He had almost caught up with Mary when a sharp pain stabbed through his left shoulder. It stopped him in his tracks. A slight dizziness came over him and he put his head down. As the pain subsided, he walked forward slowly, massaging his shoulder.

"What happened, Joseph?" laughed Mary. "Did you stop to let me win? You know, you look a little pale. What's wrong with your shoulder?"

"I'm sure it's nothing serious, maybe a pulled muscle or something. Come on, let's catch up. We don't want the kids thinking that we're getting old."

By now, Jesus had stopped. James and Salome were hanging onto his arms, breathing hard, and laughing with flushed faces. Joseph and Mary walked arm in arm until they finally caught up with them.

"And what was that all about?" questioned Mary.

With a broad smile and a thoughtful loving look in his eyes, Jesus answered, "To help you dry your tears, Mother."

AFTERWORD

His Story is Your Story

Hello, Reader! Thank you for accompanying me on this enhanced journey through the Christmas Story. I hope that you have found it as inspiring and thought-provoking as I have. Before we part company, I would like to engage with you briefly on a few compelling issues.

The first one is the blending of history and fiction, as it occurs in *The Stable*. I regard the four biographies of Jesus' life, which are included in the New Testament portion of any Bible, to be authentic, reliable, historical documents. Two of them, Matthew and Luke, recount Jesus' birth.

You met Luke, the first-century Greek physician, in the Foreword. His research was remarkably thorough and he eventually presented it to his patron, Theophilus, as an orderly account of Jesus' birth and public life. Matthew was originally a Jewish tax collector. His life was radically changed by meeting Jesus and he became one of his twelve messengers. Matthew records four of the eleven miraculous interventions while Luke records seven.

The Stable is much more than an orderly account. It dives between the lines of the reports written by Matthew and Luke, and attributes to a purely fictional character by the name of Sappheire the creation of all this extra, heart-warming material Fact and fiction are inseparably inter-twined here. The only chance you have of distinguishing one from the other is to personally read Luke's and Matthew's accounts. What they wrote is fact. Everything in *The Stable* that is added to those manuscripts is fiction.

Some of you may already hold deeply-seated convic-tions about the Christmas Story. For you, this is sacred ground and, admittedly, *The Stable* walks all over it. If, on some issue, you take offense, I fully understand, and even expect it. Opinions about Mary, for example, vacillate wildly throughout the religious world today. I have the most pro-found respect and admiration for Mary and hope that every reader will close this book having been emotionally stirred by her moving display of womanhood and spiritual maturity.

So, where did Sappheire and all this extra material come from? Aside from my own imagination, I regularly consulted two additional sources in developing the speculative content of *The Stable*. The first are the sacred writings of the Jewish religion. These are found in the Bible under the title, Old Testament. The roots of the Christmas Story are deeply en-twined in these ancient writings and they provide us with promises, prophecies, and even pre-recorded conversations between Jesus and his Father in heaven. I first read them through sixty-one years ago and have never put them down since.

The second source includes the hundreds of scholars and historians whose research and commentaries provide us with a wealth of information about Jewish life, culture, history, and geography in the first century. Among them all, I proba-bly reached for *The Life and Times of Jesus the Messiah* by Alfred Edersheim more than any other.

Actually, no one knows what really took place between the recorded lines of scripture. For sure, a great deal did take place, so *The Stable* might be closer than we think. If in any way I have violated the spirit or the letter of Matthew, Luke, and the Hebrew Scriptures, I apologize. My intentions were otherwise.

Of what value is Jesus' birth story with all these additional conversations, story lines, and human emotions? Hopefully, they will serve to convince the reader that Jesus is for real. Traditionally, we have been encouraged to put our faith in Jesus in consideration of his death and resurrection. *The Stable* presents Jesus' birth as another, solid, and profoundly beautiful basis for faith. After all, it was enough for Mary, Joseph, the shepherds, foreign dignitaries, and elderly worshipers of God at that time.

For many years, my faith in God was primarily rational and defensible. After immersing myself in Jesus' birth, my faith has become more emotional. I love him and I love his parents more than ever before. Dare I tell you this? I have rewritten the Closing Scene many times. But to this very day, I can't get through it without my eyes becoming blurred with tears over the final episode outside of Bethlehem.

This first printing of *The Stable*, is providing a window of opportunity to gather some feedback from you, the initial readers. The publisher has activated the following email address to help me gather any helpful comments, questions, or suggestions that you may have.

thestable@familyfusioninc.org

If additional printings are called for, this email address may be altered or discontinued in consideration of a larger target audience. You may also contact us at the publisher's mailing address that appears in the front of this book.

Here is the final compelling issue. To whom does this story belong? It occurred among the Jews in Israel but their leaders have not accepted it. It is not the property of the Christian religion because that tradition was not in existence at the time it took place. This story was such a well-kept secret, in my understanding, that when Jesus stepped into public life thirty years later, none of the religious leaders of his day, none of the villagers where he lived, and none of the brothers in his house even knew about it. Figure that one out!

After many years of listening imaginatively to the participants in Jesus' birth story and penning *The Stable*, my conclusion is that this is God's story and it explains how he became King over a host of human followers from every tribe, language, people, and nation. Since Mary "treasured these things in her heart," and passed them on to Matthew and Luke, then through her and them, this story has become God's gift to the whole world.

The Christmas Story is an adventure beyond all others because it brought heaven and earth back together again. *"God was in Christ, reconciling the world to himself,"* penned one of Luke's colleagues. Jesus' birth was accompanied by an outpouring of miraculous interventions and spiritual truths that are far beyond my powers of description. So, in whatever language this story is translated and, by whatever people, race, or religion it is read, this story belongs to you, the reader. It is yours to own, to enjoy, to believe, and to embrace. Have a wonderful life and may it be eternally impacted by this, the greatest story ever told.

Daniel Greene